Life is
Always
Aimless

.... *Unless You Love It*

Life is
Always
Aimless

.... Unless You Love It

Ratnadip Acharya

Srishti
PUBLISHERS & DISTRIBUTORS

Srishti Publishers & Distributors
N-16, C. R. Park
New Delhi 110 019
srishtipublishers@gmail.com

First published by Srishti Publishers & Distributors in 2013
Copyright © Ratnadip Acharya, 2013

ALL MAJOR CHARACTERS IN THIS NOVEL ARE 100% FICTITIOUS ANY
RESEMBLANCE TO ANYONE LIVING, DEAD OR TO BE BORN IS PURELY
COINCIDENTAL

Typeset in AGaramond 12pt. by Suresh Kumar Sharma at Srishti

I have spread my dreams under your feet;
Tread softly, because you tread on my dreams.

W. B. Yeats

This book is for my beautiful mother, Lila Acharjee. She was my first English teacher.
This piece of work is also dedicated to the loving memory of my father, the late Ranjit Acharjee.

Author's note

First of all, deep regards and love for Chandra Mohan Jain, widely known as OSHO, for touching my life with his love, silence and laughter and changing it forever.

My brilliant sisters, Mahua and Madhumita and my brother-in-law, Manoj, for reading and loving many of my short and long stories. They would be immensely happy to see this book published.

A big thanks to Bhaskar Maity (though he does not care for it), a best friend of mine, for always standing by me for last many years through thick and thin, for being ever ready to hear every story I devise. I really cherish those long afternoons we spent together, discussing art, life and it's mystery with our inseparable friend, *Signature* and *salted peanuts*.

My sincere thanks to Ujjal Ghosh, Subhashini Rajagopalan and the late Vivek Parashar – for helping me learn the beauty of editing my work and also for liking my stories. Among them a special thank you to Vivek Parashar. On many occasions he told me with deep conviction that one day I would live a more meaningful and fruitful life rather than doing a 8 am to 5 pm job. His sincere words are etched on my heart and inspire me even now. Unfortunately, he is no more alive to see my first novel getting published.

I am very grateful to Shobhaa De, noted author and columnist, for being unusually kind to me for last many years. For the very obvious reason, most of the well known authors are highly unapproachable. Surprisingly, Shobhaa De is an exception. She is always ready to snatch her valuable time to read my stories. What is more, she is generous enough to tell me that I have a real knack for writing and that I must continue writing no matter whether my stories get published or not.

A very special thank you to Sangita De, whom I called Boudi, the first reader of my many short stories. Her comments on my works were always sincere and genuine. To have a reader like her can be any writer's delight.

A heartfelt thanks to the editorial team at Sristhi publishers. They were always prompt to respond my mails. Without their cooperation this book would not have emerged from its manuscript.

A big thank you to Shiva Kumar, Valentina D'silva, Sr. Josephine Rozario, Bernadette, Sandee, Tulica for reading many of my stories and speaking words of love for them. It is indeed a satisfying feeling when someone tells you that your story has brought tears of love and joy to his or her eyes.

A big thanks to Sunil Jha, my friend for almost last two decades. He would be delighted to see this book published. I really cherish your friendship, brother.

And last but not least, two persons, who are the integral part of my life: Akash, the *Sky* of my little world and my Maria Fernandez, without their presence around me, I could not have written this book. They know who they are. And as you read this book, you will also get introduced with Maria Fernandez.

It is said that the language of love, prayer and silence travels beyond the boundary of time and distance. This book is written with utmost love and sincerity. While reading this work if you experience love deep within your being I would consider that my effort is successful.

At last I want to end this author's note with a beautiful saying by *Ann Landers:*

IF YOU HAVE LOVE IN YOUR LIFE, IT CAN MAKE UP FOR A GREAT MANY THINGS YOU LACK. IF YOU DON'T HAVE IT, NO MATTER WHAT ELSE THERE IS, IT'S NOT ENOUGH.

Regards,

RATNADIP ACHARYA

30th September, 2012, Mumbai

Prologue

Akash rushed down the flight of stairs, taking two steps at a time. Only after climbing down two floors he remembered that he could have used the lift. He was on the fourth floor now. He, however, did not bother to check the position of the lift and ran down three more floors to reach his flat on the first floor. He was panting as he opened the door. He did not want to waste a single moment to record the sense of inexplicable bliss that overwhelmed him. In fact he was scared that with the passing moments the exquisite feeling within him might melt away.

Reaching his study table he opened the notebook and poised the pen on the paper. For a moment he was at his wits' end. He was certain that the surging emotion and the overflowing love within him was enough to make his pen move. But he was proved wrong. The pen remained in his hand like a lifeless object. He brought the pen close to him and inspected it closely. There was a small ball on the tip of the refill, slightly smeared with ink. As the ball moved on the paper, it made a thin line of ink trail the path it had trodden. And those thin lines, if guided properly to construct meaningful sentences, spoke so much to us, about us. It evoked every possible emotion within us. Suddenly that ten-rupee-worth ball pen appeared to him as one of the most powerful weapons that human intelligence had ever invented.

He held the pen more tightly and resolutely than before and was determined to put down every thought that might pass through his mind. But then all of a sudden a flicker of doubt crossed his mind. Would he do justice to himself just by noting down his present state of mind? However ecstatic his feeling at this present moment might be, he must record all those apparently insignificant incidents, which moulded him, and write about all those people – his friends and *yaars* - whom he loved and liked, who had left indelible marks in his mind. He then thought about Maria and involuntarily his heart escaped a beat. Maria Fernandez.... Maria

Fernandez..... Maria Fernandez.....he whispered the name many times before silence took away her name from his mouth and kept it somewhere deep down within his being. A peaceful and agreeable silence filled him. Suddenly he felt very grateful to life. Yes, he thought, how he could write anything without writing about the person who made him experience a different dimension of love, which transcends all sorts of physical love. Something that was so close to a spiritual experience.

Yes, he would write about his friends, Maria and others as honestly as he could. They had recounted so much about themselves to him that he could write well about them without colouring any incident with his imagination. Then he looked at the table. On the left side there lied piles of manuscript of his short stories rejected by almost every publisher of the country. It was the testament to his last five years' hard work. But the heap of manuscript spoke of nothing but his failure. However, for now, he did not look at it with a sense of dejection.

He knew it was the first time he took up the pen without caring at all whether anyone would ever read this piece of write-up. It was his story, Maria's story, story of Sandip and Chirag. Now as he looked at each of their story, they all seemed to be complete and perfect in their own way. Each story had something to offer. Most importantly, how beautifully and intricately they were interwoven with each other.

As he placed the pen on his open notebook again an inspiration struck him, presenting him a key to open a treasure-trove. A treasure-trove that preserved all the bitter-sweet memories of last five years, precisely since the day he had joined ICL as a young trainee of twenty-two years of age. And the key to open the treasure trove was love and sincerity.

As memories came flooding to him, his pen, determined to record everything honestly, ran effortlessly on one page after another. All the time Akash could feel two innocent, limpid eyes watching him loving. Those eyes belonged to an otherwise unattractive woman of twenty-five. Maria Fernandez was her name.

1

'**F**uck, this is what they call furnished bachelor accommodation. This room is as awful as my college hostel's room,' said Aniket Mahapatra, slumping down on his holdall, after sweeping everything in the room with a disappointing gaze. He was visibly disappointed.

'If I do not leave this bloody goddamned place within six months just remind me of this afternoon,' said Aniket, pointing his finger at Akash as though Akash was responsible for the bad state of the room.

I would be happy if you leave the room even before, thought Akash and nodded slowly. He could not bring himself to like Aniket who would be his room partner for next one year.

No doubt the room was not in a good state. Its' walls were wet; the ceiling was laced with cracks. Papery scrolls of paints dangled from many places. The room was bare barring two wrought iron beds, two wooden tables and two metal-tube folding chairs. Yet the room was not really uninhabitable. Besides, Akash was not much fastidious about furnished accommodation. He looked at Aniket, trying to size him up.

Aniket was tall with sharp features. He had a fare complexion, broad shoulders and clean-shaven face. But something indiscernible in his face endowed him an air of subtle haughtiness.

He asked Akash, looking at him over his shoulder, 'What do you think of this cubbyhole?'

'Well,' said Akash slowly. 'It is not that bad.'

'Gone mad,' cried Aniket. 'This is the problem with most of us. We are ready to settle for something much less than what we deserve. And there are hundreds of bastards who are taking advantage of our *chalta hai* attitude.' Aniket stopped for a moment and continued, 'We are engineers, man, passed out from NITs, National Institute of Technology. We deserve the best, *yaar*. They cannot treat us like shit.'

'But nobody is treating us like shit. This is the ICL hostel for engineer trainees and we have been allotted a room in it, simple.' Akash tried to reason with Aniket.

Aniket goggled at Akash. How could this boy feel at home at this fucking place? thought he. Unlike him Akash was of medium height. He had curly hair and a broad forehead with a strange sparkle in his eyes. There were two big moles on both sides of his lips. He was pleasant to look at. His features were regular. But the most prominent thing in him was his fingers. They were very long and well-shaped, exactly like that of an artist. The aggressive air which was so prominent in Aniket was completely absent in Akash.

This morning they had reached ICL hostel and immediately had been allotted the same room. Akash had passed out from National Institute of Technology, Jamshedpur as an electrical engineer and Aniket from NIT Calicut as a Chemical engineer.

However, deplorable condition of the room and, what was more, his insipid roommate left Aniket in an irascible mood for the rest of the day. His communication with Akash was bare minimum. He had taken an immediate dislike to Akash for no apparent reason. Late in the afternoon when they went out to Chembur Camp to get a duplicate key for their room lock they hardly talked to each other. While Akash was busy watching new people, new eateries, Falooda centres, studios Aniket was engrossed in deep thoughts about his future. Joining a public sector like Indian Chemicals Limited (ICL) was rather a stopgap measure for him. He knew for certain that soon he would get through a reputed IT company. Moreover, he would leave no stone unturned to score well in CAT. How beautiful life would be if he got admission in one of the IIMs. After all, a blasted place like ICL could not be for him.

While returning to the hostel that evening Akash suddenly stopped in front of Ashish theatre. They were not very far from their hostel. 'Aniket, you have your key now. Would you mind going to the hostel? I would come after a few minutes,' asked Akash, somewhat absentmindedly as though his attention was somewhere else.

'It's okay, but where would you go?' asked Aniket.

Akash did not respond but indicated an old shrunken woman, selling boiled eggs, squatting on her haunches.

'Do you want to have boiled egg?' Aniket asked in a matter of fact way.

'Not really, but she has only two boiled eggs left. If somebody buys them she can leave at once,' said Akash, without averting his eyes from the old woman.

Aniket puckered his eyebrows. 'It's strange, man. If she wants to sell those eggs she should sit until she gets a customer. Why should you show pity on her? Will you buy last two eggs from her every evening?'

'I am not showing pity. I simply feel like having those eggs from her. I cannot logically prove you why,' said Akash in a tone of finality in his voice.

3

'As you wish.' Aniket shrugged his shoulder. 'Is it okay if I leave?'
'Yeah, very much.'

Aniket left with long strides and before taking the right turn towards the hostel he stole a furtive glance at Akash and the egg seller. This Bengali boy seems to be over sensitive, thought he.

The old lady removed the eggshell carefully while Akash watched her minutely. She kept the shell in a plastic bag next to her and placed the eggs on a piece of folded newspaper. A sharp knife now passed through the eggs, bisecting them and then a pinch of salt and freshly ground pepper was sprinkled on the yolks and whites. Now an old shaky hand with wrinkled skin raised and, holding the eggs on a piece of paper offered it to Akash. Akash collected it from her when she gave him a toothy smile. The boiled eggs were warm and Akash indeed liked them. After finishing the eggs Akash crumpled the paper and was about to throw it when the old lady spoke, 'Do not throw it here. Give it to me.'

She took the crumpled paper from him and stowed it away in another plastic bag.

'I sit here every evening. I do not want this place to be dirty,' said the old woman as she began to pack her things up.

'I am sorry,' said Akash.

'Do come here in the evening whenever you feel like having boiled eggs.'

'Yes, I will.'

'Thank you,' the old woman smiled. She looked at Akash for a moment and then offered her hand to him to help her get up. Akash held her hand right off and helped her stand. She was a small woman.

'You know, I always wish that hit films are always screened here,' said she, indicating Ashish theatre behind her.

'Why?'

'Because then the selling of boiled eggs goes up,' smiled she as her face contorted and small eyes almost disappeared.

'How many eggs do you bring usually?'

'Not more than a hundred. But if there is a hit film may be up to one fifty,' replied the old lady and asked as an afterthought, 'why do you ask me all these things? Normally no one talks to me more than two to three words.'

'I do not know,' said Akash.

The old lady did not say anything to him but gave him a long stare and after giving him a faint smile left with two plastic bags. As the diminutive figure of her disappeared in the crowd soon Akash experienced warm-heartedness within. He walked towards ICL hostel in silence. It was good that Aniket was not with him.

Within a month or so the hostel was bustling with life. No fewer than twenty more engineer trainees joined ICL and had been allotted different rooms on second and third floor. As weeks sped by the boys found their like-minded friends and moved about on weekends in a group of three or four. They would watch films together, frequent pubs and sometimes spend hours in the evening, sitting in the hostel canteen.

However, in the afternoon most of them would meet in front of the hostel entrance and share their day with others. They discussed their seniors in the office, talked about their idiosyncrasies and laughed at their expense.

'Gawde's scooter is no less than a good twenty-year-old. It farts so terribly once he starts it. It is enough to put the best *diwali* cracker to shame,' said Shashank Bhatti, a product from Beneras Hindu University.

His comment sparked up a hearty laugh among the friends and once it subsided Sujit Hota began, 'You guys must visit my plant to meet Mr. Pathak, the HOD of instrument department. That bugger is no less than fifty. Most of the time his hand his inside his pants, scratching balls shamelessly.'

'Most probably sometimes his shrunken dick retracts into his body and the poor fellow just tries to pull it out,' another boy rejoined.

'Have you ever shaken his hand, Sujit?' asked Swapnil.

'Not since I had seen him fiddling with his cock for the better part of the day,' replied Sujit.

'You guys must meet Masurkar from my plant. It is rumoured that he does not even spare a *kamwali Bai*. All he wants is a new cunt, no matter how much used it is. And just imagine he is a senior manager in Heavy water plant. I heard that his wife left him long back because of his regular sleeping around. He, however, continues new ventures every week.'

This piece of information made all the boys cock an ear at the speaker.

'How do you know?' asked one of the inquisitive listeners.

'Simple, from the operators. What work do they have apart from sitting in front of DCS panels? If you became friends with them they would give you information like hell.'

Now all of a sudden their loud voice slid into a lower pitch as they watched Aparna Pandit and Sujata Sharma entering the hostel premises. They both had joined as Engineer trainee in IT department a couple of weeks back and till now their communication with none of the boys was more than a customary 'Hi' and 'Hello'. Sujata and Aparna passed the bunch of boys in a hushed whisper, not really unaware that their presence made the boys more silent than before. And they indeed enjoyed it.

'Sujata has a terrific bum, man,' Sailesh gasped as Sujata disappeared behind the staircase.

'But I have heard that this year she is planning to tie a *Rakhi* to you. Then you will be your Rakhi-brother,' commented a boy.

'Never mind, then I would turn a sister-fucker,' Sailesh quipped.

Again the discussion became as animated as before. Most of the days Akash joined the after–office-discussion though he did not speak much. He loved to hear Sujit and Sailesh's funny one-liners which they produced at the drop of a hat. His roommate, Aniket, however, found those gossiping sheer wastage of time and after coming from office rushed to his room to sit with the study material for CAT. Combined Admission Test was just a month away.

'Running uphill is one of the most powerful exercises. It is a must for those who want to go for a real trekking,' said the panting Sandip.

Akash looked at Sandip. Beads of sweat were glistening on his forehead. He was not fair but there was a glow of confidence and simplicity on his face. He was Akash's height but had a very well-toned body. He had thinly chiselled features, sensitive nostrils, marked jaw line and eyes deep in their sockets. Though he had thick curly hair he tried to part it in the middle. He was clean-shaven and whenever he spoke his prominent Adam's apple bobbed up and down.

They were sitting on an iron bench near Star Guest House, located on a small picturesque knoll inside ICL township premises. In front of them was a winding road sloping away towards the main township where tall buildings for ICL employees were spaced out. Looking out over the Mumbai city from the height of Star Guest House was a pleasant experience.

'Why do not you try to jog with me at least once? The distance from below there up to the guesthouse is hardly two and a half kilometres,' Sandip said to Akash, wiping sweat from his forehead.

'Gone mad, I will expire out of breath. I come here with you only because I love this place. It commands such a beautiful view. But do not expect me to jog,' Akash smiled, looking at his friend. It was more than four months since he had joined ICL and found a friend only in Sandip.

Something in Sandip was so unique that Akash was automatically drawn towards him. Unlike most of the boys, never did Sandip discuss career related things, further studies or official matters with anyone. His passion for travelling was very evident. Though during the training period they were entitled to only 12 casual leaves Sandip had already availed fifteen leave-without-pay.

Once he said to Akash with a small smile, 'How can I make anyone understand that travelling is a part of my being. Putting my career in ICL at a little risk for it is not really a scary prospect to me. What do you think, Akash?'

'But does not it bore you to travel alone? Besides you always go to new places. Is not it risky to travel all alone?'

'Sometimes I do feel bore but most of the time I love being alone. But why should I be scared of travelling alone, that too in my own country? You must see European and American backpackers, hardly twenty or so, hitching a ride in a new country. That's real courage, Man.'

It was no more than a month since Sandip had started practising running uphill, as he had planned to go for a trekking from Rishikesh to Valley of Flowers next month. This evening he had brought Akash with him but in spite of his best effort he failed to make Akash Jog even for half a kilometre.

'Exuding sweat happily is one of the best ways to remain mentally and physically fit. Strange that you are not interested in it,' said Sandip.

Akash did not reply. Darkness fell and the stillness of the evening was very comforting. A peaceful silence ensued for a long moment, occasionally punctuated by Sandip's deep breathings.

Akash spoke after sometime, 'Does your mother know that you are going to the Himalayas for a long trekking, that too all alone?'

'I told her that I would be going to Uttaranchal for a couple of weeks. There is no point in telling her anything in details,' answered Sandip.

'Is not she worried about your expedition?'

'Not more than a widow should be for her only child,' Sandip said indifferently and then added, 'as soon as I am allotted a flat in the township after the end of training period, I would bring my mother and keep her with me for good.' Suddenly remembrance of his mother softened the rigid lines on his face.

'Let's go back. It is already 8,' said Akash.

'Yeah, anyway Akash you often ask me as to why I am not careerist like the other boys. I can also ask you the same question.'

'If I say to you honestly,' began Akash as a thoughtful expression came to his face, 'I have an intuition that I can do creative works and for that I should not be a part of a rat race.'

'What sort of creative work?' asked Sandip, raising eyebrows questioningly.

'I really do not know. But I always have a gut feeling that I understand people much better than others. I think I can use it as a fodder for creative work.'

Sandip nodded in silence, contemplatively.

Akash wished he could have said to Sandip that he wanted to be a writer but he lacked confidence to voice his innermost desire.

Aniket was in a sulky mood for last few days since he had come to know of his percentile in CAT. Apart from his roommate Akash he had not told anyone that he would appear CAT.

This evening when Akash entered the hostel room he found Aniket sitting on the bed, leaning against the wall, looking vacantly at the ceiling fan. His laptop was lying open on the bed by him. There was an air of depression about him.

'Did not go to your plant after lunch?' asked Akash.

'No,' Aniket replied curtly.

'Why, not keeping well?' Akash asked, unlacing his shoe.

'Venkatesh Rao joining Texas University next month. He scored well in GRE.'

'Who is Venkatesh Rao?' asked Akash, furrowing his forehead.

'That fucker was my batch mate in Calicut NIT. Just imagine, he used to come to my room, to me to understand thermodynamics and Mechanics of Solid. And now he is going to Texas for M. Tech and I am screwing myself in this fucking place.' Aniket's voice was pregnant with depression.

'How have you come to know?' asked Akash.

'Facebook,' said Aniket, indicating his laptop.

'Never mind, Aniket, you will have more opportunities soon. What is more, scoring well in GRE or CAT is not the last thing in life,' Akash tried to reason.

'Please leave me alone. I do not need your Sympathy.'

There was no point of telling anything to Aniket, thought Akash left the room after taking a bath. Since Sandip had left for his trekking expedition no more did Akash go to Star Guest House to enjoy the silence of the evening. As he reached in front of the hostel building he found the discussion between his friends, huddled together near the hostel entrance, was in full swing.

'Where are you going, dickhead?' asked Sujit. He and Akash had passed out from the same college.

'Chembur Camp, some small work, coming?'

'I know where you are going,' Sujit said with a mischievous smile on his lips.

Akash raised his eyebrows, looking quizzically at Sujit.

'Sujata has left hostel just a couple of minutes back, swinging her lovely ass. I know you are sniffing around her.'

'Then what are you doing here?' smiled Akash.

'What can I do, *yaar*?' Sujit wore a wistful expression on his face, 'other than shagging, thinking about her.'

'Keep it up,' smiled Akash and set off at a leisurely pace towards Chembur camp.

Near Ashish theatre as he was crossing the road his eyes met the old lady's who sold boiled eggs. Old lady's dull eyes suddenly glinted with delight as she recognised Akash at once.

This boy had had boiled eggs from her many evenings and in many times he refused to take the change from her. But she liked the boy not because he often paid her more than she deserved but because he talked to her with love and affection. She waved at him when a bright smile spread over her face. Akash raised his hand to reciprocate her greetings, which she confused as his assurance to meet her on his way back to the hostel.

On reaching Chembur Camp Akash loitered about aimlessly for sometime. Once he left Bharat medical store after buying a shaving cream and reached the main street a motorbike zoomed past him. It drew Akash's immediate attention, as he knew the bike rider as well as the pillion passenger who clung to the rider, draping both her arms around him, resting her head on his strong broad shoulder. Sujata was the pillion passenger and the rider of the bike was Jasvinder Singh, known as Jassi among his friends. He was from IT department in ICL and was a few years senior to Akash. He was tall with a well-proportioned body. His hazel eyes, cleft chin, well-defined features and above all his grizzled wavy hair made him a perfect Adonis. Being a trainee in IT department most probably Sujata was under Jassi's tutelage and he seemed to be taking all care to train her in every possible way. Akash had heard from one of his inquisitive batch mates that Jassi was well-known in ICL for his occasional flings. Most probably Sujata was another easy prey for him, thought Akash yet their moving about as lovebirds struck an arrow of envy to it his heart. Probably none of the boys know that Sujata is hanging around with Jassi, thought Akash as he walked back to the hostel.

'*O Saab.*'

Akash heard that a frail woman's voice was calling him as he was about to take a turn towards his hostel. It was the old egg seller. Akash gave her a smile and went to her. She had only two eggs in her straw basket.

'I am waiting for you, *saab*,' she said to Akash, starting to shell an egg for him.

'Why?' asked Akash.

'Did not you ask me to wait while going towards Chembur Camp? Otherwise all my eggs were sold out around half an hour back. But I have kept these two eggs for you,' she announced proudly, offering the eggs to Akash.

Her simple and candid statement touched Akash to the core. She could have left half an hour back, selling these two eggs to someone else. Yet she had waited for him with patience for she thought that he would come to her for the eggs. The exhibition of deep love in this apparently small incident left Akash speechless. He remembered his first day in Mumbai when he had bought the last two eggs from the lady.

After finishing the eggs when Akash gave her money she refused to take it. 'Many a times you gave me much more than I deserved. Please do not give me money this time.'

'Well, in one condition,' smiled Akash, without insisting further, 'in that case from now on you have to call me by my name. My name is Akash.'

'*Gaon khidar hai tumhara?* Where is your hometown?'

'Bengal, *me Bangali hun,*' replied Akash.

An affectionate smile came to old woman's wrinkled face. Akash stood by her, watching her packing her things. This evening before leaving the old woman ruffled his hair.

'*Bhagavan tumko khush rakhe, may god bless you,*' said she, before leaving.

A strange feeling of bliss filled Akash once the old lady departed. He immediately dialled Sandip to recount this loving encounter to him. But Sandip's cell phone was beyond reach. Sandip must be in some tent in his way to Valley of Flowers, thought Akash.

'There are five prayags in Uttaranchal,' began Vinay Singh, the tour operator and the proprietor of Himalayan Rafting and Mountaineering in Rishikesh. 'Sonprayag, Deoprayag, Rudrapreyag, Karnaprayag and Nandoprayag. On our way to valley of flowers we would pass through all the prayags except for Sonprayag.' He stopped and looked at all his listeners. They were only three. Sandip and a young Belgian couple who spoke English decently well. Vinay himself spoke English with an accent which most of the people in tourism business did. He was apparently proud of Uttaranchal and its rich heritage. He was not in tourism just to make some quick buck but loved his job.

Slowly Vinay delineated the entire trip to them. 'It would take you guys eleven days to reach Valley of Flowers and our last halt would be at Govind Ghat. But there are a few things I would like to tell you although you all seem to be experienced in trekking. Don't carry too much thing in your backpack. Always carry a torch and a bottle of water with you. And if you find a small or big waterfall anywhere on the way, don't hesitate to replenish your bottle with water. The water from the worst waterfall here would be better than the best packaged water of the country. Rocky Sherpa, your guide, is the best guide I have. He is very well versed in everything about this tour so please always listen to him.' Vinay Singh joined his hands and gave his guests a *namaskar.* They all rose from the chairs.

Vinay offered locker to all his tourists so whenever someone went for a long trekking he did not need to keep hotel room booked for keeping his luggage. Vinay charged very nominal for the lockers.

Sandip gave his hand to Vinay before leaving, 'I loved talking to you. You seem to love your job a lot.'

'When your job always keeps you close to her how can you dislike it?' said Vinay, indicating Ganga flowing in front of them. Himalayan Rafting and Mountaineering commanded a breathtaking view of Ganga. Unlike in Haridwar, Ganga was much clean here. The whole place was breathing with life yet there was an overwhelming tranquillity in the air.

'I envy you your job,' smiled Sandip.

'I take your statement as a compliment,' Vinay shook Sandip's hand profusely.

Leaving Vinay's office Sandip found the Belgian couple waiting for him on the other side of the street.

'Do you want to check with other tour operators?' asked the guy. He was no less than six feet. His eyes were bluish and hair golden.

'Why?' asked Sandip.

'Do you think this fella is reasonable?'

'Yeah, seven thousand for eleven days is damn reasonable,' Sandip said in a clear voice.

The boy looked at his girlfriend. She shrugged her shoulders. She had a broad face with beautiful almond eyes. Her wavy hair was tied with a yellow silk scarf. She had a strong body and was carrying an unusually big backpack. She wore a green sleeveless T-shirts and a pair of demin jeans torn near the knees. She gave a smile to Sandip. Her teeth were regular.

'Well, meet you soon, man,' said the boy, patting Sandip on his shoulder.

'Yeah,' said Sandip, giving the couple a friendly smile.

'Hey buddy, what's up?' There was a tap on Akash's shoulder. Turing around on his heels Akash found Chirag Patel standing in front of him.

'Hi Chirag,' said Akash, passing an envious glance at Chirag. Among all the boys joined ICL as trainee engineers Chirag Patel was a confirmed misfit. He rather looked like a promising upcoming model who had come to ICL to conduct a training program on personality development. He was tall with a well-proportioned body. His deepest eyes, gleaming with wit, thin lips, and clean-shaven face gave him an irresistible personality. He was Sandip's roommate though so far he had not spent more than one or two nights in the hostel. He stayed in Ghatkoper and preferred coming to ICL by riding his bike. Though he shared an amicable relationship with all the boys none of them knew much about him. Nobody really knew as to why Chirag had got a hostel room allotted for him.

Sandip, however, welcomed Chirag's not staying in the hostel. He, for some reason, found Chirag's behaviour ostentatious as though in a subtle way he wanted to draw others' attention.

'Where is Sandip? I do not see him anywhere,' asked Chirag, after passing a searching glance around.

'He is on leave, went out for trekking.'

'Where?'

'Valley of Flowers, it is somewhere close to Badrinath.'

'When?'

'I think four days back.'

'Fuck man, I wish I had known it before. I told him to inform me whenever he is going out for more than a day or two days.'

'Why?' asked Akash curiously.

'This Sandip is a strange guy. Anyway, it was bad of him not telling me about his going out,' said Chirag as though he was talking to himself. Akash felt slighted as Chirag did not bother to answer his question.

'Well, see you, man,' said Chirag, walking away from Akash. On reaching near the entrance to the training centre he got his expensive cell phone from his pocket and made a call while Akash watched him, somewhat disapprovingly, standing on the corridor. However, Akash did not have to wait much to know why Chirag wanted Sandip to inform him about his going out for a few days.

Akash came out of ICL factory gate at 5 pm with two more boys and walked barely a few steps when suddenly an old scooter screeched to a halt in front of him. The driver of that almost decrepit vehicle was a burly Sardar with a genial smile on his lips. Without any word he signalled Akash to sit behind him. Akash hesitated for a moment as he did not feel like leaving his friends walking while he would enjoy a free scooter ride up to the hostel.

'If one day I buy a car I would drop all your friends to the hostel,' Sardarji said to Akash as though he had read Akash's mind.

'Bye *yaar*,' Akash said to his friends and clambered on to the scooter. Sardarji shifted the gear, the scooter grunted and moved forward.

'*Kaise hon*? How are you?' asked Sardarji, turning his head sideways when a few droplets of spittle from his mouth travelled with wind and hit Akash's cheek. Instinctively Akash pursed his lips lest a tiny spitball might enter his mouth.

'*Thik hun*,' he said after a moment.

'How is your training going on?'

'It's okay. It will be for another few months.'

'Good. After confirmation you would be a big *saab*. Then you would not take a lift from me anymore,' said Sardarji. There was a strange kind of sadness in his voice and Akash could feel it.

'I do not know,' said he, somewhat evasively.

Sardarji did not ask him anything more. Sitting behind him Akash remembered his first encounter with Sardarji.

ICL hostel was about two kilometres from the factory and most of the trainees preferred to hitch a lift from the passing vehicles as auto rickshaw and BEST buses did not frequent this road much. It was a week or so since Akash had joined ICL. Akash and Aniket came out of factory gate that afternoon together.

'Why should not we try for a lift rather than waiting for a bus or auto rickshaw?' Akash proposed.

'If you wish you try. Somebody may say no. I do not want to give an opportunity to a two penny bastard to say no to me,' Aniket gave a wintry smile to Akash.

Akash, however, had expected more or less the same answer from the vain and self-absorbed Aniket.

Ignoring Aniket's caustic remark Akash was all set to ask for a lift. In his college days in NIT, Jamshedpur he always preferred a lift from college campus to Jamshedpur city to travel in college bus crammed full of students.

The first two motorbikes ran past Akash ignoring his request for a lift. And then came Sardarji with his old scooter. He stopped the scooter near Akash and looked at him questioningly.

'Would you drop me near Ashish theatre?' asked Akash.

'No, I do not give lift to anyone,' replied Sardarji in a gruff voice and put the scooter into gear.

No sooner had the scooter left than Aniket dissolved into laughter. 'This is exactly why I do not ask any bastard for a lift,' said he.

Akash swallowed down the humiliation and around fifteen minutes later reached the hostel by a BEST bus.

A week later he met Sardarji again while waiting for bus. This afternoon Akash averted his glance as soon as he saw Sardarji. Sardarji, however, recognised Akash and stopped his scooter near him and inspected Akash minutely for a while.

'Sit,' said the Sardarji abruptly. His voice was authoritative yet coated with affection and though Akash was miffed with him, he could not refuse his offer. It took them five to six minutes to reach the hostel and none of them spoke during the ride. And since then Sardarji had given a lift to Akash no less than thirty times but rarely had he spoken to Akash.

This afternoon once they reached near the hostel Sardarji stopped the ignition. Akash got down from the scooter and was about to thank

Sardarji as he usually did but something in Sardarji's face silenced him. His face was composed, eyes moist and lips pursed in a thoughtful way.

'If you buy a bike one day drive carefully. Very very carefully. Never try to impress anyone with your driving skill,' Sardarji's voice was distant.

Akash remained silent without knowing what to say.

Sardarji heaved a deep sigh of agony and held Akash's left wrist. His palm was damp.

'I had a son. He looked like you. If he were alive he would be your age,' Sardarji paused and began again. 'Two years ago he died while racing bike with his friends in Jalandar. In Punjab many young boys are crazy for bikes and go for a race late at night. And it cost me my son. You remind me of my son, *beta*.'

Sardarji started the scooter and left without anymore words. Akash remained in a state of shock for a few minutes, wondering about a lonesome father, weighed down by the sadness of his son's death.

'What happened, man? Why do you look so disturbed? Did that asshole Sardar tell you anything?' It was Aniket who had just reached the hostel gate.

'No, nothing' said Akash curtly and, then looking at Aniket a strange feeling occurred to him. Most probably a self-centred Aniket and the likes could never have empathy for other peoples' pain and pleasure.

That evening Akash remained all alone for a long time on the roof of the hostel, contemplating on what Sardarji had told him when, out of the blue, he hit upon an idea.

A widowed man lived with his only teenaged son.....the son was everything for him....one day the boy died of a bike accident....the bereaved father became almost demented......then one day he chanced upon a boy who asked for a lift from him......the boy was his son's lookalike.....he started giving lift to the boy regularly........and the

19

presence of this boy again gave the man a reason to live life to the fullest.....but one day the boy bought a bicycle and stopped taking a lift from him...... again the man retired to his depressive life.....and then at last there was a pleasant surprise-ending where the man and the boy met again.

So thrilled was Akash with this idea that he thought of jotting it down right off lest later he might not find the idea exciting enough.

He rushed down to his room and sat at his table, opening a notebook. Soon Akash realized that story writing was much difficult than devising a plot. He, however, undaunted, continued his effort to write the story, which later became his first full-fledged story of eight-thousand-words. He named the story *An unexpected encounter*. On the same night, however, some more surprise was in store for him.

A fit of giggles coming from the staircase along with the sound of unsteady footfalls made Akash immediately conscious. It was half past eleven. Aniket was sleeping on his bed, curling up his legs.

It cannot be Aparna, Sujata or any of their friends, thought Akash, tiptoeing over to the door as the curiosity got the better of him. He opened the door almost soundlessly for an inch and peeped out carefully. Two figures were climbing up the stair in front of him, holding each other's waist.

It was Chirag Patel with a girl. Akash had not seen her before but her dress sense was so revealing that for a moment Akash felt like sprinting to her to hold her from behind. As she climbed the stair her beautiful butt swung. She was wearing low-waist jeans and every time she lifted one of her legs her lacy panty peeped out. She possessed a curvy body and was generous enough to expose it. Her transparent bra strap clung on to skin near her shoulder. She wore a small T-shirts, As they disappeared Akash closed the door carefully. He knew they went to Sandip's room. For a moment he was seized with a desire to go upstairs to Sandip's door and eavesdrop on Chirag and his friend. However, the first thing he did was to rush to the bathroom to release himself from excitement. Vivid imagination played a considerable role and helped him reach a climax almost in no time.

Once he left the bathroom he felt that his limpness had taken away his desire to listen in on the moaning that might issue from Sandip's room now.

That night the story of the lonesome man did not proceed any further.

The room was minimally furnished, giving a distinctive impression of the person stayed there. A stack of National Geography magazine was lying in a corner. Cobwebs had woven intricate modern art on the ceiling. The crumpled bed sheet on Sandip's bed was stinking. A book on travelogue lying half-closed on his bed as though he would come to read the book at any moment.

'Interesting,' said Kritika suddenly, sweeping her eyes around the room.

'What, the room?' asked Chirag.

'No, your friend,' said Kritika. Her lips were set in a pout. Suddenly a stab of jealousy hit Chirag. He already disliked Sandip for no good reason. There was always an air of nonchalance about Sandip as though his mind always dwelt somewhere else. It made Chirag feel that Sandip was a sophisticated pretender.

'He is a very lousy fellow,' Chirag said sternly.

'Jealous?' asked Kritika archly.

'Why should I?' Chirag shrugged his shoulder.

'Well, well, let's not discuss your friend. I have already lied enough to spend this night with you,' said Kritika, sitting on Chirag's bed. The bed creaked under her weight. A mischievous smile came to her lips.

'Do you think the bed would creak all night?' she asked Chirag, winking at him.

'It's not creaking, *yaar*. It's moaning with orgasmic pleasure as your ass touched it. Believe me, you remove that goddamned jeans and sit on the bed, it would creak harder. After all, It's my bed.' Chirag gave Kritika one of his seductive smiles. Kritika slowly walked towards Chirag and once she was in his embrace she whispered to his ear, 'You know something, you are a bastard.' She bit his earlobe playfully.

'But only a bastard can have a bitch like you,' said Chirag, smelling and then licking the nape of her neck. Kritika groaned with pleasure. Soon they helped each other undress themselves and dragged their almost conjoined naked bodies to the bed.

Like an experienced masseuse Kritika made Chirag lay on his bed and mounted on him. She guided both his hands to hold her firm breasts. As his hands automatically squeezed her gravity-defying assets Kritika bent her head down and kissed Chirag's lips. Soon their tongues entwined, sought divine nectar from each other's mouth. They were both, however, well prepared for this moment and had done enough homework to enjoy this moment to the fullest. Chirag had popped a few balls of mouth freshener and Kritika had applied *Diva,* an imported lipstick, generously on her lips. Her job in Epicentre, a well-known call centre, made her well informed of many cosmetic products, which, otherwise, she might not know of.

Slowly as they breathed harder Kritika led Chirag inside her. A sigh of ecstasy escaped both of them. The experienced Kritika gradually started giving powerful thrusts letting Chirag enjoy deeper penetration.

'Do you love me, dear?' her voice was deep and low. She was running her nails on his waxed bare chest.

'Yes, yes, I do love you,' whispered Chirag.

'I love you too, dear. I never loved anyone as much as I love you,' said Kritika lovingly, her eyes half-closed with the pleasure of an about-to-come-orgasm.

Though Chirag's mind was drugged with a kind of bliss all of a sudden he remembered an advertisement for used BMW car. The advertisement had earned some prestigious award for its sheer creativity and thus became a widely circulated email.

It depicted a beautiful teenage girl with flossy golden hair and seductive eyes looking at the camera with an inviting smile on her lips. On the left corner below her photograph written on bold letters was:

YOU KNOW YOU ARE NOT THE FIRST
BUT DO YOU REALLY CARE?

On the right corner there was a small logo of BMW car with its tagline – Sheer driving pleasure.

Kritika's repeated whispering — I love you, I love you — he knew, was nothing but like that slogan in BMW used car's advertisement. He knew for certain that she had said it to many boys before. But he could not attribute blame to her for nobody knew better than him that he had used this mantra '*I love you*' to no less than twenty girls. This mantra, however, qualified him to win over no fewer than fifteen of them and what was more, most of them had not hesitated much to shed their clothes once the mantra cast a spell on them.

But now he could not think more as past, present and future were dissolving in this rare moment of bliss. He was coming, squirting warm semen within her.

A few minutes later Kritika was cuddling up against Chirag, playing with his limp and wet toy, lying between his legs. She hoped that her caress would bring it to life. Though she enjoyed the love-making with her present boyfriend she had come to meet him with some other plans up her sleeve. This afternoon when he had called her to tell that this entire night they could spend together Kritika had done two things at once.

The first one was to tell a blatant lie to her mother that she had to go to Epicentre this evening though it was her weekly off. And the second thing was to interchange the SIM cards of her mother's cell phone and her own.

'Mamma, from now on you would use my cell,' said Kritika to her mother, giving her a kiss and hug.

'But if I use your cell phone what will you do? Besides I can hardly operate this phone, *beta*. I do not understand this touch-screen and all that,' said the mother, holding an almost-new cell phone with a large display.

'For a day or two I would manage with yours one,' Kritika paused and added, 'and then, I hope, I would get a new one.'

'You will buy a new one or you will get a new one?' Her mother looked askance at her.

'Oh, mamma, you ask too many questions,' said Kritika, a bit irritably.

Kritika's mother did not ask anything. She was not really unaware of the fact that her daughter had many boyfriends with whom she had had physical relationships as well. In the beginning she had been scandalized by Kritika's confession. She was only seventeen at that time. And now her daughter was earning. She was a confident self. Even her husband looked up to his daughter since she had financially helped him buy a Maruti Alto. Kritika's mother often felt that her daughter was fabricating stories yet she remained silent for, she knew, her words of advice would hardly matter to Kritika.

'See it is not responding to my fondling,' said Kritika, slowly stroking Chirag's manhood.

'Most probably it is yearning for someone else's fondling now,' Chirag quipped.

'You bastard,' Kritika shouted with feigned anger and then added as an afterthought, 'wait a minute, dearie, I think I have got an SMS.'

Yes, this is the most opportune moment to show him what an old cell phone I have, thought Kritika and reached into her purse. And here it was - the old much-used Nokia cell phone of 2002. She fidgeted with the cell phone for a long moment, pretending to check the INBOX for SMS when Chirag asked her, 'Why are you using this fucking old cell? Where is your cell?'

'Lost it last week, it's mom's.'

'Why did not you buy a new one, *yaar*?'

'I will, let's next month's salary come.'

'Fuck you, don't tell me that you do not have enough cash to buy a new cell. Besides, you have a ICICI credit card.'

'I will buy one soon. I know you feel embarrassed to be seen with a girl who carries such an old cell,' Kritika said slowly, lowering her eyes, pretending to be hurt.

'Are you free tomorrow evening?' Chirag asked in a matter of fact tone. A steamy lovemaking always made him generous.

'Why? Will we come here again?' Kritika asked innocently though she knew very well what Chirag really meant.

'We will go to R Mall, Ghatkopar. We will get a new phone for you.'

Mission accomplished! Kritika's heart leaped with joy although she

25

tried to maintain a woebegone expression on her face.

'I really do not need a cell phone now, dearie. Please do not waste your money on me.' Kritika's voice honeyed with affection.

'The chapter is closed. Tomorrow you will wait for me near MacDonald's at 6.30.'

Kritika nodded in silence. She lied beside Chirag and started to coax his member to hardness in a much-determined way. Chirag really deserved another round of violent lovemaking with her, thought she.

As Kritika was busy with her job suddenly Chirag's attention was drawn to the wall next to Sandip's bed. On the wall Sandip had drawn a small mountain and the sun rising from behind it with HB pencil. Beneath the drawing he had written '*I love what I know and I know what I love.*' For a moment Chirag wondered as to where Sandip might be now.

The pathway was bumpier than Sandip, Christen and Alberto had expected. Moreover, it was tortuous, leading upwards. Though there was a chill in the wind they all three had already sweated profusely. It was the fourth day on their way to Valley of Flowers and everyday they were trekking for no less than ten hours. Last evening they had reached Rudraprayag and this morning heading towards Karnaprayag. The trek was physically exhausting but offered a due compensation. The enigmatic beauty of the foothills of Himalayas was breathtaking. Another thing that caught Sandip's attention was cluster of small hutments, made of stone, dotted the slopes of the hill. Outside the huts busy mothers could be seen giving a bath to their naked children, men smoking *bidi*, sitting on a piece of stone with an enviable contentment on their face. But the most heart-warming thing was the bunch of Grehwal children who gathered near the trekkers, sprinting out from their huts, and waved at them. They were well-versed in uttering a few sentences like, 'Wish u a happy journey'......'Welcome to our village'....'Enjoy your trekking'...'Do you want water?'.

Soon the trekkers understood that such greetings were made with some expectation. Christen was the first one to feel it. She called one of those small girls and tied her scarf to her hair. It's effect was astonishing as no less than ten children surrounded them at once. They were all looking at the trekkers, chiefly at the white-skinned couple, with hope and expectation. Alberto's quick wit helped them deal with the predicament right away. He distributed two packets of biscuits among the children and they dispersed, somewhat disappointedly as they had expected some exclusive gifts for each of them.

'Good riddance,' said Alberto with a hearty smile.

'Do you have many more packets of biscuits?' asked Rocky Sherpa. He was visibly amused by Alberto's biscuits-distribution.

'I think three to four more packets are left. But why?'

'Because we would encounter many more bunches of children on our way,' Rocky smiled genially.

'But I have only one more scarf and I need it for myself,' said Christen, affecting seriousness.

They all smiled. Late at that afternoon they stopped for a while after trekking for a couple of hours at a stretch. They settled on a huge boulder when christen went behind a nearby bush to relieve herself. Alberto removed his shoe and lied on the stone.

'It's so relaxing,' said he, looking at the azure sky where whitish clouds were scudding peacefully.

He got a cigarette out of his pocket, lit it and puffed at it twice. Meanwhile Christen came back. She sat on her haunches and took the cigarette from Alberto.

'So far am I from home yet so much at home I feel here. This place gives me a feeling that I was here before. A strange feeling that I cannot explain,' said Alberto in a distant voice.

Sandip smiled and so, too, did Alberto.

'We have to cover another four kilometres before sunset. So please...' Rocky Sherpa instructed them.

Sandip had already come to know that Rocky Sherpa was not his actual name. Being a great admirer of Sylvester Stallon and his Rocky and Rambo series Brijmohan Singh introduced himself as Rocky and Sherpa was an appellation for knowing the foothills of the Himalayas very well.

They were about to get up when something caught all their attention. It was the most fascinating chirping of a bird they had ever heard. Involuntarily they all passed a curious searching glance around them, hoping a catch a glimpse of the singing bird. Above them branches of the tall trees joined together from both sides of the pathway. Shafts of afternoon sunlight were coming down through the gaps in the canopy of the leaves. There were no human beings except for them in the immediate vicinity. There was an eerie sound of the rustling of the leaves accentuated by the soulful calls from an unknown bird.

'Do you know which bird is this?' Alberto asked Rocky in a whisper as though he did not want the bird to fly away.

'Yeah,' Rocky replied simply. 'In our language we call it Disha.'

'Deesa, nice name,' said Christen.

'Do you want to see it?' Rocky asked Christen playfully.

'Yeah,' said Christen and Alberto in unison. 'But how?'

Rocky smiled. He was happy to get an opportunity to display one of his rare skills.

'See,' Rocky began in a conspiratorial tone. 'I would try to bring her somewhere closer but please remain silent if you really want to see her for a long moment. She is a multihued bird and such birds are usually very fearful.'

'How do you know it is a *she*?' Alberto asked curiously.

'It is a she, calling for her mate,' Rocky said a bit irritably and placing his forefinger on his lips signalled they three to remain silent and if possible, motionless.

He then blocked his mouth with his cupped hands and awaited the next call from Disha.

They all waited for a minute when each second seemed like eternity and then there was an enchanting cry from the bird. But this time no sooner had the bird's cry stopped than there was another melodious cry as if a response to the bird's calling for its mate.

Speechless and mouth agape Sandip, Alberto and Christen looked at Rocky Sherpa, who was taking the preparation to respond the next call from the bird. A few rounds of cries went on between the Disha and her human mate for a few minutes before the bird could locate its mate and then suddenly it became silent.

'It is coming,' Rocky said in a muffled voice.

They three waited eagerly, muscles tightened, face expectant and breathings soundless. And they saw it. It flew almost silently and now perching on a branch of a tree in front of them.

It had a long colourful large beck with a relatively smaller body. The most mesmerizing thing about it was its multicoloured bright feathers which were slightly puffed up in the present condition.

The bird sat in silence for a few minute, looking for her mate and then, without finding him, gave a cry again. Sandip felt that there was an element of desperation in her call. But this time her mate did not respond. She continued her futile effort for a few more times before, dejected and dispirited, she flew away.

Alberto and Christen were very pleased by the whole drama enacted before them and were surprised to find a sign of disappointment on Rocky's face.

'What happens, buddy?' Alberto asked Rocky.

'Feeling bad. I should not have done it,' said Rocky, somewhat regretfully.

'Done what?' Alberto raised his eyebrows.

'In a way I have deceived a Disha. We call it Disha because in Garwal region we believe that this bird shows us the right direction and way when we are lost in a jungle. Disha means direction. It is a rare bird. I should not have done it. I have broken a bird's trust. I am feeling bad now.' Rocky remained silent and repentant.

Looking at Rocky a strange feeling came to Sandip. This simple boy, who was no more than his age, was conscience-stricken for pretending to be a bird's mate just for a few minutes, whereas in his hostel, office everyday he met so many selfish pretenders whose conscience never smote them.

As they continued walking Sandip said to Rocky after a while, 'I am very lucky to meet you. They say travelling is educative and I think it is only because we can meet people like you who have such a big heart.'

Rocky did not reply but shook Sandip's hand gratefully.

Next morning on reaching office Akash realized that it was not only he who had watched Chirag last night. As the boys assembled in the training centre before lunch Chirag's sexual escapade was the topic of discussion. In Chirag's absence the discussion was in full swing.

'Nowadays everybody is bloody screwing, yaar, except for us,' said Shashank. 'Chirag getting a girl to the hostel, Sujata is hanging out with Jasvinder. Aparna is a vapid sot. We have no girls, man. My hand is tired of doing all mechanical job every night.'

'You and your roommate can do it for each other, just for a change,' someone suggested.

'We are not bloody gay like you. Besides Swapnil Sharma is my roommate. Every night he reads Hanuman Challisa before sleeping and every morning I wake up by his irritable mantra chantings, *yaar*.'

'How do you know Sujata is hanging out with Jasvinder?' asked Rakesh Mohite. He was a studious type.

'I think most of us know it because we do not go to our room and sit to study just after coming from office,' Shashank said tersely. He did not like Rakesh.

'It is very bad of Sujata. She belongs to our batch. We should have been given the first preference, but see, she is fooling around with that Jasvinder fellow,' said one.

'That's life, dude,' said another boy sympathetically. 'Do not worry, every dog has his day.'

'*Arre yaar*, let's go to canteen. We are already late by ten minutes. I do not think any chicken leg piece is left for us,' said Sujit, consulting his watch.

The name of chicken leg piece made all the boys move.

Akash did not feel like taking lunch in the canteen and headed towards the factory gate. He had already taken to a small restaurant near Chembur Camp. Vaishno Punjab was it's name and it offered delicious Punjabi dishes at a very reasonable rate. After coming out of factory gate Akash looked around expectantly, hoping to get a lift soon. It was not the time for Sardarji to come, thought Akash and remembered to complete the story on a lonesome person.

Now a motorbike stopped near him. A middle aged tall man with an engaging smile called him. He was wearing ICL's uniform.

'Where do you want to go?' asked the tall man. There was a kind of calmness in his eyes.

'Chembur Camp,' said Akash.

'Sit,' said the man. His voice was soft.

Once they reached Chembur Camp the gentleman stopped the bike near a traffic signal and Akash got off the bike.

'Thanks,' said Akash, smiling affably.

'Have you joined ICL recently?'

'Yeah, I am an engineer trainee. Akash Chatterjee is my name.'

'Daniel Fernandez,' said the man and extended his hand to Akash.

Akash shook his hand and asked, 'Do not you stay in ICL Township?'

'No, I stay in Bhandup, Kamalsagar Housing society, but planning to shift to ICL colony soon. Nowadays I am finding the commuting from Bhandup very taxing.'

'Then we would keep meeting,' said Akash casually.

'Yeah, hope so,' said Daniel and started the bike.

Nice man, thought Akash as he was entering Vaishno Punjab. Not in his wildest dream did Akash imagine that one day he would be deeply connected to Daniel's family.

They were on their way back from Valley of Flowers to Ghangria where they would spend the night. Sandip was walking in silence and on and off looking back over his shoulder, slowing down his pace.

'Do not feel like leaving this place?' Christen asked him.

'The best place ever I have visited. But it happens to me quite often. Whenever I like a place, parting from it is always a heart-rending experience.'

'You are not the only one to have such an experience, buddy. It happened to us too. Last year we were in Maldives for more than a month. Every day there passed like a dream. We went for long walks to the villages and the villagers often welcomed us with tea and biscuits. When we left Maldives we had a painful feeling as though somebody was cutting our umbilical cords, separating us from our mothers permanently. Yet now we often sit together and watch those photographs on laptop together. It is so nostalgic,' said Alberto.

'In Maldives the old women have a notion that if you take a baby on your lap and the baby pees on you it means the baby has accepted you as its own,' Christen began reminiscently. 'Every afternoon as we went for a long walk to the nearest village, Mandu, I used to take kids on my lap. Almost every afternoon one or two children peed on my skirt or jeans. It was such a sweet feeling.'

'You can enjoy this sweet feeling again, as many times as you want,' said Sandip, smiling at Christen and Alberto, 'just get married and have a child.'

'No marriage is on the cards. Forget about children,' replied Alberto.

'We cannot afford to live a life the way we wish to with a kid,' said Christen. 'We already have our travelling plans for the next two years provided we come into some money.' Christen gave a candid smile.

Rocky Sherpa was waiting for an opportunity to speak for some time. Now he asked Alberto, 'Have you been to Switzerland?'

'Yeah, I did, but long back. May be I was fifteen at that time. But why?'

Rocky dithered for a moment and asked, 'Is Switzerland and its snow-clad mountain more beautiful than our Valley of Flowers and the Himalaya?' Earnestness was evident in his voice. Alberto remained silent for a long moment.

'Switzerland is small. It is very beautiful and clean. But your Himalaya is Himalaya, brother. It is incomparable and so is your valley of Flowers.'

A proud smile came to Rocky's lips. Late in the afternoon they reached Ghangria. It was a very small place and throbbing with life. From every second shops and eateries devotional Punjabi songs were emanating. Every second tourist here was a Sikh for a six kilometre trail from Ghangria took one to HemKund, identified as the spot where the Sikh guru Govind Singh had meditated in a former life.

After a bath they walked for a while and then had a quick dinner. It was hardly 9 pm when spine-chilling silence came over Ghangria as though everybody had retired early tonight. Sandip tried to read the Valley of Flowers by Frank S. Snythe for sometime but felt a deep urge to go out and walk alone. Who knows he may not visit this place again, thought he. When he went out from his room it was half past nine. He zipped the jacket upright to the neck and tied the hood tightly. He slipped his hands into his jackets pocket and walked in a slow and a languorous pace.

The sky was clean and a crescent moon flooding everything around with a golden glow. There was not a single living being on the narrow pathway, partly covered with stony soil. Small shops, closed for the night, stood on both sides of the road looked vulnerable once one looked at the mountain, girdled this sleepy village.

As Sandip walked he could hear his footfalls distinctly. Occasionally it gave him an uncanny feeling that somebody was following him. On and off he looked back, over his shoulder to ensure that no one was behind him.

Suddenly the silence of the night was shattered by a sharp screech of a bird as if Sandip had uninvitedly invaded its region. The sudden surprise rooted Sandip to the spot as he tried to see the bird. The bird gave another cry; a less impatient one than the previous one. Sandip decided not to budge even an inch and strained his eyes to see the bird. Wings fluttered and then he saw it, sitting on bamboo fencing not very far from him.

Sandip took no time to understand that it was a *Disha*. He gazed at it unblinkingly, remembering what Rocky had said about this bird. Yes, in a way, he too was a traveller who had lost his way. He wanted to travel all his life, meet new people, see new places, and savour new foods. He never craved for money, fame or social status, nor did he crave for a family. He knew how difficult it would be to lead such a life with a full-fledged job. How would he live without travelling? Sandip looked at the D*isha,* hoping that in this unknown place, at this odd hour, it would show him the right direction.

The bird pecked at the bamboo, gracefully turned its neck both sides and let out a cry. Sandip observed how different its cry now was from its cry for its mate.

Now the *Disha* flapped its wings noisily, flew from one tree to another randomly in the search for something and disappeared all of a sudden.

Most probably, the message for me, thought Sandip, is to travel aimlessly from one place to another in the search for beauty and then one day disappear from the hustle and bustle of life happily.

It was the most serious after-office-discussion they had since they had joined ICL. There was a solemn expression on all their faces expect for that of Sandip, who, surprisingly, joined this afternoon's discussion. They were on the verge of completing their training period of one year but by now only eight trainees were left. Most of the boys got through Infosys, Wipro and TCS and two through Satyam Software.

Akash had also appeared the written tests for IT companies but could not clear a single written test. He was disheartened but not as much as other boys were.

'In a few years there will be a yawning gap between the boys who left ICL and us. Man, if they go to the US for an offshore project even for a year they would save no less than ten lakhs. If we remain here it would take us no less than six to seven years to save that much. Just imagine,' said Shashank Bhatti

'The chief thing is that their life style would change completely. What is more, they would get more opportunities to use their intelligence,' said another boy.

'But one thing is very strange, *yaar*,' began Sandip as all the boys paid heed to him. It was because Sandip spoke very little and most importantly, whatever he said was his original thoughts although sometimes other boys found them provocative and impractical. 'Until none of the boys among us got through any IT companies, never had we compared their lifestyle with ours. Never did we think that we were paid less and felt the pinch. But now all of a sudden we are downhearted because we are comparing ourselves with the boys from IT companies.'

'But unless until we compare ourselves with our fellow mates we would never know what we really deserve,' said Shashank.

'But comparison does not pay in anyway, *yaar*, apart from giving unnecessary headache and heartache. Besides, fortune will smile on all of us. It is merely a matter of time,' said Sandip.

'See the crux of the matter is that as we are all engineers and have to do a job for a living. So it is always advisable that we should strive for the best job,' said another boy.

'But some of us may have knack for something else. No doubt as an engineer we can get a better jobs but what if someone of us have a talent for something, say, painting or singing. Who knows if he hones his talent for that creative field, one day he may make a decent living from it,' said Akash in a roundabout way, without telling anyone of his dream of becoming a writer. At once all the boys looked at him.

'I do not know anyone from our batch who has an exceptional talent for anything. Are you talking about yourself anyway, Akash?' asked a boy sarcastically.

'No, no,' protested Akash vehemently. 'It was just a general statement.'

Once the discussion was over and all the boys except for Akash and Sandip dispersed, Sandip looked at Akash.

'I have a gut feeling as to why you made that vague statement on talent and all that,' said Sandip.

'Why?' breathed Akash. He could not remember ever telling Sandip about his dream of pursuing a literary career.

'I think you want to be writer,' Sandip said plainly.

'How do you know?'

'I know because I like you.'

'Do you think I can write well? I mean good enough to make a living,' Akash asked earnestly.

'I do not know whether you can make a living from it. But I know for certain that you would write with love and sincerity. Because you love people,' Sandip gave a small smile.

'Thank you, brother,' Akash held Sandip's hand.

2

A fit of persistent cough from the adjacent room woke her up. She checked her cell phone. It was 1.30 pm. She got up and walked on tiptoes to the neighbouring room. Her parents were sleeping there. Her father's protective hand was on her mother. She was cuddling up against him.

Dada must have coughed in his sleep, thought she. Through the open window a sliver of moonlight was entering her parents' bedroom but it was enough for her to see her parents' face. Her father's face was calm and collected. His mouth was slightly open and he was snoring.

Her mother was a small woman and looked like a little girl lying next to her father. She was fair with regular features and as she inhaled deeply her nostrils swelled slightly. She wore a *bindi* unlike other catholic woman she knew.

A surge of love overcame her suddenly as she saw her parents sleeping lovingly, completely as peace with each other. But then a sense of emptiness filled her as she remembered her spat with her mother this evening. How difficult it was for her to make her mother understand something that was so obvious to her. Why could not she understand that her daughter was bad at pretending, that she could not hide her feelings or speak something that she really did not mean just to earn a personal benefit? Well, such attributes might be the sign of maturity, might help one win the battle of life. But what was the point of winning such a battle if it made one hate oneself.

She knew as to why her mother was always after her to make her more careerist and ambitious. She wanted her daughter's life to be success story like that of her siblings' children. So downhearted was she once she knew that her daughter had scored only 65% in B. Com.

'How will you get a job? Listen to me and join a software course for six months. You would get a decent job,' said her worried mother.

She remained silent. Career, job, competition – the whole thing seemed so daunting to her.

'Did you hear what I said?' asked her mother, raising her voice.

'Yes, Mummy,' said she.

'Then why do not you respond?' the mother demanded an answer.

'Give me a week to think, Mummy,' she said.

'All your cousin brothers and sisters are doing well in life. They have respectable jobs and are well-paid. And my daughter has scored only 65%. What would I say to your Glancy and Kathy aunty?'

'Say whatever you wish. I do not owe an explanation to them for anything,' she said as anger welled up within her. 'And if at all I do not get a job I would join a Call Centre. I would not ask anyone for any financial help.'

'Do not ever think of joining a Call Centre,' yelled her mother. 'I know what girls and boys do there.'

Her mother stopped and studying her critically for a long moment began again, 'If you take a little more effort you would look more presentable.' Her voice softened, 'I told you to apply sliced cucumber for those dark circles beneath your eyes but have you ever listened to me? You bite your nails; they are never properly manicured. See, life is no more as it was thirty or forty years back. Now everywhere there is a competition and you have to be a part of it to survive. If you style yourself with a little taste you will look beautiful, take my words for it.'

'I am already beautiful, Mummy. If someone does not find me beautiful it is his or her problem,' said she, fighting back her tears. It was not the first time her mother hinted that she did not approve her look.

Her mother came to her, walking across the room in long strides. 'When someone is so determined to remain stupid even Jesus could not help her. And you are one of such silly girls,' said her mother and stormed off.

She heaved a deep sigh and went to the drawing room where her younger brother was sleeping on a divan. He was 16 and was unusually fat for his age. Yet in his sleep he looked like a small child. His hair was curly and golden. For a moment she felt like running her fingers through his hair. Yet now he applied Johnson and Johnson baby powder and she loved the smell his body gave off. Her brother was the apple of her parents' eyes. Her mother was never tired of preparing delicacies for him. Everyday as he returned from school she rushed to open the door. He was unusually fair and a little exposure to sunlight turned his cheeks red. Her mother would dab at his face with a wet towel, asking him all trivial questions, which spoke of her motherly concern and affection.

She did not remember her mother ever treating her with so much affection and care once she had returned from school.

As she retired to her room in silence a sense of self-doubt filled her. She was not good-looking. Her academic career was never above average, in fact much worse than that of all her cousin brothers and sisters. For a moment she felt herself unwanted as though her parents and her brother, John, constituted a perfect family without her.

Tears welled up in her eyes. She stood by the window, resting her hands on the windowsill. It was a small room and had enough space for a single bed and a study table. She wiped her eyes with her left forearm and looked out through the window. She is unwanted, unsuccessful in everybody's terms and undesirable in a way. Then what was the point of living? thought she and looked out to seek and answer from the silence and the darkness of the night. And it was the first time she saw him! The wall clock from her parents' room struck two.

It was hardly a couple of weeks since they had shifted to the leafy township of ICL from Bhandup. Her father was tired of travelling everyday from Bhandup

She hid herself behind the curtain lest he might see her looking at him and observed him carefully. He seemed to be completely lost in his own world, totally oblivious to everything around him. He was walking slowly with an enviable delicious languor as though no worry of the world could penetrate his state of ecstasy.

He was of medium height with curly hair and an oval face. He was healthy but not stout. Though she strained to see his face the streetlights were not generous enough to quench her desire. She, however, stood by the window and watched him walking along the narrow road that ran along the series of six storey buildings, named after famous Indians who were now rather a part of myth than history. They were on the third floor of Aryabhatt and on the right side of that six-storey tower were two more apartment buildings, namely, Shree Krishna and Chanakya.

He must be staying in one of these buildings; she did a mental note. Does he work in ICL or it is his father, she wondered. But if he works in ICL why is he out so late at night. Most probably he works in shift.

He was now right beneath her window, ambling towards Shree Krishna. He wore a denim jeans and a half-sleeved turtle neck T-shirts. He was fair and black suit him well. If black is his favourite colour it would the first common choice between us, she told herself and leaned against the window to watch him from more closely.

At the very instant her father gave a violent sneeze, breaking the silence of the night. Instinctively he looked up. She hid behind the curtain in a flash. But before that she succeeded in stealing a glimpse of his face. He had a broad forehead, big nose and thin lips. But the most beautiful thing on his face was his eyes. They were long and limpid with a strange glint in them. A shiver of curiosity and excitement ran down her spine. Now she came out from behind the curtain and watched him retracing his steps towards Shree Krishna. She could not see exactly in which building he stayed as all the buildings were in the same line.

She, however, did not go to bed immediately, harbouring a faint hope that he might come for another stroll. But he did not. Presently a bunch of new thoughts flashed across her mind, elbowing out the vexing thoughts which had weighed on her mind just a few minutes back.

What if he does not stay here, but has come on a vacation to one of his relatives place? No, it cannot be. He seems to be completely at ease here. He cannot be a visitor; her chain of thoughts was active. Well, if he is staying here why he is out for a walk at wee hours. Most probably he is preparing for some competitive examination like CAT or GRE. What if he leaves the township in near future to pursue further study? A queer fear filled her as she thought so. Then an absent smile came to her lips. How strange her mind was. It was scared of losing something that it did not even possess.

She went to bed very late at night and early in the morning when the golden sun glided up to the indigo sky and the birds were chipping merrily, heralding a new day, a new beginning, she had a sweet dream.

She saw him walking late at night. The road was well-lit but deserted and strewn with leaves. He was playfully kicking the foliages on and off. He seemed to be so much in peace with himself. She then saw herself walking towards him with determined stride. He stopped as she reached near him. She looked up at him and introduced herself, 'Hi, I am Maria, Maria Fernandez.' Her voice throbbed with love and joy of meeting him. He smiled at her as if he had been expecting her to come and meet him. 'Myself....,' his voice faded away.

Her sleep broke as a small sparrow twittered, sitting on the windowsill next to her bed. It's song appeared to Maria as a challenge to come out of the daydream and face the real world with courage and determination.

Thunderstruck, Akash remained silent for a while, looking at his laptop screen with a vacant expression on his face. It was half an hour past midnight and just now he had opened his Gmail inbox. There were two unread messages in Inbox and as he read the subject of the first mail his heart escaped a bit. It read: your proposal. The sender was woodpecker publishers. He clicked the mail open. It was a three-lined mail written in a very formal way. It said:

Dear Mr. Akash Chatterjee,

We were very happy to receive your proposal. We went through it and loved it. But, unfortunately, it does not fit our recent publishing requirement. Our best wishes are with you for placing your proposal to the editorial department of the other publishers.

Regards,

The editorial team, Woodpecker publishers.

Akash read and reread the mail as he felt that something within him was dying, withering away. He signed out his Gmail account, took a shutdown and snapped his laptop close. For a moment he did not know what to do. So certain had he been that his proposal would be accepted by Woodpecker publishers and that soon they would ask for his complete manuscript that a prompt rejection from the publisher dealt a blow to him. He then opened the laptop and started it again as a flicker of hope crossed his mind. He might have misread the message. He had a very faint hope that the content of the mail from the Woodpecker publishers might have changed in the span of last five minutes. But, unfortunately, miracle did not happen. The mail was exactly the same.

Suddenly a sense of betrayal swept over him as though he was a victim of injustice. Why did they reject my work? Each story I sent to them had a surprise ending. They were all different from each other. And above all, all the stories were about life and its beauty.

So much time had he devoted in writing and editing Random Thoughts – a collection of his short stories. So much he loved the stories as they were all about ordinary people with an extraordinary beautiful mind.

He left his flat at Shree Krishna at a quarter to two. It was no more than four months since he had shifted to ICL Township from the hostel. Sandip and Chirag were in Chanakya which was on the right side of Shree Krishna. Akash reached the main road in front of his building and walked past Aryabhatt, which was on the left side of Shree Krishna.

What should he do now? Should he send the proposal to the other publishers or sit in silence, accepting his defeat? What if all the leading publishers of the country rejected his work? Akash was lost in his maze of thoughts yet he had a strange feeling that somebody was watching him with curiosity. Several times he looked behind but there was no one in the vicinity in the dead of the night. Quite often Akash went out for a late night walk and sometimes even up to Star Guest House, hoping that the quiet of the night would help him devise more stories. His working in shift afforded him more time to read and write. Sandip and Chirag, who were on the same floor of Chanakya, were also in shift and they both used their spare time in what they were best at.

As time passed by Akash experienced a kind of courage within him. What if a publisher has rejected his first collection of short stories? He could work on another collection of short stories. A long stroll brought a new ray of hope to his disappointed heart.

Once he was walking back to his flat he heard someone sneezing as he reached in front of Aryabhatt. He stopped for a moment and looked up. Suddenly he felt somebody standing near the window on the third floor stepped back and hid behind the curtain.

This flat was vacant for last few months. Somebody must have shifted here recently, thought Akash, walking towards Shree Krishna while he felt that a shadowy figure was again watching him.

He stopped in front of his building and looked up. He was on first floor and except for his flat in only one flat light was glowing. Jasvinder Singh stayed there and Sujata came to his place very often. Akash had heard that they would get married soon. He went to his flat and closed the door. Next day he had an evening shift and he could take the liberty of sleeping as late as he wanted. Before going to bed he thought of writing a mail to Woodpecker Publisher demanding his manuscript back. However, he did not need to write an email as next day at midday he received a courier, containing his proposal and a rejection letter from Woodpecker Publisher.

Maria felt exhilarated as she saw him again. She had not expected to be rewarded so early. Soon her heart leaped with joy of many reasons. He was wearing ICL officers' uniform so least this was certain that he was not a guest at someone's place. He was available at one of her neighbouring buildings and she could feast her eyes on him everyday.

Another thing she observed was that last night he had seemed to be aloof and distant, lost in his own world. But this afternoon in broad daylight she found him lively and animated young man who was really not unapproachable.

She checked her watch. It was 1.50 pm. Most probably he was going to an evening shift, in that case he should return from office at 10.00 pm, she thought and did a mental calculation. Her parents were staunch Catholic and every evening both the siblings had to sit with their parents for a long rosary followed by the reading of at least one chapter from the Holy Bible. However, such long spiritual meetings often pushed their dinnertime to 9.30 to 10.00 pm. and Daniel always made sure that they all four had their dinner together.

This afternoon as Maria saw him, down her building, sitting on his new Pulser motorbike, talking with a three-year-old boy from the ground floor, a queer fear struck her. What if she cannot see him while he comes back from office, thought she and suddenly her mind revolted against the hour-long Bible-reading. At any cost she must make herself free before ten tonight. If required, she would tell her mother that she did not feel like eating and retire to her room before ten.

She wished she could see him from closer but for now she was careful not to be seen. The little boy insisted on sitting on the bike for a ride while he tried to convince the boy that he was getting late for office.

'Tomorrow I will take you to Star guesthouse. It's a promise,' said he in a crisp voice. 'But now you have to spare me, *Beta.*'

The little boy thought for a while and then let him go, stepping aside from in front of his motorbike. He kick-started the motorbike and pressing the clutch put the bike into gear. The bike glided forward almost soundlessly.

'Bye Akash uncle,' shouted the little boy and suddenly Maria felt grateful to the little boy. So Akash was his name. Akash looked back over his shoulder and waved at the little boy. For an instant Maria felt an irrepressible yearning to wave back at him. She saw his eyes again. They were large and beautiful but this afternoon she observed something more about him. His fingers were very long and artistic.

She sat on the bed, mind clouded with thoughts. He looked studies type. What would she talk to him if one day she got an opportunity? What if he found her a bore? But at first she must make a whole-hearted attempt to introduce herself to him, no matter how daunting it might appear. Yes, she would not do anything in a hurry otherwise he might think that she was desperate to tag along with him.

Why has she suddenly taken to Akash, Maria asked herself, is it because of her sense of depression and the feeling of being unwanted makes her feel the need of someone who would feel and understand her? If so, then it is merely a passing infatuation. Whenever she felt full of life again she might not need Akash anymore. Maria remained silent for a long time while an absent smile made its way to her lips and then spread around her face. No, it is love, not an infatuation, she told herself. She did not know how deep it was but she had not doubt that it was love. Once her mind demanded a logical explanation for this sudden falling in love her heart failed to give a satisfactory answer but repeatedly declared, in its language of silence, that it was nothing but love.

Now she stood by the window and watched the little boy playing down while his grandfather chasing after him with a bowl of food. The old man was no less than seventy-five years of age but quite agile for his age. The bowl he carried contained two pieces of fried fish and it took him no less than half an hour to cajole his grandson into eating the fried fish.

'See if you do not eat food I would ask Akash uncle not to give you

Dairy milk anymore. Did not he tell you to have food on time if you want a ride on bike?' said the grandfather in Marathi. Like an obedient pupil the little boy opened his mouth while the grandfather wasted no time to place the last morsel of food into his mouth. The little boy chewed at the fish for a minute, contemplatively. He then went near a roadside plant and pulling his small pants down up to his knee, he peed, wetting his pants partly. His grandfather watched him urinating with evident pride. He walked across the road to him, helped him lift his small pants up and, then bending down planted a kiss on his cheek. The little boy rewarded his grandfather with a cherubic smile. He then took the boy on his lap and went towards his flat.

Maria enjoyed herself watching the deep bond of love between the grandfather and the little boy. But she was happy for another reason, too. She felt that through the little boy and the grandfather she could achieve a breakthrough in meeting Akash. But first of all she must get a Dairy milk for the boy this afternoon.

The doorbell rang. Her mother had come home. She had got a job of a schoolteacher in St. Sebastian's, a convent school, as soon as they shifted to ICL colony. Maria opened the door, expecting her mother to start grumbling about her staying home all day, doing nothing constructive.

Her mother entered the drawing room and gazed at her for a long moment. Somewhat surprised, Maria asked, 'What happened, Mummy?'

'Did you go anywhere out?' asked her mother, Helen.

'No,' replied Maria, more surprised than before. 'But why?'

'Because I see some change in your face. I cannot say what exactly it is but I can feel it.'

'What change, Mummy?'

'You look unusually happy for a girl who is lazing away throughout the day when she should study or earn a living,' said her mother sternly.

Though her mother's statement provoked anger within her, for now, she was determined not to lose her cool.

That afternoon while Maria was going out her mother asked, 'Where are you going?'

'Apna Bazar, do you want anything?'

'Check if they keep chicken nuggets. Got cash?'

'Yeah, anything else?'

'Two packets of Parle – G. What are you getting for yourself?'

'Nothing. There is a small cute boy on the ground floor. I thought of getting a packet of dairy Milk for him.'

'I know them. His name is Atharva. They are basically from Satara. Atharva has an elder sister, Ankita. Their father works in Accounts department with your father and the mother with LIC.'

'How do you know so much about them?' asked an astonished Maria.

'One must know one's neighbour. They will come to your help before your relatives. That's why I always suggest you become more social.'

'Well, Mummy, this buying a Dairy Milk for Atharva may help me know my neighbour better,' said Maria with an enigmatic smile and left the flat. Once she was out of the building the afternoon sunlight kissed her, infusing hope and expectation into her.

Why did she lie? He would have gifted her a cell phone if she asked for one. Why did she devise such an ugly scheme to get a cell phone from him? thought the wounded Chirag, lying on his bed, his head pillowed on his arms. There was an aching emptiness in his heart. He had been deceived, cheated and, what was more, by someone whom he had trusted. In his twenty-four years of life he had slept with no less than a dozen of girls. But never had he gone to bed with anyone without a mutual consent.   Besides, he had never wanted any girl to have it with him for any tangible benefit; because such an act could be attributed to prostitution.

He remembered all the girls with whom he had been in relationship and later for some trivial reason they broke up. Most of the time over a period of time they lost interest in each other or any one of them took a fancy to someone else but such separation had never hurt Chirag. None the girls had ever schemed against him. He knew for certain whether Kritika apologised or not he would never feel like talking to her again. From this afternoon Kritika made her way to that list of girls who were a part of his past now.

He switched on the laptop and opened his facebook account. In no time he removed her name from his friends' list. He checked his account for a few more minutes. Aniket Mahapatra had loaded the photographs of his recent trip to Niagara Falls. Aniket had joined Infosys more than a year back and was now in the US for an offshore project. He was about to logout but then thought of checking for Sandip's account again. He typed Sandip's name and surname but Sandip had no account in Facebook, at least in his real name.

He was not on speaking terms with Sandip anymore. Once they completed their training period his communication with Sandip narrowed down to *hi* and *hello*. Incidentally, they both had been allotted flat on the same floor of Chanakya. Soon after they had their own flats both stopped talking to each other. But though Chirag disliked Sandip he was curious about him. Sandip's holding himself aloof, talking extremely less, travelling all alone for weeks often made Chirag jealous of him. However, he could never lower himself to ask their mutual friends like Akash about Sandip to garner information on him. So on and off he searched for Sandip on facebook but every time his search gave no fruitful results. Apparently Sandip had not opened an account on facebook or twitter. He kept the laptop on the table near his bed and looked down through the open window, remembering his meeting with Kritika and her mother last Sunday at Shopper's Stop, Ghatkoper.

'Wow, what a pleasant surprise,' Kritika beamed with joy. 'But what brought you here? You do not shop from Shopper's Stop usually.'

'Looking for a perfumed candle; a friend of mine told me that they have it in Shopper's Stop,' said Chirag with a smile, appreciating Kritika's ravishing beauty.

'Listen,' said Kritika, lowering her voice to a whisper. 'See, Mamma is standing there. I will introduce you to her but tell her that you work with me.'

'Ok, but why?' asked Chirag, placing his hand on Kritika's back, feeling the hook of her bra with the tip of his fingers.

'You horny bastard, we are not in your bedroom now. Now be on your best behaviour and follow me.'

After the brief introduction Kritika left Chirag and her mother alone and went to Solitaire section.

Chirag talked to her mother, haltingly, for a few minutes, when her cell phone buzzed. She reached into her purse and got in out. To his utter surprise, Chirag discovered that it was the same cell phone Ktritika claimed to have lost. Within no time he understood that Kritika had lied to him, devised an ugly ploy just to get a new cell phone from him. Yet he asked her mother, to remove the last vestige of his doubt, once she had finished talking on cell phone.

'Is it the same cell phone Kritika used to use?'

'Yeah, she gave it to me since she got a new one. But I am not yet accustomed to this touch screen thing,' replied Kritika's mother.

Suddenly Chirag experienced a searing pain within him. He gave Kritika a long stare. She was standing a little distance off, examining a solitaire minutely. Even five minutes back her curvy body would have sent him into a maze of wild imagination but now he felt her like a venomous snake that breathed out poison.

'Does she work well in her office, beta? I am often worried about her as weeks after weeks she works on night shift,' suddenly Kritika's mother asked Chirag, assuming that Kritika and Chirah worked together. There was an air of anxiety about her as if she was nervous about Kritika and her future. This simple question made Chirag feel how much care his mother would have taken of him had she been alive now. Most probably, in that case his life would not have trodden such a bumpy road.

He gave a dry smile to Krititka's mother and said, 'Don't worry, aunty, Kritika is a very smart girl. She can get away with anything.' He then excused himself and left without meeting Kritika. Once he reached the parking lot to collect his Royal Enfield he was at a loss.

There was a call from Kritika. How on earth could one imagine looking at this beautiful face of this girl that she is a cheat?, thought Chirag and received her call.

'Where are you?' asked Kritika, her voice was impatient.

'At the parking lot,' replied Chirag impassively.

'Are you leaving?'

'Yeah.'

Silence for a long moment and then her voice changed.

'Why?'

'Because my work is done.'

'Why are you speaking so frostily?'

This time silence on Chirag's side. 'I am happy that you gave your mamma the cell that you had lost,'

Chirag said at last.

Again a long silence.

'So?' asked Kritika in a hushed voice.

'Nothing, I curse myself for being gullible enough to trust in you.'

'I will phone you soon, dearie. Mamma is awaiting me,' said Kritika in a placatory way and cut the phone.

Chirag got a call from her that evening but did not receive the call. Another call from her just after two minutes. In the next 30 minutes his cell phone was reading 12 missed calls. Then came an SMS from her.

I am ashamed of what I did. Please forgive and forget.

No response from Chirag. Next message came after fifteen minutes.

Don't stop talking to me for my small folly.

Again no response from Chirag. No message for next two hours. Then came the third text message.

I m free 2morrow. Which shift do u hav? Plz replace dose stinky pillow covers. Luv u.

Chirag read and reread the message. He knew very well what she really tried to imply. But he doubted he would ever feel excited to sleep with her again.

Next day a few more calls from her went unanswered.

That evening she sent a new SMS. Mamma and me met with an accident. Mamma seriously injured. Wud u care 2 call?

Chirag made no reply. Then came her call from an unknown number. But Chirag cut the call as soon as he understood it was Kritika.

For next few days no call or SMS from Kritika nor did Chirag bother to call her. At last this evening an SMS from her. u d'nt deserve me. i regret wasting my time with u.

But this SMS too failed to provoke Chirag. Lying on his back, with his legs apart, Chirag gazed at the ceiling for a long time. Suddenly he felt like going home at Ghatkoper where everything would be familiar but then a sense of loneliness descended upon him. What would he do going there? His father would be busy at his Clothes' shop and even if he were at home Chirag preferred avoiding him. His elder brother, Vinod, always with a preoccupied mind to augment his business, was in Surat now to strike a deal with Dinesh Bhai, a leading garment merchant from Surat. Chirag was never comfortable in confiding his loneliness to his brother. He thought of phoning Akash who stayed in the neighbouring building. He was a silent type and most importantly, a good and sincere listener. He was a slightly strange fellow but not a bad sort. He picked up the phone to call Akash unsurely but then stopped at once as he could hear Sandip talking with a woman just outside his door.

Curious, he tiptoed to the door and peeped out through the peephole. There was Sandip, wearing a shorts and a casual T-shirt, carrying to large suitcases to his flat. Close to the main door to his flat, standing was a middle-aged woman whose receding hair was plastered to her head. She was of medium height with fair complexion. She wore an ordinary cotton sari, draping herself with the *pallu*.

Her eyes were unusually calm and face serene. She was the mother incarnate. Once both the suitcases were brought in, Sandip held his mother by her shoulder and led her to his flat. The door closed behind them.

Chirag returned to his bed in silence. Rarely had he felt so lonely. He forgot calling Akash and switched on his laptop. In Yahoo Messenger a few friends of him were logged in. He began chatting with them disinterestedly and soon found Maina Barua log in. He had been introduced with this bespectacled girl a few weeks ago in Roseberry, a leading pub in Juhu. Maina worked in PR with Warner Brothers and was full of petty information about film stars, which she purveyed to her listeners with evident interest. For some strange reason she took a fancy to cuss words and in every second sentence loved using words like *fuck, fucking, asshole,* or *oh god, I am fucked.*

She was on the plump side with a voluptuous body. Though Chirag and Maina had exchanged their phone no at once none of them had ever called each other. However, a few days later he received a note from Maina, inviting him to join her friends group in facebook. Since then they often met on line and chatted for a while on casual things.

But this afternoon Chirag started chatting to her to ward off his loneliness and soon understood that Maina was not really unapproachable. He could easily ask her out. But this time he would be cautious not to be an easy prey.

Maria held his hand. It was small enough to disappear within her fist. She checked for lines on his palm. There were no more than four lines on his palm. She pressed his knuckles playfully. They were soft and vulnerable. Suddenly he gave her a mischievous smile and pinched her hand. Maria looked at his cherubic face when a thought struck her. Her purpose of meeting Atharva was to pave the way for her to know Akash but she felt that she had already liked the kid.

'Do you like Dairy Milk?' she asked him.

Atharva gazed at her. His eyelashes were long and the white of his eyes were white. He rocked his head to say yes.

Maria opened her purse and gave him a king-sized packet of Dairy Milk. The boy immediately snatched it from her.

'Say thank you to the aunty,' said Atharva's grandfather, standing near him.

The boy, however, did not bother to thank Maria rather was busy with opening the packet of Dairy Milk.

'Give it to me. I will open it for you,' said Maria to the boy, extending her hand. But Atharva refused to give it to her. He preferred giving the packet to his grandfather who opened it carefully and tore open the golden wrapper inside the packet and gave a cube of Dairy Milk to the little boy. Atharva collected it from his grandfather and started munching it at once. Soon he smeared his lips with melted Dairy Milk.

'What is your name?' asked Athrava's grandfather to Maria.

'Maria Fernandez,' Maria replied.

The old man was wearing a loose cotton shirt and a pair of much-used trousers. His hands were long and veins stood out of his skin. He wore a small amulet, hung from a black thread, loosely tied around his neck. His receding hairline contrasted the dense growth of hair around his ear. As his eyes met Maria's she felt his watery eyes bore despair.

'Where do you stay?' he asked her, taking the boy on his lap, beginning to walk slowly.

'On the third floor,' replied Maria, trying to take Atharva from his grandfather's lap. But the boy refused.

'There is another Christen family in the building. Do you know them?' he asked after sometime.

'Mr. And Mrs. Levin Alves?' asked Maria. She was matching with the old man's languid pace.

'Yeah, they stay on the fourth floor. They are from Hydrabad,' informed Atharva's grandfather.

'I know. They came to our place once. My parents and they go to the same church here.'

'You don't go to church?'

'I do, but not as regularly as my parents go,' said Maria and began after a pause, 'I always see Atharva with you. You feed him lunch, take him out for playing. He is very close to you.'

'As you grow old nothing is a better entertainment than playing with your grandchildren, watching them grow, feeding them with your own hand, changing their dipar, hug them against your heart once they cry,' smiled the old man.

'So you are one of those lucky grandfathers to be with his grandchild.'

'Yeah,' said Atharva's grandfather dryly. 'So long as his father wishes.'

Maria was taken aback by his answer. 'But his father means your son,' she stammered in a way.

'But more than that he is someone's husband. Besides these small 2BHK flats in Bombay do not have much space for old parents. We need them only when we are in need of them but we do not need them when they are in need of us,' said the old man in a pained voice.

Maria remained silent. She wished she could say something to elevate the old man's mood.

'But one day everybody will grow old,' said the old man as though he was speaking with himself.

They had already walked around 100 meters off their building. Now they turned and started walking towards Aryabhatt.

'Does he like Dairy Milk a lot?' asked Maria, hoping to change the topic.

'Yeah, but the blame goes to Akash,' said the old man.

Maria's heart escaped a beat. 'Means?' she asked innocently.

'Akash is a young engineer, staying next to our building, a nice boy. He gives Dairy Milk to Atharva regularly and now he is addicted to it.'

'He is a Maharashtrian?' asked Maria, holding her breath. She was worried not to give an impression that she was curious about Akash.

'No, he is a Bengali. Akash Chatterjee is his name. He shifted to the colony just a few months back. Whenever he meets Athu, Athu demands for a bike ride and the poor fellow obliges him most of the time.'

By this time they reached in front of Aryabhatt.

'Say bye-bye to Maria didi,' the grandfather said to Atharva.

'Ta ta,' mumbled the boy.

'Ta ta, Athu, tomorrow again I will get a Dairy Milk for you,' said Maria smilingly, waving at the boy. She was about to enter the building but felt that someone watching her from the fourth floor. She looked up instinctively. It was Flora Alves, the wife of Levin Alves, looking at her disapprovingly. Maria disliked the Alves couple from the very first day they came to their flat. She found them orthodox and conservative to a fault. Their hatred for other religion was evident and their chief religious activity was to be with the associations which encouraged conversion of poor Hindus into Christens.

Though Mrs. Alves came to Fernandezs' flat a few times, after their first encounter Maria always avoided Flora consciously.

Maria entered her room. She was happy with the progress she had made this afternoon. What was more gratifying that the old man had confirmed her that Akash was nice boy. It gave her new impetus to her endeavour.

Evening wore on heavily as she sat on the bed in her room with *A modern approach to verbal and nonverbal reasoning* by Dr. R. S. Aggarwal without any intention to go through it. The book was a sort of buffer against her mother, who, otherwise, would ask her hundreds of questions on her whiling away the time. Every time she heard the sound of a motorbike passing by, she felt like rushing to the window. What if he came from the office a little early this evening?

Her mother peeped into her room twice. Though she cast her a dubious look, finding her poring over a fat book, did not say anything to her. Rarely had she seen her daughter reading with manifest interest. This evening the bible-reading was curtailed considerably and the dinner was over much before ten. As wall clock struck ten every second passed was like an hour to Maria. As another ten minutes elapsed her excitement and fear mounted up. She was excited as the time to see him was approaching, and yet scared she was for what if he did not come. And at last she saw him. His motorbike passed in front of window in a slow pace, as he had already shifted the gear into neutral.

She now returned to her bed and imagined doing him all the household things that he might do after coming from office. Her imagination conjured up a picture where she saw herself feeding him with her own hand and him eating food with gusto. She closed her eyes as the picture in her mind became more and more vivid and clear, overwhelming her with a soothing feeling. She saw his room minimally furnished. A few uniforms were hanging from pegs at one corner of the room. He slept on a single bed where a few books were scattered around. His pillows were oil-stained. Next to his bed there was a mirror, rested on the windowsill, leaning against the window. Suddenly she felt that the room was inviting her, asking her to spruce it up and make it more habitable for Akash and also for herself. She felt a sense of warmth about her heart.

'Are you sleeping, Maria?' asked her mother sharply. 'It is not yet eleven.'

'No, Mummy, just closed my eyes for a moment,' replied Maria with an inward smile. Then finding her mother frowning at her she wondered whether her mother had ever experienced the sublime beauty of love. She had a handful of female friends who studied with her in the same school and college. Almost all of them had boyfriends with whom they had had physical relationship. Maria had had crush on many boys since her school days but never succeeded in establishing a slender relationship with any boy. She attributed her failure to her small stature and features which were not at all attractive. Yet some latent pride within her always forbade her from smartening herself to be accepted or loved by anyone. No boys had ever proposed her, nor was she courageous enough to tell a boy that she had taken to him.

Yet she wanted to be loved, cherished and needed by someone as life was not worth living otherwise.

A little after midnight when her parents and brother went to bed she switched off the light of her room. But she was wide awake. She harboured a hope that tonight again Akash might come out for a late night walk. She stood by the window, looking outside with expectation and eagerness while minutes ticked away.

And at last when the mists of sleep made her eyes close she heard a light footfall, which, along with the rustling sound of the foliage, reached her ear like a melodious music. Maria rose to her feet in an instant. It was Akash, walking in such a relaxed manner as if he led a completely idyllic life. Maria gazed at him lovingly as a strong desire seized her. She felt like running down the stairs to him. She wanted to walk by him in silence. She had a strange feeling that he would accept her as she was and that she could be exactly herself with him. It was around half past two while drugged with a pleasant dream, Maria fell asleep.

This time Chirag was determined to be cautious about the money he spent on Maina. Standing by the doorway he watched her from behind. She was standing by the window, looking out. They were in his flat on the fourth floor of Chanakya. It was a Saturday afternoon. On the other side of the road two cuckoos were singing merrily, perching on a branch of a Banyan tree. Maina looked at the cuckoos with manifest interest. She stayed in a skyscraper near R-Mall, a famous shopping Mall in Mulund, where tall buildings outnumbered trees. A leafy, verdant township like ICL colony was a picnic spot to her. She liked the place and also the guy with whom she was at present in a relationship. She knew his purpose of inviting her to his flat and she was okay with it.

She wore a long skirt and a sleeveless T-shirt. Her hair was in a bob and every time she bent her head a bunch of unruly hair came in front of her glasses, making her look attractive and seductive. Never did she make an effort to replace her hair.

How beautiful she looked, thought Chirag and walking across the room, he reached her and held her from behind. He smelt her flaxen perfumed hair. His fingers locked against her stomach, his scrotum area pressed against her well-rounded hip. A shiver of excitement ran down his spine up to his manhood, hardening it with virility. Most probably, Maina could feel his hardness as she placed her left hand on his shorts and with her right hand she caressed his crisscrossed fingers. Slowly she slipped her hand into his shorts and then into his Jockey underwear. She took his member in her hand and fondled and stroked it. Chirag placed his head on her shoulder and licked the salty film of dust, sweat and deodorant from her neck. Maina yielded to all his affection with a smile.

'Look at them, who says only human being can make passionate love?' Maina said after a few minutes, indicating the two cuckoos, billing and cooing, sitting on the same branch.

'We should not be left behind,' whispered Chirag, slipping his hand inside her skirt.

'In that case you have to be innovative,' she teased him.

'I can be, provided I am given a fair opportunity to explore all the territories you possess,' Chirag quipped, while his hand grabbed what it was searching for inside her skirt. She released a moan of pleasure.

'For now all the territories are yours, Mr. Adventurer. Let me see how successful an expedition you perform.'

'If all the territories really belong to me I would rather prefer to take them on my bed,' said Chirag, lifting Maina with both his hands while she draped her arms around his neck. She gave him a disarming smile.

'You are a darling,' she whispered.

'So are you,' Chirag murmured.

Soon Chirag found that unlike Kritika, Maina was more receptive type on bed. Kritika rather loved to dominate the whole game. She had always guided his hands, decided the moment when he should enter her. While orgasmic pleasure throbbed her she would bite his fingers, often hold his neck tightly as if she was about to strangle Chirag.

But Maina was more silent and calm on bed; belying the first impression she had given him in Roseberry. Chirag loved her receptivity and after the lovemaking held her tightly for a long time. She lied comfortably in his embrace, sticking her cheeks against his. Pressing her against him Chirag experienced a strange sense of solace, something that a steamy physical love could never give him.

They were silent for a while, then Maina asked him, 'Your bedroom is very spick and spun for that of a bachelor. How many girls had visited your bedroom before me?'

'It seems you know a lot of bachelors' bedroom. How many bachelors' bedroom did you visit before coming to mine?' retorted Chirag.

'Not many guys in Bombay are lucky enough to have his own bedroom. I loved your flat,' smiled Maina.

'But you have not answered my question.'

'Do not be nosy. Are not you enjoying this moment with me?'

'Yes, I am. Actually I asked you just out of curiosity,' Chirag defended himself.

'Well, the most audacious lovemaking I did was not in anyone's bedroom but inside an Innova, parking the car near Bandra Band Strand. All the sliding windows of the car were of frosted glass and we felt ourselves safe inside,' she began reminiscently. 'That evening we were returning from a premier while Kasthub offered me a lift to drop me Mulund. He was working with Warner Brothers at that time before leaving for the US to learn film-making. We had our dinner at Café Sea Side near Band Strand. Once returning suddenly he stopped his car by the road. It was drizzling outside and vehicles on the road were far and few between. I was a bit surprised and looked at him questioningly when he showed a small boy, selling popcorn. He wore a long raincoat of some ordinary see-through polythene sheet. The raincoat was quite large for him. He was no more than fifteen years of age.

Kasthub slid the window glass down and beckoned the boy with a wave of his hand. The boy came running to him.

'How many packets of popcorn do you have?' Kasthub asked the boy now.

'Around fifteen,' replied the boy.

'How much does a packet cost?'

'One for five, three for ten,' said the boy, without knowing where the conversation was leading.

Kasthub gave him a crisp note of hundred and said, 'Give me all the packets.'

The boy gave him a long disbelieving look and counted the number of packets. He did a mental calculation and said, 'There are seventeen packets. I can give it for fifty.'

He handed a large polythene bag to Kasthub. Droplets of rainwater were dancing on it. The boy was about to return fifty rupees to Kasthub but with a wave of his hand Kasthub told the boy that he did not want the money back.

'Keep it with you. Do give me packets of popcorns when I have no money with myself,' he smiled at the boy.

'Thank you, saab,' mumbled the boy with mist of tears in his eyes.

Kasthub again waved at the boy and the window glass rose up. Kasthub now looked at me, turning his head. Love for life was glinting in his eyes. I felt so nice sitting by him. He had been my colleague for last many months but never had I seen him acting with empathy for an unknown. I knew for certain that his display of affection was not to impress me but natural.

'Want popcorn?' he smiled at me.

'Yeah,' I said.

We munched popcorn from two separate packets in silence while the whirring of the air conditioner and the purr of the engine played a rhythmic music.

He kept his left hand casually on the gear handle.

'I often think how little we know of one another. More surprisingly, how easily we lead ourselves to believe that we know everything about other's nature,' I said slowly.

'That's really philosophical,' he teased me.

'I am not joking,' I said with feigned anger and playfully hit him on his left hand. He did not say anything. I did not know what happened to me but could not take my hand away after hitting him. My right hand remained on his left for a while. It was so comforting. Remember it was never sexual. Slowly I rubbed my hand against his. I knew that he already had a steady girlfriend to whom he was apparently faithful. I did not want to seduce him. Actually suddenly I wanted to surrender myself to him, to his love for others.

I do not remember how it started but after a few minutes we were on the backseat of the car, making one of the most passionate love-makings of my life. It was short but extremely sweet, probably because it was not premeditated. We did not exchange a word for the rest of the ride. Once he stopped his car near R-Mall, I got down from his car and mumbled thanks to him.

'I never knew that kindness might be rewarded in such a nice way,' he smiled.

I smiled back, a bit awkwardly.

However, he had never mentioned that evening again when we were together, nor did he make a pass at me. We both counted it as our slip which time and situation had demanded from us,' Maina paused and then asked Chirag, 'bored to death by my story?'

'Not in the least,' said Chirag and added as an afterthought, 'once I saw you in Roseberry for the first time, I was shocked at your swearing. Never did it occur to me that you can speak so sensibly, so beautifully.'

'Thanks,' she said with an answering smile.

'I had a girlfriend. Kritika was her name. She used to come here. He spent a lot of good time together until one day I came to know that she was a cheat,' Chirag said slowly.

'So you deserted her at once?'

'Yeah, what else could I do?'

'Never did you feel like taking a revenge on her?'

'No, but I had a searing pain within me for weeks. It is so difficult to trust people once you are deceived.'

'But that is the only way to live life. We all need people whom we can trust on, rely upon,' Maina said, snuggling her head against his bare chest.

He held her and related the whole Kritika episode to her as she listened to him with sympathetic silence. As Chirag finished telling her the whole story a happy feeling filled him as though somebody had taken a load off his mind.

'Thanks for listening to me,' he murmured.

She patted him on his back in response. She then dropped to sleep after sometime.

Late in that evening once Chirag left his flat with Maina he met Sandip's mother outside his flat. His eyes met her calm eyes. Soon she opened the door and went inside. Suddenly Chirag felt a stab of guilt inside him. Most probably like other conservative mothers, she disapproves my spending time alone with others girls in my flat, thought Chirag.

'Who is that lady?' Maina asked him as he kickstarted his Royal Enfield.

'My colleague's mother.'

'She has an adorable personality.'

'How do you know without talking to her?'

'I do not know it but felt it as I saw her.'

Chirag remained silent. He wanted to talk about his own mother but did not discuss her while driving. He hoped someday he would tell Maina how often he missed his mother.

Without turning back Maria knew that it was Akash's motorbike. For last one week she had been awaiting every afternoon and night to hear the grunt of his motorbike. And now she could recognise his motorbike just by the whirr of its engine. It was two in the afternoon and Maria knew that this morning Akash had his first morning shift. For very obvious reason she had joined Atharva's lunch session in front of their building.

Akash stopped the bike very close to Atharva as though he was about to dash the boy and gave him a smile.

'Dairy Milk,' said the boy at once, trying to clamber up the bike.

'Did not I give a big packet yesterday? No Dairy Milk today.'

'If you do not give Maria didi will give me,' said the three and half year old boy.

Akash looked at Maria with an unsmiling smile. Maria looked into his eyes and suddenly everything around her and Akash disappeared; time came to a stop and breathing became an arduous task. So at last he was in front of him.

'She is Maria, recently shifted to this building with her family,' Atharva's grandfather's words came to her rescue in a way for; otherwise, she did not know what to say.

'Hi, myself Akash,' said Akash. His voice was ordinary.

'Hi,' said Maria. She wanted to say something more but fumbled for words.

Unwillingly she dragged her eyes from him on to Atharva but before that she had engraved his bright eyes, broad forehead, sensitive nostrils into her mind.

He was wearing a full-sleeved shirt. A thin film of grime peeking out from the collar of his shirt. The shirt was not properly ironed and must have already been worn several times. There was a speck of dirt on his trousers near his ankle. He did not seem to pay much attention to his uniform. Suddenly a wave of affection swept over her. She shot him a sideway glance. He was looking at Atharva, watching him play with the rim of the wheel of his bike.

'It is dirty, *beta*. Do not touch it,' he said to Atharva who took no heed of his instruction.

'He is so cute,' said Maria to no one in particular. She desperately wanted to make some original statement but standing in close proximity of Akash she felt that her mind was not working.

'Yeah, he is,' said Akash casually and added, 'you must have heard this saying *'there is only one beautiful child in the world and every mother has got it.'* '

'Yeah, I did,' Maria lied. Never before she was ashamed of admitting her ignorance.

'I think this statement is incomplete,' said Akash Jocularly.

'Why?' stammered Maria, without knowing what Akash really meant.

'Because the remaining part of the statement is missing; so I devised it. It says… *and there is only one unfaithful husband in this world and very wife has got it,*' smiled Akash and asked Maria, 'have you heard it before?'

'No,' Maria said softly, looking at him in melting eyes.

'Just kidding,' said Akash and released the clutch. The motorbike moved forward.

Mesmerized, Maria gazed at Akash so long as she could see him.

And when she was out of her reverie she found Atharva's grandfather looking at her. There was an amused look on his face.

'He is a very nice boy, I like him,' he said, referring to Akash, somewhat irrelevantly. It surprised Maria to think that the old man might have read love for Akash in her eyes.

'I have got to go now,' she said.

'Bye Maria didi,' Atharva waved at her.

Maria waved back at him. Before entering the building she passed an envious glance at her neighbouring building. She was irrationally jealous of the building for possessing her lover.

How beautiful love is, just a couple of minutes' meeting with your beloved is enough to keep you in a buoyant mood for all day, thought Maria and felt a deep urge to do something constructive. How could she tell Akash that she was an ordinary B. Com. graduate, doing nothing, killing time at home? She stood by the window, looking out when love and an unknown fear filled her heart. Time and again she remembered her minute-long conversation with Akash. Yes, she was certain that never before her heart had beaten for anyone like this.

'Sit, make yourself comfortable,' said the dapper man whose baritone voice belied his small stature. The only enigmatic thing, Maria found, in his features was his deep-set eyes. They gave Maria an impression that just with a glance at an unknown person he could know about him more than other people could.

'Thanks,' said Maria, sitting on the swivel chair, somewhat diffidently. It was the first time she was appearing an interview.

The small man passed a cursory glance at her resume and smiled all of a sudden as if he remembered an old joke.

'What do you mean by working knowledge of Microsoft office? That's what you have written on your résumé, I understand?' he asked and looked at Maria. There was a twinkle of amusement in her eyes.

'Actually I have not worked much on Microsoft Word, Excel or Power Point. But I am very much willing to learn and given me a chance I would try my best to meet all the responsibilities I might be entrusted with.'

She was at Ecole Mondiale world school, Juhu, appearing to a job interview. The recruitment was going on for several posts and Maria had applied for the post of Assistant accountant.

'Do you know that our hiring an Assistant accountant may be a provisional arrangement. After a year or so we may not need your service. Besides, we cannot afford a stipend more than seven thousand. Are these conditions okay with you, Maria?' The small man's voice was kind and fatherly. He was on the verge of sixty.

Maria remained silent for a moment when she remembered Akash, her love, her mother's occasional caustic remarks and her spending days at home, in a way killing time.

When she began after a few seconds there was a tone of finality in her voice, 'Sir, so far I have not worked anywhere. Working here would help me learn new things and this experience may count later if I try for another job. And I am okay with the stipend.'

The small man, whose name Maria came to know later, was Cyrus Paperwalla, gave a small smile.

'The formal offering letter will be couriered to your residential address in a day or two. Do come to office from the coming Monday.'

'Thank you, sir,' said Maria gratefully. She had not expected that the interview would end so early.

'Another thing, if you ever face any trouble in working here, any sort of, do not hesitate to meet me,' said Mr. Paperwalla and raised his assuring hand up.

'Thank you, sir,' Maria breathed and rushed out of the room.

For a few minutes she was on cloud nine but then a fear struck her. What if Akash laughs at her for the paltry sum she gets as a stipend? What if he avoids her thinking that she was much inferior to him?

She did not know much about him but did not want him to avoid her at any cost. She did not even mind lying for it. She decided to lie to him about her salary. If one day she felt that he did not care about her status, job profile or salary she would make a clean breast of the truth to him. But until then she had to take help of an innocuous lie, she decided as she walked towards the bus stop.

'My mouth is in fire,' said Sandip's mother, gulping down the last of the water and then raising the glass to the waiter, asking him to bring more water.

The waiter hurried with a jug of water. He filled her glass and was about to take the jug back when Sandip's mother said to him, 'Why do not you leave it here? I would need more water for such spicy foods.' The waiter left the jug somewhat unwillingly. Sandip's mother got the handkerchief from her bag and wiped her teary eyes.

'Do you boys have this food regularly?' she asked Akash and her son.

'Not very often, but we do not find it spicy. We are okay with it,' Sandip said.

'I prefer going to Vaishno Punjab. Food is much better there. But he does not like that place,' said Akash. 'Someday I will take you there. They have a separate AC family room.'

'I am quite comfortable in non AC restaurant as well, Akash. I did not see electricity for the first fifteen years of my life,' said Sandip's mother crisply.

'I hate going to Chembur camp. It is so crowded,' said Sandip.

'You are so much like your father,' said Sandip's mother to her son, then turning to Akash she said, 'his father was also scared of going to crowded places. He preferred staying alone, isolated.'

'But I think Sandip has taken after his mother,' Akash said, smiling at his dearest friend. There was a natural ease, an air of confidence, a collected composure about Sandip's mother. Rarely had Akash witnessed all these qualities in a widow who was on the wrong side of fifty. Sandip was profusely endowed with all these rare qualities.

'Really?' said Sandip's mother. 'But I am always happy to think that he is like his father. He was one of the very few men I was in awe of even after knowing him from very close. As you go nearer to a person you may discover many ugly things about him. It is very difficult to look up to someone whom you know very closely. But his father was an exception.'

Akash and Sandip remained silent. They were having their dinner in Gurudev, a modest vegetarian restaurant outside ICL Township. It was more than two months Sandip's mother was staying with him.

'His father also loved travelling?' asked Akash to Sandip's mother.

'He did, but at our time travelling was a luxury which we really could not afford. Anyway, I do not remember him travelling all alone for weeks as my son does,' Sandip's mother looked at her son affectionately.

'Marry him off, it will put a stop to his travelling all alone,' Akash suggested playfully.

'Why? Does he like any girl?' asked Sandip's mother.

'I do not know, ask him,' smiled Akash, shrugging his shoulder.

'Why do not you tell Mamma about the girl you have taken to?' Sandip asked Akash.

'Gone mad. I have not taken to any girl,' Akash defended himself, knowing very well that Sandip was referring to Maria.

'What about Maria then?' asked Sandip.

'What can I do if she comes to talk to me whenever she finds me taking walk in the evening? Besides, she is an ordinary girl. I do not have any special feeling for her,' Akash said casually, remembering Maria's ordinary look and small stature. It was beyond him to imagine that he might fall for an uninviting-looking girl like Maria.

'What do you mean by an ordinary girl?' Sandip's mother asked Akash directly. Akash fumbled for words for a sensible answer while Sandip enjoyed watching him caught off guard.

'Well,' Akash said at last. 'I call someone ordinary if speaking with him or her bores me to death.'

'You may feel bored to death talking to someone, but what if he or she loves talking to you,' remarked Sandip's mother. 'There is a possibility that we all love to talk to someone who finds us bore and ordinary.'

Akash remained silent. Sandip's mother's statement reminded him of Maria and the eagerness with which she used to tell him the trivial events of her life.

'Actually, so far I understand, Akash, none of us are ordinary. We are all special for someone and ordinary for someone else....' Sandip's mother could not complete.

'Mamma please, Akash does not like anyone preaching at him,' interposed Sandip.

'Am I getting preachy?'

'No, not at all, rather I loved what you said,' said Akash.

'Let's go,' Sandip said. 'I have got to get up early tomorrow. That's why I hate morning shift.'

'Bye, Akash. Do come to our flat. My son likes you a lot,' said Sandip's mother.

'Yeah, I know,' smiled Akash as he saw Sandip's mother sitting on the pillion seat of her son's bike with natural agility.

Akash started his bike after Sandip and his mother left. After a few minutes, as he was riding past Aryabhatt, he saw a shadowy figure of Maria, standing by the window of her room. The room was dark yet the light offered by the nearest lamppost was enough to see her face.

As Akash's eyes met her for an instant, he noticed that her eyes glinted with joy as if she was happy to see him return his flat safely. Though Akash had no special feeling for her it gladdened him to feel that he was important for her.

3

Akash watched the key maker with evident interest to make the duplicate key for a filing cabinet whose key had lost a few weeks ago. He had his last morning shift followed by a weekly off. Srichan Jagiasi, the key maker, inserted a small piece of metal into the keyhole and rotated it delicately clockwise for several times before taking it out. The piece of the metal was the size of an ordinary key without any slots in it. Srichan inspected the metal piece minutely and again inserted it into the keyhole. The same operation was exercised again. Then he slowly pulled the metal piece out and observed it carefully for a long moment. Soon a satisfactory grin came to his lips.

He had a wrinkled face and was of medium height. A stench of beer and sweat was emanating from his overused clothes. His nails were long and layer of dirt harboured there. Though everything about him gave him an unpleasant personality Akash took an immediate liking to this man. He could feel that the key maker, Srichan Jagiasi, lived life on his own terms. What was more, no matter what other people thought of him, he was completely at ease with himself.

Never before Akash had seen anyone making a duplicate key to a lock.

'Wherever the impression comes we would file and grind that place until the slots in the duplicate key matches with that of the lock. This job requires a lot of patience but not really difficult to perform,' the key maker gave a toothy smile to Akash, displaying his uneven teeth. He took a small file from his bag, containing all the paraphernalia for key-making, and started filing the metal piece while Akash asked him a volley of questions about his life and strange profession.

Once the key–making was over, the key maker kept the keys on the table in front of Akash and went to the door. But suddenly he stopped as something struck him. He turned back and looked at Akash critically for a long moment.

'May I tell you something?' he asked to Akash.

'What?' asked the puzzled Akash.

'You may a good engineer but I do not think you enjoy your job,' he remarked.

'Why?'

'Because I think you are curious about people, their life and thinking. I think you would enjoy a job where you can work with people and their life,' the key maker said simply.

'Why do you think so?' Akash asked surprisingly. Nobody could ever tell him this simple truth about himself.

The key maker gave an enigmatic smile in response.

'God bless you,' said he and left off.

Suddenly this small encounter with the key maker boosted Akash's confidence in working towards his dream of becoming a writer. With renewed enthusiasm he decided upon working harder to produce fresh stories, edit them again and again, and send them to different publishers, magazines and upload them to different sites.

He left office at 2 pm on the dot as his shift reliever reached on time.

After reaching his flat he made do with the previous night's leftover and went out for a walk. He had an indefinable feeling that if he remained alone for sometime, silent and peaceful, he might hit upon a unique story about a key maker. The road was almost deserted as he walked slowly, remembering his conversation with the key maker. Slowly his mind drifted into a state where he could never reach with conscious effort. Soon a singular story about a key maker and his little world started germinating in his mind. So lost was he in his pleasant state of story making that he was not aware of Maria walking towards him from behind with slow but determined strides. For her it was a treat to catch Akash alone.

'Hi Akash,' said Maria as she reached Akash.

Akash spun on his heel and was not really happy to find Maria, standing next to him. She was a diminutive figure beside Akash. A bag was slung over her shoulder. Her face was small but eyes large and innocent. Her lips were dry and a few drops of sweat accumulated above her upper lip. She looked small and vulnerable. She was so different from the other girls her age.

'Hi Maria, coming early from office,' asked Akash courteously.

'Yeah, some cultural program was there. I did not join it,' said Maria and looking at Akash's face asked him, 'Have I disturbed you? I mean, you wanted to be alone.'

'Not exactly,' said Akash. He had a strange kind of sympathy for Maria as he always felt that Maria loved to walk with him, talk to him. She hanged on every word he said, treated them with immense importance and remembered them for a long time.

'May I walk with you?' asked Maria.

'Yeah, why not?'

They walked in silence on the main road that divided the colony into two equal parts.

Maria never uttered a word. She was more than happy to walk by Akash. Everyday her love for Akash was mounting yet never could she muster courage to voice her innermost feelings to him. Rather for last six months her only objective was to improve herself in all aspects so as to deserve Akash. As yet never had she changed herself to be admired by anyone. But with Akash all her calculations and equations dissolved. Just a simple touch of his finger was enough to send her in a world of ecstasy.

'This morning I met a strange man in my office. Though he looks ordinary I call him a strange person because he has many unique stories to offer. I think he understands people much better than a psychiatrist.'

Maria was already accustomed to hearing Akash's sudden narration on people and their idiosyncrasies and the strange occurrence in the world. He spoke English with excellent command. He was extraordinarily well informed about world at large. Yet, strangely enough, he did not seem to have any interest in pursuing further studies. It often occurred to her that he was a misfit in a public sector like ICL but then she told herself, with a chuckle, she could not have met him if he were not here.

'Who was that man?' She asked him curiously.

'He was key maker. What I felt that he lives his life with gay abandon. In everyday life we do not meet people who live life so passionately. Surprisingly he told me something about me, which, people who are with me for more than a year could not even guess.'

Is he giving me a challenge? Is there anything that I do not know about him, thought Maria and was suddenly jealous of the key maker. She loved Akash. Her mind was always full of his thoughts. Did not he understand how much he meant for her? Did not he understand that his such a casual and indifferent remark hurt her like anything. The key maker might have made some interesting comment on him but she was ready to surrender herself completely to him. Did not it mean anything to him? If he was really a sensible guy why could not he experience her love for him? Every time they met she always sought for an opportunity to show him how much she cared for him but had he ever given a chance to her? A long chain of thoughts passed through Maria's mind as tears welled in her loving eyes. She looked at the tall trees stood on the both sides of the street when two drops of tears rolled down the contour of her dry cheeks.

How painful it is when your loved one does not understand the depth of your love for him, thought she, secretly wiping her eyes with the back of her hand.

'I have got to go,' she said to him at last as her voice throbbed with emotion.

'I will also leave now. It is almost four. I have some personal work,' said Akash, without any knowledge of the emotional turmoil Maria was battling with within her.

'Okay,' Maria said. She was dying to know what his personal work was but something within her stopped her from asking. They walked in silence and once they reached in front of Aryabatta Maria walked to her building without a word. It was very unlike of her and Akash was surprised by her behaviour. He walked towards his building in a quick pace. He wanted to jot down the basic idea of the story on the key maker in his red leather bound notebook before he forgot. He was about to enter the building when he heard a loud sound of slamming the door. Within a second he heard someone thumping down the stairs. He stood by the staircase and looked up. It was Sujata Sharma, Jasvinder's wife, running down the stairs agitatedly. Her unkempt hair, teary eyes told Akash that she had had a fight with Jasvider. Akash was already aware of Jasvinder and Sujata's occasional fight as from their flat he often heard the sound of loud shouting, banging of the utensils issuing. Sujata ran down the stairs at a breakneck speed without looking at Akash. She then headed to the parking lot from where she collected her Scooty and soon disappeared, sitting on it.

Slowly he climbed the stairs, thinking about Sujata and her troubled married life. As soon as he entered his flat he received an SMS. It was from Maria. Akash read it at once.

Our true friends shower their affection on us only when we open ourselves to them.

Akash thought for a while. These words seemed to be her own, thought he, though he could not find any relevance of this sudden SMS. He typed a text message at once and pressed the send option. A few seconds later a message flashed on his cell phone screen. *Delivered to PUCHU.*

In Bengali a small boy or girl is often affectionately called *PUCHU*, which particularly has no meaning. Maria, however, would have felt flattered to know that Akash had given her such a cute name.

As her cell phone beeped twice Maria's heart missed a beat. She knew that it was an SMS from Akash. She picked up her cell from her study table. *1 message received* – said the display screen with a sign of an envelope. Maria opened the inbox. It was an SMS from MySkyMyLove. She opened Akash's SMS and read it.

But does not true affection of our friends make us open our bare soul to them?

She read and reread the text message. Rarely had Akash sent SMS to her and she treasured all the SMS sent by him. Every time she felt low, every time a nagging doubt chased her that Akash would never understand her love for him she went through his SMSs. None of those SMSs were the jokes circulated among young friends. Whatever he sent to her was his own words, own thoughts and she loved it terribly. Unknowingly she had often pressed her cell phone against her lips after reading a text message from Akash.

But the present SMS took her in a contemplative mood. Does Akash mean that if I shower more affection on him, he would open his heart to me, she thought. But how can I do? Most of times he is so silent, lost in his own thoughts. Slowly a sense of helplessness filled her. She passed a quick glance at the neighbouring room where on a four-poster bed her mother was sleeping comfortably. Several times she had seen her daughter and Akash walking together but very time she averted her eyes from them and later on never discussed Maria's meeting Akash regularly. Her father, Daniel, knew Akash much before they had shifted to ICL colony and never raised objection to Maria's walking with him. It always gave Maria a sense of comfort that every time Akash and her father met they would acknowledge each other with a nod or a friendly smile.

She lied on her bed and turned and tossed sleeplessly for half an hour before she heard her mother say, 'Why have not you changed your clothes yet?' Maria looked at her mother who appeared to be in an interrogative mood.

'I will, Mummy, just feeling sleepy,' said Maria evasively.

'Happy with your job?'

'Yeah, I am.'

'Do not you think you should study more to get a better job?'

'If I earn experience from the present job I will positively get a better job.'

Her mother stood by the door, hesitated for a long moment and then left without a word. Maria remained on her bed for a while, wondering on her present state. The journey to win Akash's heart seemed to be an impossible task.

She knew most of her friends went to bed with most of their boyfriends within a month from their first meeting. They even changed their boyfriends in a fast pace. What astonished her the most was that after splitting with their boyfriends within a week or so they managed to get a new man in their life. And every time they confirmed that the new man possessed everything that their ex-boyfriend had not had.

She, however, loved a guy who had not even given a chance in last many months to tell him that she loved him. Yet it was beyond her imagination that she would give up effort of owning him. There was an element of enigma in his personality which Maria always found irresistible.

Suddenly Maria sprang to her feet as she heard Akash talking to Atharva down. Instantly she ran to the window and there he was, bending his head down, patting Atharva's cheeks. He was wearing a turtleneck black T-shirts and a pair of denim jeans. Again a wave of affection and love swept over her. From up there she could see the thick bush of his curly hair, his long fingers, lithe body and all of a sudden a desire to hold his head against her bosom seized her. She wanted to smoother him with kisses, whisper all the loving words to his ear, dissolve him into her embrace. She could feel her breathing become heavier as she was overflowing with love. At the very same moment he looked up as though some invisible element in the air had carried her feeling to him. As her eyes met his for a brief moment he gave her a smile. She reciprocated with a wave of her hand. He then walked towards the main road. She knew he was out for a walk. Should she go out and be with him although he had not invited her, thought she, slumping on her bed, torn between her self-respect and the desire for being with him.

Now her cell phone beeped. 1 message received. Yes it was from her

Mysky Mylove. It said: R u free now?

She replied immediately: yes, very much, why?

Within a minute another SMS on her cell : wanna join me at Tastings after fifteen minutes.

Maria's hands shaking, heart drumming against her ribs as she read the text message. So far never had Akash asked her to meet anywhere. As yet she had not met him anywhere outside ICL Township.

would be there on time : she typed and sent the message at once.

Now suddenly Maria was at her wit's end. She did not want to wear any casual T-shirts and Jeans on the special evening. She opened the fitted wardrobe in her parents' room and checked her salwar- suits. She did not have many salwar suits and none of them seemed to suit the present occasion. They were all either too gaudy or extremely ordinary. Suddenly she felt that the second's hand in the wall clock was running very fast. She had already wasted five minutes undecidedly. She knew Akash was extremely punctual and did not want anyone to keep him waiting. All of a sudden she remembered a beautiful kurti that Glancy aunty had gifted her on the last Christmas. So far she had never worn it. It was not because it did not fit her properly but she had vowed never to wear it as she immensely disliked Glancy aunty.

Every time Glancy aunty visited their flat she was always full of praise for both her daughters, for their beauty, their splendid academic qualification and for the respectable jobs they had. Every time Maria's mother would listen to her elder sister with silence and occasional nod. Her daughter had nothing in special to sing her praises to others. Aftermath of such discussions between the sisters was never sweet for Maria as her mother would start finding fault in everything about Maria and, most annoying for Maria, would compare her with her cousin sisters. Maria hated her mother's meeting her elder sister.

This evening, however, she forgot all her dislike of Glancy aunty and her vow as well. Pressing the Kurti took her another few minutes. She knew that she would get late to reach and sent and SMS to Akash.

Would get slightly late to reach.

She received a quick reply. It's okay. already reached.

She wasted no time now. She sprinkled water on her face, neck and nape of her neck. She then dabbed her face with a cotton towel, hoping that it would help her look fairer. For the first time after many months she applied a thin film of lip gloss on her lips. She now looked at her reflection on the mirror was not really unhappy with it. She picked up her purse and headed towards the main door. From the shoe rack, standing beside the main door she got out a pair of shoes with 2 inch high heel. Her mother had bought it for her from Regal at Dadar TT. The lipgloss, shoes were among the many more things Helen had got for her daughter to make her look more presentable. So far, however, never had her daughter used all these things to do herself up.

'Where are you going all of a sudden?' her mother asked surprisingly.

'To meet one of my friends, will tell you later, Mummy,' Maria replied hurriedly, telling herself that she had enough time to fabricate a story for her mother.

'Do reach home before the Rosary starts.'

'Yes, Mummy,' Maria went out and closed the door behind her.

The lift took her no more than twenty seconds to reach the ground floor but in that span of twenty seconds she consulted the watch for three times. Every moment a fear chased her. What if suddenly the lift comes to a stop for some electrical or mechanical problem, thought she though she knew that her fear was unfounded. She came out of Aryabhatt in a quick pace and fortunately got an auto rickshaw right in front of the building. She wasted no time and hopped on to it.

'Tastings, near Diamond park,' she gasped, breathing deeply, as the rickshaw driver turned the meter on.

As the rickshaw was turning towards the main road, Maria saw Atharva's grandfather sitting on a slab of concrete by the road. The slab was strewn with foliage and Atharva's grandfather was sitting amidst it. His shoulders hunched and both his hands lying feebly on his lap. He was looking at the ground, digging the imaginary earth with his toes. His posture bespoke nothing but deep melancholy. The sound of auto rickshaw made him raise his head and for a moment his eye met Maria's before he averted his eyes. All Maria could read in those eyes was sadness and helplessness. She wanted to talk to the old man, listen to him and if possible share a few words of hope with him but for now her meeting with Akash was her first priority.

She looked at the straight avenue in front of her. Soon the auto rickshaw left ICL Township and ran towards Diamond Park.

'*Arre madam, Paisa to ley lho,*' said the auto driver to Maria as she almost ran towards Akash without taking her change from the rickshaw-walla.

'*Nahi nahi, raheno do,*' said the exhilarated Maria, raising her hand to the rickshaw driver, without looking at him. How could she look at something else when her Mysky Mylove was right in front of her, sitting on his parked motorbike, looking at her smilingly?

'Sorry, got late,' she said.

'It's okay, I reached here at least ten minutes back,' said he, getting down from the motorbike.

They were at the parking lot near Diamond Park. Evening walkers were taking walk along the cemented path around the park. Kids were playing on the swings, slides, see-saws and jungle gyms inside the park under their parents' strict supervision. In front of them was a busy street leading to Chembur station and on the other side of the road was Tastings, one of the most respectable cafes in chembur. College-going lovebirds usually thronged there for the better part of the day and spent their time over the mugs of thick cold coffee, served with a straw.

'Let's cross the road,' Akash said.

'Yeah,' she said and followed him, walking slightly behind him.

They ordered cold coffee, veg grilled sandwich and French Fry and occupied a table overlooking the highway.

'Did you come here before?' Akash asked Maria.

'No, this is really a nice place. Do you come here regularly?'

'Once or twice a week, I love the creamy cold coffee they serve.'

'Alone?'

''No, I normally come with my girlfriend,' said Akash with a mischievous grin.

Light extinguished from Maria's face at once. Suddenly the fountain of her dream shattered. She ran her tongue on her lips thinking that they must have got dry like her throat. She tried to smile but a sob caught in her throat.

'Just kidding, I come here with my friend, Sandip, and sometimes with Chirag,' smiled Akash. He seemed to be amused to see the transformation on Maria's face.

Maria gave a sheepish grin, knowing that she had been caught. Akash, however, made no reference to it.

'You very often talk of Sandip and once you told me that *he is smitten by wanderlust.*'

'You remember the exact words I used, strange,' said Akash. He was visibly surprised.

Maria remained silent. She wished she could tell Akash that she remembered each and everything he had said to her.

Meanwhile cold coffee and grilled sandwich were served.

'Do you know why I suddenly called you to join me here?' Akash asked her.

'No.'

'I thought you would like this place.'

'This place is very nice. The food is awesome, too,' said Maria.

Akash nodded, munching the grilled sandwich when a BEST bus screeched to a halt near the traffic signal. Almost immediately a group of school children climbed the bus. Each of them was trying to enter the bus before others and thus created an obstruction for other passengers to climb the bus.

Akash gave a small smile, looking at the kids and drew Maria's attention to them. 'Look at those kids, giggling for no reason. At this moment they are happier than any king of the world,' said Akash, sucking cold coffee through the straw. Maria gazed at the kids when a reminiscent smile hovered on her lips. She met such kids every morning while catching a bus for her office.

'I meet such kids every morning,' she said to Akash after a while.

'How?'

'They catch the same bus with me. In fact I am friends with one of those kids. Usha is her name. She is a nine-year-old pony-tailed girl.'

'How did you make friends with her?'

'It is a long story. It may you bore.'

'Sometimes I love getting bored.'

Maria smiled. 'Those kids catch the bus with me from Golf Club bus stop and get down near fine Arts Society. I think there is a municipality school behind Fine Arts Society. One day I saw one of those girls distributing toffees among her schoolmates in the bus. She appeared to be a hero among all the kids. I was sitting on an aisle seat, close to her. As a few toffees were left after distributing among her friends she offered me one. I looked at her. She had beautiful eyes, sparkling with innocence and beauty. I loved her at once. Usha was her name. They were all staying in different chawls scattered around Chembur camp. Almost all the kids fawning over Usha as she gave toffees to them at least once a week. Soon I came to know the source of the toffees. Usha's father had a pan-bidi shop near Chembur Naka. Every time the bus ran past Chembur Naka she proudly showed me her father's stall. It was a very small stall stood on the pavement. The stall was empty except for a few bottles of biscuits, toffees and cigarettes. Her father, sitting behind those bottles, on a straight-backed chair was a frail man. He had a shrunken face and thin limbs. He might not have anything that one could be proud of, yet his daughter used to show me proudly, 'See, that is my father and it is our shop.' Sometimes she would call her father from the bus and her father would wave at her. I was very much touched by her innocence.' Maria suddenly paused here and asked Akash, 'Am I boring you?'

'Please continue,' Akash said briefly.

Maria knew Akash was listening to her with the utmost attention and she was happy with it.

She began with renewed enthusiasm, 'However, mishap struck Usha and her family a couple of months after I came to know her. BMC often ventured into cleaning the city. The outcome of all such ventures is all the small shops like Usha's father's shop are razed to the ground. Since then I have not met Usha. But I often miss her,' Maria stopped, her eyes glistening with tears.

Akash remained silent for a long time, sipping coffee absentmindedly and then said, 'Your story touched me. I think I would like to work on it.'

'Means?' asked Maria.

'Nothing,' Akash gave an enigmatic smile. 'Lei's go.'

'Yeah,' said Maria. 'I should not be late for the Rosary.'

As they were about to cross the street suddenly a motorbike zoomed past them. Instinctively Akash held Maria's wrist and did not leave it until they crossed the road safely. Akash is holding my hand, thought Maria and felt that she would faint with happiness. She wanted him to hold her hand forever, lead her whenever he wished to, but, unfortunately, her ecstasy was short-lived as Akash left her wrist once they crossed the road.

'Thanks for coming. In fact I was feeling a bit lonely this evening,' said Akash.

'Thanks for calling,' said Maria.

Akash smiled.

'Wait a moment,' said Maria and headed towards a banyan tree near Diamond Park.

Beneath the tree a few idols of Hindu god and goddess were kept. They were leaning against the gigantic trunk of the tree, which was smeared with vermilion powder. Beside the clay idols of the god and goddess some big stones were kept. An old man religiously worshipped these stones and the idols every evening. His apparent devotion to god and goddess drew the attention of many passers-by and they often spent a couple of minutes, praying to the idols before dropping a few coins to the offertory box kept near the idols. It was very obvious that the old man took the offertory box along with him every night.

Maria stood in front of the idols, bending her head down, joining her hands in a prayerful gesture while Akash watched her in wonderment.

She returned after a few minutes, her face calm and peaceful.

'I think, I would give you a surprise within a week,' Akash told

Maria once she got down from the bike.

'What is that?'

'That's a surprise.'

Around fifteen minutes after reaching home Maria received a text message from Akash: What did you pray to god?

She sent a reply in no time: your good health, long life, happiness and ......

Next SMS from Akash was: what was that and .....?

Response came to Akash at once: that you call me for a coffee every time you feel lonely.

But rarely do I feel lonely – it was Akash's response.

Then may I invite you every time I feel lonely? – she wrote him.

May be, good night: typed Akash and sent to her.

Maria was not very happy with Akash's last text message. Sitting alone in her room she lost in a deep thought as to what surprise Akash would give her.

When Akash had evening shift on Saturdays and Sundays, weekend was agonizingly dull for Maria. Since her last meeting with Akash in Tasting four days had passed by. Yet now she had no idea what surprise was awaiting her. Time and again she feared that Akash might have forgotten his promise.

It was a Sunday evening and Maria was taking walk alone. Whenever she was alone in the evening she made sure to walk for forty to fifty minutes. Her cell phone and its hand's free always accompanied her. She would tune her cell phone in to some radio station and listen to the songs. Earlier she was too shy to take brisk walk all alone amidst so many confident-looking evening walkers who came in hordes to ICL township every morning and evening from all over Chembur to enjoy walking. Earlier, like many other women, she was unsure of herself and every time a casual glance from a self-assured person was enough to make her diffident. But since she came into contact with Akash slowly she felt that his attitude, way of talking and thinking instilled confidence into her. His presence in her life brought tremendous change to her outlook.

This evening she could walk barely 200 meters when a depressing sight brought her to a standstill. Atharva's grandfather was sitting alone on a slab of concrete where Maria had seen him a few days ago. There was a dispiriting air about him. He was gazing at the ground unblinkingly. On and off his whole body shuddered and Maria doubted, most probably, he was trying to control an ungovernable sob. Without a second thought Maria walked across the road and reached him. She sat by him in silence. He cast her a depressed glance for a moment and again stared vacantly to the ground in front of him.

Maria was determined to do her best to enliven the old man's mood although she was not sure what caused old man so much pain. For once, she missed Akash not for herself but for Atharva's grandfather. There is always some magic in his words. He could perk him up in no time, she thought for a moment and made an effort to persuade the old man into talking to her.

'Where is Atharva, uncle?' she asked after a while.

No replay but a drop of tear fell on the old man's hand with a silent thud.

'Why do you sit here alone? The other day also I saw you sitting here. Come, we will walk together,' said Maria, gesturing to lead the old man to walk.

No reply from the old man. Suddenly Maria remembered Atharva's grandfather had told her once, in a roundabout way, that he was one of those neglected parents. But this evening determined not to leave him alone, Maria sat by him in total silence, keeping her elbows on her knees, her chin rested on her cupped hands, hoping that soon he would speak on his own. Her intuition, however, proved correct as the old man opened his month after a few minutes.

'I have only one hope now; that is to die with dignity,' he began haltingly. 'Here at my son's place all I needed was a small divan to sleep on and two regular meals. Sometimes I felt feverish or weak but never had I told anyone of my problem. All I wanted was to be with my grandson, Atharva,' the old man paused. The remembrance of his grandson made two rivulets of tears run down his eyes. 'My days are numbered now. Being with my grandson, I literary relive my childhood; in him I see myself growing again. This delightful experience cannot be expressed in words. But now everything is over.'

'Means?'

'Means my daughter-in-law has already given me a hint that I am no more welcome here.'

'Why should you care what your daughter-in-law says? This flat belongs to your son. Besides, if you leave who will feed lunch to Atharva?'

The old man gave a wintry smile. 'My daughter-in-law voiced her husband's wish. I think, Sanjay, Atharva's father had no guts to tell me directly to leave this place.'

'Why?'

'Because he knows how much he owes me. My wife died when Sanjay was only nine. My mother and I reared him, did everything for him that we could so that he did not feel the absence of his mother. It pains me to feel how he can forget everything so easily,' Atharva's grandfather stopped.

'What will you do now?' asked Maria and the very next moment regretted asking such a childish question.

'I will be leaving on coming Wednesday. May be for good,' he heaved a deep sigh.

After a few minutes of mutual silence he began again, 'You know, I am not scared of staying alone. I have enough money to see through me for next twenty years. But life is empty back home at Satara as my heart is always here, with my little grandson.' His voice quivered with emotion.

'In life we always need someone on whom we can shower our love and affection unconditionally. It makes life worth living. Tell me, otherwise what is left in life?'

'Yes, uncle,' said Maria absentmindedly, considering her life and love for Akash.

Slowly talking to Maria steadied the old man's nerves. 'Let's walk, too many mosquitoes are here,' he said.

'Yeah, may be for the culvert down there.'

They walked for a long time when the old man told Maria about his wife's death, the pranks his son used to play in his childhood, his pilgrimage to Trombokeshwar and Char Dham.

'In Trombokeshwar, I slept outside a temple with a few more pilgrims. It is a holy place so the chance of pilferage was almost zero. Moreover, none of us were carrying anything of much financial value. However, once I got up early in the next morning I was taken by a pleasant surprise. Somebody had stolen my sandal. It was a month-old and did not cost more than one fifty rupees. But so considerate was the thief that he had left a pair of old sandal for me. I loved that thief with ethics and used that pair of sandal he had left for the next one year,' the old man stopped and laughed. It was a natural and hearty laugh. It was the first time Maria had seen him laughing this evening. She also laughed.

Around an hour later once they headed towards Aryabhatt Atharva's grandfather stopped suddenly, 'I feel much better after talking to you, beta,' he said to Maria.

'Tomorrow I will try to come from office early. We will again walk together,' said Maria.

'Thank you,' said the old man and added, 'where is your Akash?'

Your Akash - the words Atharva's grandfather had chosen made Maria blush.

'Akash has an evening shift today, till Wednesday he has evening shift,' Maria informed.

'In that case I may not meet him again. My train is in Wednesday morning.'

'If you have any message for him you can give it to me. I would relay it to him.'

'Tell him that he would not get a better wife than Maria Fernandez if he wants to marry one day. Tell him that it was my parting words for him.'

Suddenly Maria's pent-up emotion and worry gave voice to her innermost thought.

'I love him, very very much. But I often doubt whether he understands my love. Sometimes he is so indifferent to my feelings.'

'_Shradha shaburi_ – Respect and patience – these are the keywords. Besides what is the fun of winning the love of someone who accepts your love in the very first meeting.'

'Thank you, uncle,' said Maria as her face lit with hope.

'I shall rather give you thanks,' said the old man.

After seeing off Atharva's grandfather Maria climbed up the stairs slowly, lost in her own thoughts. Talking to Atharva's grandfather at length, emboldening him in a way, she experienced a sense of satisfaction.

For the next two days she spent her evening with him while the old man told her many small and apparently insignificant events of his life that he recollected vividly. Every evening at the time of parting he would thank her, saying that without her presence he might not even remember those beautiful incidents of his life. Every evening he would remind Maria to pass his message to Akash without fail.

'Yes, I will. But let me meet him first.'

The cold coffee was creamy and thick, grilled sandwich fresh and crispy yet Maria did not enjoy the food. On this-much-waited-Sunday, two weeks after their previous meeting at Tastings, when Akash SMSed her, asking her to meet him at Tastings, she cherished a hope that he would come with some surprise gift for her. But, to her dismay, she found that Akash was carrying nothing. He was wearing a pair of denim jeans and a half-sleeved black shirt. He carried nothing except for a long envelope in his breast pocket. The envelope was so thin that she could not imagine it containing any surprise for her.

Akash, however, was in his element and more talkative than usual.

Time and again she thought of giving Atharva's grandfather's message to Akash but every time she experienced an awkwardness within as though she was begging for herself.

Around fifteen to seven Akash got up, 'Let's leave. I have a marriage invitation tonight.'

Maria got up somewhat unwillingly. As they reached the parking lot Akash got his bike, he sat on it and asked Maria, 'Do you remember once I told you about a surprise I would give you?'

'Yes, I do,' breathed Maria.

'Here it is,' Akash gave the envelope from his breast pocket to her.

'It is the surprise,' she said weakly as the size of the surprise dampened her spirits.

She wanted to open the envelope but Akash forbade her.

'Do not open it in a hurry. Open it only when you have an hour to spare.'

'Okay,' said Maria and climbed on to the pillion seat. She was somewhat intrigued by what Akash told her. She planned to open the envelope after dinner.

In the beginning Maria could not make head nor tail of it. Under the heading 'the first shaft of realization' four pages were full of paragraphs typed in Arial narrow, font size 12. She leafed through the pages and on the last pages beneath the last paragraphs two hand written lines arrested her immediate attention.

For my little sweet friend, Maria, whose keen observation inspired me to write this piece of work.

Regards......

Akash

She could not afford to waste a single second now and began to read one paragraph after another.

THE FIRST SHAFT OF REALIZATION

THE TREE WHICH MOVES SOME TO TEARS OF JOY IS IN THE EYES OF OTHERS ONLY A GREEN THING THAT STANDS IN THE WAY.

- WILLIAM BLAKE -

It was a sheer stroke of luck that one morning I reached the bus stand ten minutes before usual and caught another BEST bus to go to my office. This morning I found myself among all new faces. Unlike the BEST bus which I normally caught this bus was crammed with school children. I literally had to wade through a throng of school children -

ranged between eight and twelve – to reach the ladies' seat. When I seated myself comfortably and the bus sped up for the first time I paid my attention to those school children whose clamour and giggle filled the bus. They were all wearing the uniform that was the common uniform of all the municipality schools in Mumbai. The boys were in navy-blue shirts and deep blue pants and the girls in navy-blue shirts and deep-blue skirts. Most of their uniforms were crinkled and washed-out. Buttons of many of the boys' shirts' were missing, exposing their smooth skin. The multihued buttons which replaced the original ones attracted my attention more than the ones missing. Few of the children were barefoot and, later, I was surprised to know a few of the barefoot children carried their sandals inside the empty compartment of their satchel for they loved to move about barefoot.

However, without further digression, I must go now to that pleasant morning when I caught a No. 399 bus at ten past eight o'clock. Though I always preferred the window seat this morning the only available ladies seat was an aisle seat. I sat there hesitantly for I did not want to sit when so many children were standing. They, however, were not interested in sitting and were engrossed in an animated discussion on the matters which seemed to have immense importance in their life. The window seat beside me was occupied by a fat middle-aged lady. Her regular breath and closed eyes told me that she was one of those rare commuters who fall asleep as soon as their commute starts. Her deep sleep was soon punctured by a roar of laughter of a bunch of children standing close to our seat. The lady was miffed and rebuked the children for spoiling her sleep, "Every morning you disturb me. Have your parents taught you to scream and shout when the elders are sleeping?" The children maintained silence for a long moment, looking at each other mischievously and again they dissolved into another bout of laughter.

Unlike other mornings this time I did not feel like removing the newspaper from my bag. A smile lingered on my lips as I continued looking at the children and all of a sudden a smile on a little girl's face held my attention. It was the first time I witnessed a child who could smile with her eyes. When my eyes met hers she smiled at me. Her eyes shone and lips parted, exposing her white regular teeth. In the beginning it was a shy smile but once she found me smiling at her she giggled. Now I paid attention to her look. She must have been around ten years of age and was tall for a girl of her age. She was dark and lean. Her hair which she wore in pigtails was oiled and plastered to her head. The whites of her eyes were completely white and her eyelashes were very long. Her ears were large and nostrils small. She was not at all beautiful but her lovely eyes and innocence that her candid smile exuded made me like her almost immediately.

"What is your name?" I asked her. She was standing close to me. But before she could reply anything suddenly a man's voice materialized from nowhere. I looked about. The bus had just pulled in to a bus stop near Chembur naka. The man's voice was crying loudly, "Usha, Usha......." I saw the little girl standing beside me, whom I had already liked, responding loudly, "Papa here I am, here I am." And within a fraction of second something happened which took me by surprise. Suddenly a ball thrown by someone from outside the bus shot right in front of my head and the girl whose father had called her as Usha caught it with natural grace and dexterity. I was open-mouthed and could not make out that it was not a ball but a small pouch, full of candies, wrapped carefully till Usha came up to me to offer one. I could not thank Usha or talk to her further as all the children got down at the next stop. There is a municipality school behind 'Fine Arts Society'. They must be on their way to school, I told myself. I opened the wrapper of the candy. It was half circular in shape and widely known as orange candy. To the best of my knowledge it was the cheapest candy available in the market and, honestly speaking, had I been offered by anyone else on any other occasion I would not have eaten it. I, however, popped it into my mouth and the next moment an orangey flavour filled my mouth.

I reached the office a bit early and the next morning again I found myself boarding the same bus. An unaccountable desire to meet Usha seized me.

This time again I found her in the same bus and it was really not difficult to talk her into a conversation. Some silly questions were enough to break the introductory ice and soon she evinced an oratory skill. "What is the meaning of your name, Usha?" I asked her. She did not reply immediately but observed me critically. "Did you like the candy I gave you yesterday?" suddenly a question was shot at me. "Yeah, it was good, thank you very much for the candy. Does your father give you candy every morning?" "Yeah, he does," she paused and continued, "but not only for me, actually for all of us," said she, sweeping all other children with a friendly gaze.

She was standing by me, holding the edge of my seat. "What is your name?" she asked me. "Maria," I replied, smilingly. "Nice name, English name," she told me. "My name literally means dawn. Mamma told me that I was born very early in the morning and what's why I was named Usha. Do you like the meaning of my name?" When I told her that I liked it Usha was happy. "I liked your name too, Maria. It sounds like the name of some queen."

She stopped and looked at me to check whether she had succeeded in making me happy. I nodded to acknowledge her comment. She then began on her own accord, "Do you know why they all like me more than others? It's because of the candies that I distribute every morning. My father has a small stall behind the bus stop near Chembur naka. Every morning he gives me around twenty orange candies. I distribute them to all my friends out here and occasionally I have a few extra candies which I often share with all uncles and aunties who are nice like you. But some of them are very rude to us. If by mistake I step on their feet they shout at me. I never give them any candy." She stopped and looked at me. I strangely felt that her words were coated with pride, joy of giving and vindictiveness. She enjoyed the joy of giving candies to other children, took pride in the fact that all her friends liked her more than others. At same time she was unforgiving and revengeful in her own way to those who were unkind to her.

When the bus was about to pull in to the bus stop near Chembur naka I craned my neck to see Usha's father and his stall as Usha had already described it vividly to me. And I did not have any difficulty in finding the stall. It was exactly behind the bus stop, stood on the pavement, blocking it partially. It was roofed with an old corrugated iron. Three sides of the stall except for the front were covered with rusted thin sheets of iron, which, I believed, had been bought from a scrap dealer for a song. The front of the shop was open and Usha's father could be seen sitting on a stool, behind a few transparent plastic bottles. The bottles contained three or four types of sweetmeats and packets of Four Square and Gold Flake. All the cigarettes and candies put together would not be worth more than a thousand rupees and the owner's daily profit could not be more than seventy to eighty rupees, I estimated. Usha's father was a sturdy man with a thick bushy moustache, contrasting the miserable state of his cigarette stall. As the bus stopped at the bus stop for a few seconds to let the passenger board I saw that act of true parental love and affection between a poor father and his daughter. Usha shouted, "Papa, papa…" and her father traced her in a jiffy. Again a small pouch, containing orange candies, was hurled at the window of the bus and inside the bus Usha caught it with feline agility. But the act of throwing the pouch and catching it was performed with immense skill and it was understandable that both, father and daughter, had learnt it with considerable effort. When the pouch, full of orange sweetmeats, was in Usha's grasp, I saw the other children casting envious glances at it. Without any delay Usha undid the rubber band which secured the pouch of candy and kept one candy in each of the proffered outstretched palm. I did not fail to read awe and docility written on the other children's face when they collected the candy from Usha. An orange candy would not cost even twenty-five paisa but the distribution of so cheap a candy gave Usha a Robin-hood-image among her friends. When the candy distribution was complete Usha counted the rest of the candies and gave one to me and one to the bus conductor. I thanked Usha while taking the candy from her and could not refrain from asking her a question, "What if there is no candy for you after giving them all?" "Why? It happened a few times. But I always make it a point to give to all of them before I eat any. Have not you seen how much they like me?" said the ten-year-old Usha. I looked at the other children. I felt that their attitude towards Usha was not exactly friendly but rather obsequious.

Since my first meeting with Usha I found myself availing the same bus in which I could meet Usha. I loved her company every morning though it lasted hardly for ten minutes. I loved to see the beatific smile that graced her eyes and face when she gave candies to her friends. I loved to see the way other children contested to gain a lion's share of her affection. Most probably, they were under an impression that if they succeeded, Usha would favour them with an extra candy.

Days passed by. Weeks turned to months. And every morning this small meeting became a part of my daily life. If I happened to miss the same bus or if any day Usha did not show up I felt something amiss throughout the day. One morning Usha announced that she would be celebrating her birthday the next Monday and that her father had promised special Cadbury chocolate for all of them that morning. The novelty of getting Cadbury chocolate, which was arguably the best candy brand in the country, immediately caught the imagination of all the children present. Most probably rarely did those poor children have an opportunity to eat so delectable a piece of candy. The effect of this announcement among Usha's friends was quick. I could feel that they started treating Usha more deferentially than ever before. None of them wanted Usha to be unhappy with him or her lest he or she would miss the birthday treat.

And on the morning of Usha's birthday when I boarded the bus Usha held me by hand, 'Maria aunty, you sit here,' said she, indicating an empty ladies seat. "Have you forgotten that, today is my birthday and that papa will give us all Cadbury chocolate today?" "No, no, I haven't," said I, sitting on an aisle seat. But when the bus reached the bus stop near Chembur naka something shocked me, Usha and definitely the other children as well. Usha's father's stall was not there. There lying around were a few old rusted sheets of corrugated iron and a few wooden planks. It took me a few seconds to understand that one of those BMC's expeditions had been conducted the previous day. And in the name of putting a stop to illegal encroachment on the government's land the poor man's stall, like many other small stalls of tea makers and cobblers had been razed to the ground. Brihan Mumbai Municipality Corporation often ventures into cleaning the city by destroying the buildings and shops which stand on the government land, but, unfortunately, on most of the occasions poor people like Usha's father are the actual victim of such ventures.

Though the shop was completely destroyed Usha had a faint hope that her father was standing somewhere close to the bus stop and cried continuously at the highest pitch of her voice, "Papa, papa, I am here, I am here…….." till the bus left the bus stop. Soon tears welled up in her lovely eyes. A feeling of humiliation, defeat and sorrow filled her little heart. A few of her schoolmates understood it and one of them said to Usha, "Never mind Usha, you give us Cadbury chocolates on your next birthday. By that time your father will make another stall here." She laughed and the other children joined her. Each word she hurled at Usha was coated with acid. Had I not seen it with my own eyes I might not have believed that a ten or eleven year old girl was capable of making so caustic a remark. I saw rivulets of tears rolling down Usha's beautiful eyes. I wished I could do something to set Usha free from this predicament, yet I was aware of my helplessness.

A couple of weeks had passed since BMC's demolition but the stall had not been erected again. Somehow I could not bring myself to ask Usha what her father was doing nowadays. Moreover a regular occurrence since BMC's demolition tore my heart out. As Usha was no more a candy distributor, her popularity had quickly petered out. On top of that gradually most of the children made her the butt of their jokes. Only a few remained faithful to Usha. Never had Usha thought that so many of her friends who had received candies from her in a fawning way for months could suddenly become so mean.

And then sensational news was exposed to the light of day by one of the children. Soon the news spread like wild fire and became the hot topic of discussion among the children. A little girl, who perhaps was jealous of Usha, was the first to voice it, "Usha, is it true that your father's stall was destroyed because he is a thief?" Usha stared at her, shocked and speechless. Now a few children joined her, "Are you a thief's daughter?" Again streams of hot tears rolled down Usha's beautiful eyes. I was so angry with those children that I would have slapped them had I not felt at the right moment that I should not do so. The only way out, I thought, was to buy a few candies, give them to Usha and ask her to distribute it among her ungrateful friends. So one morning when I boarded the bus I gave her a small packet of candies, "Distribute it among your friends and they will never trouble you anymore," I told her with a smile. But she looked surprised and embarrassed, "It's your candy, Maria aunty. Why should I give it to them? No, no, don't give it to me." I did not insist her further and liked her more than ever for her self-respect. She was no more a chirpy girl as before but most of the time a sombre expression dominated her face. The new appellation – *the thief's daughter* – given by her friends, often made her cry. Sometimes I tried to intervene yet I knew how helpless I was to help her. And one day when Usha could not stand her friends' mockery anymore she stopped coming with her friends.

At first I thought she must be catching another bus to avoid her friends but soon came to know from one of her schoolmates that she did not go to school anymore. Her father's stall had not been erected again. Most probably poverty forced her father to stop Usha's education, thought I and as days passed by I became sure that I would ever see her again.

However, I often thought of her and whenever she came to my mind, her beautiful and innocent smile brought nothing but a combination of love, pity and compassion to my mind. Her image would have melted away from my mind and died out completely had I not run into a spectacular sight one pleasant afternoon.

That afternoon I was returning a bit early from my workplace. I got down near Chembur station and was heading for the auto rickshaw stand near Udipi restaurant when something caught my attention. Quite close to Udipi restaurant, on the pavement, a tarpaulin sheet of about five ft. by four ft. was spread. Half the sheet was occupied by a heap of fresh *mogra* flowers and on the other half around thirty to forty garlands were laid in the piles of three and four. Behind the tarpaulin, sitting on a reed mat were three people, completely engrossed in their own persuasion which they were performing with love and sincerity. It was easily understood that they were father, mother and the daughter. Their work was well-defined. The father was sitting in the centre with his legs crossed and his wife was at his right hand and at his left was his daughter whom I longed to see for so many weeks. The mother, a frail-looking woman with very long fingers, was picking up one flower after another off the heap of *mogra* flowers, inspecting them carefully, rejecting a few, and giving the rest to her husband whose needle was working constantly, making perfect garlands of the same size and shape. Once each garland was made, he inspected it carefully before handing it over to his daughter. And the daughter, with an air of a proprietor, was keeping the garlands systematically on the tarpaulin sheet in front of her. If anyone was trying to haggle with her over the price of the garlands she was simply shoving them off with a sweep of her hand.

Now I witnessed something extremely heart-warming but describing its beauty was beyond me. The man suddenly took two garlands which he had not given to his daughter, watched them carefully and placed one of them on his wife's bun and the other on his daughter's plait. The daughter turned her head, looked at her father and smiled and so, too, did her mother. It took me no time to realise the real source of the rare ability to smile with her eyes that she had. I did not know how long I stood there motionless and watched them. I did not know how long my mind was blank. I did not know for how long time came to a standstill but when I was myself again the first thought crossed my mind was '*even BMC can not destroy their small business now. Any moment, if situation demanded, they could fold the tarpaulin sheet and reed mat and leave off for a new destination.*'

But soon it dawned on me that there are many more things to learn from Usha and her parents. I understood that ignorant was I and so were we all, who thought that real happiness was proportionate to money. Usha's remembrance in conjunction with her poverty always evolved a strange feeling – an unknown combination of love, pity and compassion – to my heart. Realisation dawned on me that no matter how poor someone may be we can love them from the bottom of our hearts but have no right to pity them, for, in truth, they may be in a much happier state than ourselves. The ironic fact remains that even though their poverty may tempt us to take the liberty to pity them, we may be poorer in myriad ways which entitles them to pity and mock our miserable existence. The memory of Sunday sermons came flooding in my mind and I understood perhaps the first time in my life, what '*Blessed are the poor for theirs is the kingdom of Heaven*' truly meant.

AKASH CHATTERJEE

As she finished the last paragraph tears of love and joy were rolling down her eyes as her whole body racked with a soundless sob. What better a surprise could anyone give her? She pressed those pages to her bosom. She then kissed the last page where he had singed his name. No one but a good-hearted man could write such a heart-warming story. She was not at all into reading books. For the first time it occurred to her that she did not even know what she had been missing so long.

She wanted to take his name again and again, as loudly as possible; so many unsolved questions in her mind had been answered by Akash's story. Suddenly she understood as to why Akash had a natural revulsion against higher studies, material success and so called prestigious job. He had often told her referring to his dream that he wanted to set himself free from conventional and monotonous life. Suddenly all pieces of the jigsaw fell into place and she understood that he wanted to be a writer. She could collect fodder for his work. She could narrate to him whatever caught her attention and he could write heart-touching stories on them.

She sent an immediate SMS to him:

Ur maria is much better than me.

Akash wrote her back: liked the story?

She sent a quick reply: very much, but the author more than the story.

So happy with the surprise?

Best gift ever I have got.

Thanks, good night.

Thanks for letting me be with you.

No reply from Akash for the last SMS. Maria waited for a long time before sleep overwhelmed her.

4

'You sleep, beta,' said his mother, looking affectionately at her ten-year-old son. 'I will sleep only after your father comes home.'

'No mamma, I will go to bed only when you come with me,' protested the little boy. 'Why do you wait for Baba every night? Never does he take dinner at home.'

'Because he is your father. I should look after him,' his mother reasoned.

'But does he also look after you?' asked the boy innocently.

His mother remained silent. She had no answer to her son's blunt question.

'Mamma, bhaiya told me that baba closes his shop at 9.30 and then he goes to a secret place.'

'What did he say to you?' his mother's voice was pregnant with anxiety. She did not want her son to be aware of the crude facts of life at this tender age.

'Bhaiya said to me that,' the boy lowered his voice as if somebody might overhear their conversation although no one was there except the mother and son. 'after closing the shop baba goes to a dirty place where girls serve wine. They dance if you give them money. Bhaiya says that baba gives them a lot of money.'

Pent-up anger and frustration suddenly made his mother angry. She took all precautions so that her sons could not know how badly her husband treated her. But now she felt helpless. Her little son also knew the dark and ugly side of her husband's life. Her anger at her husband knew no bounds. All of a sudden she gave vent her rage by slapping her ten year-old son.

'Do not talk bad things about your father,' she warned him weakly.

The boy, however, could sense that his mother was not really angry with him. He hugged his mother right away and cried, 'I love you, mamma, I love you very much.'

She was at once swept over by motherly love for her son. She hid his face to her bosom and cried too, whispering words of love to her son's ear.

Hot tears rolling down his cheeks for he knew that his mother was unhappy with life. Late at night he had often heard the sound of quarrelling in undertones issuing out from the depths of his parents' room. Such quarrels usually followed by the low sound of muffled crying of his mother. However, next morning his mother would make no reference to the previous night's incident. Her eyes might remain swollen but a motherly smile for both her sons would always play on her lips.

How safe he felt burying his head in his mother's chest. He took a deep breath, inhaling the comforting smell, emanating from her heavy breast while his mother encircled him with her hands. He closed his eyes and wanted to remain in her sweet embrace forever. Now he could feel her bringing his head close to her face by both her hands, urging him to open his eyes. Slowly he opened his eyes and was at once in a state of shock. It was a young girl holding his face, looking tenderly at him. He was about enquire his mother but realized that he had had a dream.

She did not say anything to him but held him tightly to her.

All of a sudden a strange feeing struck Chirag. It was a first time in his life he was lying in a young naked girl's embrace while he experienced no carnal desire for her.

'Dozed off for a while?' Maina said after a few minutes.

'Yeah, actually felt very much at home with you,' said Chirag with a dry smile, remembering one of the recurring dreams he had had just now.

'Had a dream?' asked Maina in a mild voice.

'How do you know?'

'Because you were talking in your sleep. Your speech was somewhat slurred yet I sensed that you were talking to someone you like a lot. That's why I held you tightly against me.'

'Thanks, Maina. Thank you very much.'

Maina remained silent without asking him anything about his dream. She rather ruffled his hair affectionately. Slowly Chirag felt an urge within to tell Maina about his dream, which visited him regularly, bringing back all the bittersweet memories of his mother.

'Would not you ask me about the dream?' Chirag asked her.

'Why should I? Rather you should tell me about it if you feel like.'

'I often have that dream. It is about my mother. I lost her when I was only 12. Since then I had a disturbed life.'

'How did she die?'

'They called it cardiac failure but I knew that my father was the instrument for it. She was a neglected wife whose husband spent his nights at ladies' bar, squandering money on bar girls. My mother tried her best to change my father. She was a very dutiful wife. But all she received for her obedience to her husband was occasional beating. Gradually she withered away and then one day…. ' Chirag did not finish his words but heaved a deep sigh.

'Did your father change after your mother's death?'

'Not in the least, for a month or so he used to come home early, but then slowly old habits claimed him. You know, every time I see my mother in a dream I get up with an aching emptiness within me. Most probably, my life would have been different if she were alive now,' Chirag said thoughtfully.

'How?' asked Maina, slapping his bare hip playfully.

'I had had a lot of casual sex since I was 16. No doubt I always told my partner that I loved her. But now I doubt whether I have ever really understood what love is. Sometimes I feel all my sexual escapades were futile. They gave me short-lived pleasure yet loneliness always haunted me. And it gets intensified if you have no one to speak your heart out.'

'But I thought I am a good listener,' Maina smiled.

'You are indeed a good listener. Never did I tell anyone about my mother. I feel much better after talking to you,' said Chirag gratefully, playing with a few strands of Maina's hair.

Her face was very close to Chirag's. He slowly kissed her lips, fondling her pendulous breasts. She responded to his caressing and soon they ended up doing another round of love-making. Once it was over Maina asked him, 'Was it one of those casual sex for you?'

'Not exactly, because I wanted you to enjoy it as much as I did. I did not want it to be mechanical.'

'Why?' Maina asked in a somewhat teasing voice.

'Because I like you,' said Chirag, averting his eyes. He did not want to look directly at Maina's eyes.

There was as such no emotion commitment between them. Chirag knew very well that Maina had slept with many boys before she met him. He had no idea whether now also she occasionally shared bed with other guys. But he was sure of one thing that she was a sincere girl and really meant what she said. Over a period he had taken to her and wanted to spend as much time as he could with her. But her hectic schedule and his shift duty afforded them to meet no more than four or five times a month.

Chirag always wanted to ask Maina whether she liked him but an unknown pride within smothered his voice.

Maina asked him after a while, 'Why do you think that you do not know what love is?'

Chirag thought for a long moment and gave a distant smile, 'To know love one must be deeply loved by someone. I do not think after my mother's death anyone ever truly loved me nor did I love anyone. There is always a fear in my mind, a fear of loneliness. And I think you cannot totally love anyone so long as you are fearful of something. Loving someone totally is the most courageous act in this world.'

'I really loved what you said. It is so unlike of you to talk in such a thoughtful way,' said Maina.

Chirag continued, 'For my mother I could have done anything that my might permitted. I would have never bothered about the consequences. It is such a fulfilling feeling to love someone so completely. But no more do I have such feeling for anyone else.'

Maina looked into Chirag's eyes for a long moment. Suddenly she saw a simple, honest and vulnerable Chirag who was tired and lonely.

'You have a good heart, Chirag. That's all I can say. You may be a bit wild type. But deep down you are a better person than many of those sophisticate bastards.'

Chirag did not respond but held Maina tightly against him for a long time while he felt peace descending upon him as the restiveness within him melting away.

Akash leafed through the rejected manuscript of his second collection of short stories 'A Garland of Flowers' as he was on the verge of tears. This time he was much more hopeful than the previous for a few reasons. Two faithful readers of his work had appreciated his stories and vouched for their publishable worth. Though both his readers had no literary background yet he counted on their comments as they were sincere and honest. Sandip's comment on all his stories were more or less the same, 'No matter what you write it would be a heart touching piece of work because you love people. What is more, all your stories are different and have a surprise ending.'

Maria's reaction to all his stories, however, was very emboldening. She would send long text messages after reading his stories. Her messages were full of beautiful words for his work. Since she had read Akash's The shaft of realization around eight months back she developed a love for literature. To begin with, at Akash's suggestion she had bought a few novels by R. K. Narayan and buried herself in the novels whenever she had spare time. Yet what she really looked forward to everyday was Akash's new story. Each of his story strengthened her conviction that she would never meet a man like Akash in her life.

Two months back when Akash had told her that the proposal for his second collection of short stories was accepted by Destiny Books and that the publisher asked for his complete manuscript she was on cloud nine. The day Akash couriered the complete manuscript to Destiny Books she went to Mount Mary Church in Bandra for a prayer. Mount Mary church was one of the rarest religious places in Bombay where people of all religion, of all walks of life, went to pray as a general belief prevailed that praying here sincerely made one's wish come true.

Outside the church Maria stopped near a street vendor. The street vendor was an elderly lady with dark complexion and stoutly built. She wore a long skirt with frills at the edge and a full-sleeved shirt. Though she was on the wrong side of the fifty her backbone was as steady as a ramrod. She was sitting on a stool and in front of her on a table there were a motley collection of miniature house, car, man, woman, motorbike and purse. All these small objects were made of wax with a wick peeping out of it's top. All these things represented the kinds of wishes the visitors came with. If someone had come to pray for a flat, he could pick up a wax-made home. He would light it's wick in front of Mother Mary and prayed for a flat from her. Very obviously, someone, looking for a suitable bride or groom, would choose to light a wax-made woman or man respectively. It was a common faith among the visitors that if the wick of your chosen object remained burning so long as you were in the church, your wish and prayer would come true.

Many people, however, frequented the church just to thank the Almighty for whatever they had and they usually preferred lighting ordinary candles.

Maria passed a cursory glance at the objects on the table as an idea struck her. She was slightly disappointed for the object she was looking for was not on display. She was about to turn and leave when the lady behind the table asked her in crisp English, 'What are you looking for?'

'You do not have it,' said Maria casually.

'Do you mind telling me?' said the woman, somewhat sternly.

'A book,' Maria replied curtly.

The lady watched Maria for a long moment and then reaching into a jute bag, lying beside her, she took out a thin book made of white wax.

'It is the last piece I have,' she said to Maria.

'Thanks, it is very kind of you,' said Maria. She was genuinely grateful to the lady. 'How much does it cost?'

The lady looked into her eyes, smilingly, and then said, 'Nothing.'

'But I cannot take it from you without paying its price,' protested Maria.

'Well,' the lady thought for a while and said, 'you better go to the church now. I will take it's price once you return.'

Maria entered the church. There was a heavy silence inside, occasionally punctured by the cries from the little children. Maria kept her wax book a little away from the other candles and lit it's wick. She then genuflected, closed her eyes and prayed to Mother Mary for the success of Akash's book. Once she opened her eyes and looked at the Mother Mary's statue it occurred to her that the Mother gave her a benign smile. So solacing it was to look at The Mother and Her Son's statue. She then passed a glance at her book, which had already started melting. Its feeble flame flickering on and off yet it seemed to be determined not to extinguish easily. Before leaving the church she paid a final look at her candle. From a distance off it was difficult to locate her candle. But once she found it she was happy. It's flame was now steady and for some strange reason it was almost blue unlike the flames of other candles.

Maria left the church, cherishing a hope within her that God had listened to her prayer. She had nothing to pray for herself only if God fulfilled Akash's dream. Outside the church she met the street vendor again.

'How much should I pay you?' asked Maria.

In reply the lady asked her a question, 'Whom did you pray for?'

Maria was taken by surprise by her question. 'How do you know that I have not come here to pray for myself?'

'Because most of the people, who come here to pray have greed and anxiety in their eyes. But in your eyes I read love, deep love for someone.'

If this unknown woman can read love in my eyes why cannot Akash read it, thought Maria and said, 'He is my friend. He dreams of becoming an author. I was here to pray for his book.'

'Does he also love you?'

'I do not know,' Maria said briefly.

'What is the point of loving someone who does not feel your love, whom you have to tell that you love him?'

However correct her question might be Maria was miffed with her, thinking that she was making disparaging remark on Akash.

'I am in a hurry. I have got to go. How much should I pay?' she asked, reaching into her purse.

'Pay me only when your prayer comes true,' said the woman. Her voice was soothing and affectionate. 'You two come together to me then. I will take ten times the cost of the book.'

'Thank you very much,' Maria gasped. She loved this pavement seller for no reason. She decided not to breathe a single word to Akash about her prayer at Mount Mary church so long as his dream came true.

And now, two months later, on this Saturday afternoon, she was completely nonplussed as she read and reread Akash's text message. Manuscript rejected, absolutely devastated. Sorry if you too are disappointed.

Disappointed? It was too mild a word to express her feeling. She felt as though somebody had sliced through her heart. Yet she knew her prime concern should be to perk Akash up. She sent an SMS to Akash right off: what if it is rejected? All your stories are real gem. We will not give up easily.

A quick reply came form him: Thanks, would meet me in the evening. Feeling very low.

Yeah, of course. She wrote him.

Later in that evening they were sitting on a concrete slab with their back towards the road near Star Guest house. Behind them regular evening walkers were busy taking a brisk walk. Sitting on the top of the knoll they could view well-lit Vashi bridge which was actually no less than six kilometre off ICL colony. Cars passing through the bridge looked like small match boxes from up there. On the other side there were tall chimneys of BPCL and HPCL disgorging fire and some gas to the sky. Everything around them was busy, occupied in their own pursuit. Nobody seemed to have any time to know how disheartened he was, thought Akash, passing a sidelong glance at Maria. Yes, she really cared for me though she knows that she cannot help me anyway in the present situation.

Maria was fiddling with her cell phone as she did not want to break Akash's silence. She knew Akash was broken-hearted.

'Lets' go,' said Akash after sometime. 'Why should I spoil your mood for my failure? I really feel bad to think that I have disappointed you. You attached so much hope and expectation to my work.' Akash's voice was heavy with despair.

'That is my problem,' she almost snapped, getting to her feet while her cell phone slipped from her hand, hit a piece of brick with a dull thud and fell onto the ground.

Akash bent down at once and collected the cell.

'See, it got switched off,' said he, pressing the button to turn the cell phone on. Within a few seconds light came back to the screen, displaying Nokia's logo and followed by a welcome note. Akash was stunned as he read the welcome note. Immediately a shiver of unknown fear ran down his spine.

The welcome note on Maria's cell phone was: *love is life, life is Akash*.

Most probably this welcome note is in her cell phone since she knew me, he thought and gave her a long stare. Yes, he liked her, not only for the care, attention and love she showered on him but also for her sensitivity and kind-heartedness. He always thought of her as one of his best friends but could not feel any love for her. She was a small woman with no physical attraction and like most of the youth Akash also nurtured a secret desire that his wife (if at all he married one day) must always evoke some lustful desire in his mind. After all, one did not need a wife or girlfriend only for intellectual discussion. A good friend had her own place in life and a wife or a girlfriend had her own. These places were not interchangeable. Yes, however good Maria might be it did not qualify her to be his girlfriend. Besides, he should not be blamed for her loving him…. suddenly a set of selfish, self-centred, mean thoughts seized him. With his mind's eyes he imagined himself and Maria together as a couple and felt an immediate aversion.

He slowly turned the cell phone to her, showing the welcome note to her.

'What is this?' he asked her though he knew such a stupid question was useless.

She passed a quick glance at the cell phone and said to him calmly, 'I never wanted you to know it, Akash.' Suddenly she looked extremely vulnerable. Her lips were quivering with emotion, eyes teary. She was breathing deeply. Akash was standing just a couple of feet away from her. She closed her eyes as she did not want any eye contact with him and spoke in a trembling voice, 'You do not know, Akash, how much you mean to me. You and your work is my every morning's waking thought. It is you who remain in my mind before I sleep every night.'

These words, however sentimental might sound, were actually coming from deep down of her being. For so many months she had imagined of expressing her love for him. Slowly her love made her so courageous that she embraced him, resting her head on his chest, draping her hands around him.

'I love you, Akash. I love you. My world is empty without you. I know that I do not look beautiful or sexy. I may not be good enough for you. But believe me, I am a very good girl and whatever I have I surrender everything to you....'

She kept speaking while rivulets of hot tears coursed down her cheeks. She was not scared of anyone seeing her holding Akash in her embrace. For more than one year she had been braving everything to own him, to win his love, to smother him with kisses and now, suddenly all her bottled-up emotion exploded. She held Akash more tightly than before and wanted to merge into him. She wanted him to feel her heartbeat, to know that her heart was brimming over with love for him, to understand that she could not live without him.

'I love you, Akash, love you a lot,' she continued whispering, burying her head in his chest.

Her whole body was trembling as an ungovernable desire to express her love had seized her.

Bewilderment rooted Akash to the spot. He was completely taken aback by her sudden startling revelation. Of course he always felt that she loved him but never had it occurred to him that she loved him so deeply. Motionless and at a loss for words, he stood frozen within her passionate embrace. He wanted to say something to her but words failed him.

'Maria,' he said slowly after a while. 'See, everyone is looking at us queerly. We must leave now. We will talk later and please give me some time. No sincere decision can be taken within an hour or a day. Please.'

Like a docile girl Maria released him from her embrace and looked into his eyes with her innocent loving eyes. Most probably she wanted to read love for her in her eyes. Suddenly Akash felt he had no courage to meet her eyes lest her tender gaze might reach his heart and realize that his heart was more dry and cold than it appeared to.

'We must leave now, Maria. I know you love me a lot and I feel blessed for that. Now let's go,' said Akash, holding Maria's hand, leading her to him parked motorbike.

'I am a simple girl, Akash. I cannot play with words. But whatever I said to you came straight from my heart,' she said.

'Yes, I know, that's why I am deeply moved by your words. Now let's go,' said Akash.

As Maria followed Akash in silence suddenly she saw Flora Alvas, her neighbour, staring at her and Akash with a frown of disapproval on her face.

She must have seen me hugging Akash. But why should I care what that bitch of a woman thinks of me, thought Maria.

Akash kickstarted the motorbike and Maria sat behind him. It took them no more than ten minutes to reach Maria's building. During the ride none of them uttered a word. Once Akash stopped the bike in front of Aryabhatt, Maria got down and stood near Akash, looking at him, expecting him to say something to keep her hope alive.

'I am with you, Maria. Every time I feel low or lonely it is you I always want to be with. I also need you as you need me.'

'I need you, Akash, because I love you. I do not love you because I need you,' said Maria.

'We will talk tomorrow, Maria. I will go nowhere leaving you,' said Akash vaguely.

Why does he say every thing except for three simple words – I love you – that I am dying to hear from him. And then she remembered what Atharva's grandfather told her once. Patience is the keyword to win anyone' love.

'I would wait for you forever, Akash,' she said in a steady voice and walked towards Aryabhatt.

Helen Fernandez pursed her lips as a train of thoughts passed through her mind. Flora Ales had wasted no time to relay the message of Maria's romantic escapade to her mother, Helen. Her devotion to Christianity was on the verge of madness. According to her nothing could be severe sin for a dedicated Catholic to love or marry a non-Catholic unless he or she was ready to convert into Christianity. Many a time she had seen Akash and Maria together and a natural look of defiance in Akash told her that he would not convert into a Christian even if he married Maria one day. She hated him for earning so much of Maria's attention. Her female instinct told her that Maria was in deep love with Akash and now her only objective was to rescue Maria from the evil spell that that Bengali boy had cast around her. Yet she had no courage to tell anything directly to Maria. Though she was a small girl she seemed to be capable of answering her back.

However, as soon as she had seen Akash and Maria holding each other unabashedly in front of a dozen of evening walkers she felt that enough was enough. She put a stop to her evening walk and reached Helen Fernandez immediately.

'We must save our Maria from that Bengali boy. He looked very arrogant. He must have won our gullible Maria's heart with some sweet words. We must warn Maria now before things go out of hand. And as you already know, Helen, Maria is just like my daughter,' these were Flora Alves's parting words to Maria's mother.

After Flora left Helen Fernandez was lost in deep thoughts for a while. She was not unaware of her daughter's meeting Akash for last one year. She had also witnessed some positive change in Maria since then. She knew that she would not be really unhappy if one day Maria and Akash got married. She knew that for her less-than-average-looking and ordinary B. Com graduate girl it would not be an easy task to get a good-looking engineer with a secured job in her community. She secretly felt Akash was a good catch for her daughter. She had already garnered information about Akash from his colleagues through her husband and whatever information she had gathered was not really unsatisfactory to her. Her husband, Daniel, was also okay with Akash and Maria's occasional meeting. The only fear she harboured in her mind was what if Akash was whiling away the time with her daughter, what if he deserted her daughter after using her. This evening Flora Alves's revelation told her that she must dig into the relationship between Akash and Maria. If Akash and Maria had already decided to marry she would rather heave a sigh of relief.

This evening once her daughter came home she found her eyes red and swollen from crying. Did that boy hurt my daughter or pained her with rude words, thought Helen Fernandez as suddenly a motherly concern swept over her. She made several efforts to make eye-contact with her daughter for she wanted to read truth from her eyes but every time her daughter foiled her effort by averting her gaze. An hour after dinner when Daniel was peacefully snoring and Maria's younger brother, John, in the drawing room, engrossed in downloading a recent film, Helen tiptoed to Maria's room.

She was sitting on her bed, squatting on her haunches, resting her chin on her knee. Her gaze rested on the floor in front of her. Helen sat by her daughter in silence. Turning her head Maria gave her a brief look. For once she was not troubled by her mother's presence in her room. She knew that Flora Alves had already informed her mother everything with adequate *mirch* and *masala*.

'It is very easy to think that our parents are not our well-wishers and that they would not understand us,' said Helen after a while as though she was talking with herself. 'We do not even care to think that how much humiliated our parents feel when other people come to tell us that our children are going astray.'

Maria did not reply. Helen could easily make out from her daughter's face that she was in an emotional turmoil.

She softened her voice, 'You may not care to tell us anything but let me tell you very clearly that your father and I have no objection to your marrying Akash.'

Maria was stunned to hear her mother.

'We are just friends, Mummy,' she said slowly.

'But we do not hug our grown up friends passionately at public place,' her mother's reply was prompt.

Now Maria had no answer for her mother.

'Does not he love you too? I mean, as much as you love him,' asked her mother categorically.

'He likes me a lot,' said Maria doubtfully. She wished in place of the word *Like* she could use *Love*.

'Did he ever try to get physical with you?'

'Mummy, please,' Maria said weakly. 'Akash is very different from other boys. His dreams are unique. It is very difficult to understand him.'

Her mother gave her a fond smile. 'I am not interested in understanding your Akash so long as he marries my daughter and keeps her happy.'

Suddenly Maria felt like giving her mother a bear hug. She hated her mother every time she gave her some stale advice, compared her with her cousin sisters and prodded her into taking care of her look but now it occurred to her that nobody was really worried about her welfare as much as her parents did.

'We are just knowing each other now, Mummy,' said Maria in a clear voice now. 'But I promise that I would never do anything for which I might have to regret later.'

'But you two are talking to each other for more than one year. Do you want more time to know each other? You know very well that everybody in the neighbourhood knows that Daniel's daughter always hangs around with Akash. And many people may not think twice before making a nasty comment about you two.'

'I do not care what other people think of Akash and me. Besides what do they know of him?'

'But we care what other people say about our children. You are twenty-two now. It is a very right age to marry.'

'Please, Mummy, give us some time,' implored Maria.

'Well,' said her mother with a doting smile. 'it is very difficult to understand a mother's concern for her daughter unless you become a mother.' Helen placed her hand on Maria's head for a long moment before leaving the room.

Once her mother left Maria felt very tired. She went to bathroom, splashed water on her face and dabbed with a towel. She then returned to her room, switched off light and retired. As she drifted into sleep her mind was full of thoughts about Akash and her admission of love this evening but later at night she had a strange dream about someone she had never thought of recently.

'Do you remember my telling you about the thief who stole my sandal from outside a temple in Trombokeshwar,' said the old man to Maria. He was a wizened man now. His eyes were deep in socket but were calm and tranquil as though he had no grievance against life or anyone.

'Yes, yes, I remember,' replied Maria. She wanted to ask him why he looked so thin and fragile.

The old man gave a toothy smile, 'He has returned my Sandal, Maria.

Now I can go as far as I want by wearing that sandal.'

Suddenly Maria felt that the old man's voice was coming from a distance away although he was standing in front of her. Uncanny feeling filled her as a fear crossed her mind.

'Where will you go?' she asked to the old man.

The old man gave an inscrutable smile, 'I will go where joy and sorrow has no meaning, a place which is beyond the reach of pain and pleasure.'

'I also want to go there,' said Maria, mesmerized by what the old man said.

'You have a long way to go, Maria. Someday you will also go there. But one request to you, tell Atharva that I love him beyond life and death,' said the old man. Slowly his lean body turned into an apparition before it became a wisp of smoke and dissolved into nothingness.

Bewildered, Maria called him repeatedly as her sleep broke. The dream had such a terrible effect on her that the frightened Maria did not budge on her bed for a few minutes. At last when the soft light of the early morning entered her room through the open window Maria got up. Yet now her head was heavy with the early morning's dream. She walked across the room to the window. Outside the window, sitting on a pepal tree branch was a tiny sparrow, chirping merrily. It seemed to be oblivious to life and death, pain and pleasure.

Around a couple of hours later once her mother came back after her customary morning walk she brought the news of the death of Atharva's grandfather last night.

'Sanjay, Atharva's father, is inconsolable. Even his wife is crying so terribly as if she has lost her own father. She was repeatedly saying, 'We all wanted Baba to stay with us forever. But he was reluctant to stay in our small flat. He loved staying in his own house in his village.' ' Helen said to Daniel.

'May god rest his soul. Nowadays it is next to impossible to get a woman like Sanjay's wife who likes her father-in-law so much,' said Daniel.

Standing at a little away Maria, speechless and shocked, heard her parents' conversation.

Early morning's dream and now the sheer hypocrisy of Atharva's parents made her completely muddleheaded. Again and again Atharva's grandfather's calm and serene face came to her mind. All of a sudden she felt that all the human relationship were superficial and transitory. If people around us are so distrustful and two-faced as to tell lies about their parents then is it worth living with them, thought Maria and felt lonely and deceived in a way. She rushed to her room at once and hiding her face in her pillow cried terribly. We all talk of love, praise it for its power to act as the finest balm for any wound yet why is it so absent in us? Maria wished somebody to answer her eternal query.

5

'So what have you decided?' Sandip asked with a serious expression on his face. He was slurping coffee from a mug noisily. It often irritated Akash but he ignored it, knowing very well that the incorrigible Sandip would not change his way of drinking tea or coffee.

'It is not something that you can decide with rational thinking and that's why I thought of discussing it with you,' Akash said a bit irritably.

'I am positively not qualified to give guidance on such a matter. All I can tell you is that whatever your decision is let Maria know it soon. If a girl loves you with all her heart you must not keep her waiting to let know your decision for such a long period. One year of time is too much.'

'But Sandip, you are not really understanding my predicament. I like her a lot, not because she is head over heels in love with me,' paused Akash while deep frown came to his forehead. 'She is not a run-of-the-mill kind of girl. Well, she may be an ordinary girl in many senses but possesses a very tender heart. Around a month back she was supposed to meet me at 4.00 pm in front of Macdonald in Bandra.

You know I am punctual to a fault. I religiously reached there ten minutes before the appointed time. When it was fifteen minutes past four and there was no call from her to inform me that she might get late I called her. Her cell phone rang until No answer displayed on my cell phone. Five minutes later I made another call and then another. Just after half past four, extremely pissed off with her, cursing myself repeatedly for being on time, I thought of leaving. I got my cell phone and was typing an angry text message for her when I saw her coming. She was carrying a rucksack, which looked very heavy, as she was slightly leaning front. Seeing me from distance a sense of relief came to her face. As she came close to me I saw that the kajol in her eyes was smudged for, probably, she had cried. There was no smile on her face that she usually has once she comes to meet me. Her lips were dry and slightly parted.

I told her dryly, 'I am here for last forty minutes if you really care to know.'

'I was in Mount Mary church,' she said in a small voice.

So she was praying there or gossiping with someone without caring for my waiting for her, thought I as again anger rising within me.

'And you were so busy in praying or talking to someone that you did not bother to receive my call. I called you no less than five times in last fifteen minutes.'

'My cell was in my bag and it was not with me,' she said slowly, without revealing much. She looked disheartened.

'You know very well I hate waiting for anyone,' I said. 'By the way what caused you the delay?'

'How can people be so heartless and rude, Akash?' she asked me.

At first I thought she was referring to me but soon she revealed everything.'

'On the previous night someone had left a few-days-old girl in a wicker basket in front of the church. The child was plump and fair. Very obviously it was an illegitimate child whose parents wanted to get rid of it. And what could be better place to desert such a kid than the entrance of a temple or a church. However, the church authority took the immediate charge of the kid and named her Aakhansha. This afternoon when she went to Mount Mary to pray for me she came to know of the child and forgetting everything else spent more than an hour with the child.'

"It is such a beautiful girl, Akash. Its cheeks are red and hair curly. Once it held my finger. How can any parents be so stony-hearted as to abandon such a loving girl?' She asked me while hot tears rolled down her eyes.'

'I was speechless, Sandip, as her simple words touched me to the core. Never did I encounter a girl with such a tender heart.'

'Then why do not you accept her proposal? It is already more than a year since she had proposed you,' Sandip asked directly.

Akash dithered. 'It is so difficult to explain to you that there is a narrow line between loving someone and liking someone. I like her because she is a good person and she makes me feel special but I want to love someone who really appeals me,' said Akash, haltingly. He was not sure whether Sandip had understood his feeling.

Sandip inspected Akash for a long moment and then said slowly, 'Dear brother, I have only one request, do not mingle your intellect with love. I have a deep regard for your intellect but love is an altogether different thing. If she really loves you do not expect any better reward from life.'

Akash remained silent. 'I need some more time to decide,' he said at last.

'Is she ready to wait for your response as long as you want?' asked Sandip.

'She told me that she could wait for ages to be with me. She even said to me that her feeling towards me would not change even if I could not love her one day,' said Akash without looking at Sandip. He felt a stab of guilt in his chest as he remembered Maria's innocent face.

'Life is so strange,' said Sandip with a chuckle. 'Some people yearns for true love and some spurn true love. I am not sure who is more unfortunate among these two types of people.'

'But, Sandip, I cannot force myself to love someone. It should naturally grow within me,' Akash tried to justify his point.

'Okay,' said Sandip, shrugging his shoulders. 'Another round of coffee?'

'I do not mind,' said Akash indifferently, lost in his own thoughts.

They were sitting in one of their favourite hangout places. It was Udipi restaurant near Chembur station. It was famous for its steaming filter coffee and mouth-watering Mysore Masala dosa. Akash often brought Maria here and she liked this place as much as she liked Tastings.

Filter coffee was served soon and both the friends sipped coffee in silence.

'Akash, if Maria were good-looking with the same intrinsic qualities, would you have accepted her proposal? If it is yes then all I can say that your hesitation is only because she is short and does not look attractive. But brother, someone's physical beauty is immaterial if you have seen her inner beauty,' Sandip stopped and drained the last of the coffee.

Akash felt slightly humiliated by what Sandip said as Sandip had caught him in the raw.

'Let's go,' said Sandip, paying the bill.

'When will aunty leave?' Akash asked, hoping to stop discuss Maria.

'Next week and I am leaving on 19th, exactly a week after she leaves. Countdown has already began.' Sandip gave a lopsided smile.

'This time aunty was here for more than three months.'

'Yeah, now she wants to stay in our village home for sometime. May be after a couple of months she will be back here. Actually she does not want our house to be completely in tenants' custody for a long time.'

'Are you on two-weeks' leave?'

'Yeah, this time it was a bit difficult to get leave sanctioned. That bastard of a Patel grumbled a lot before sanctioning my leave. He is a bloody sadist.'

'But why are you going to Rajastan again? You have already been there twice,' asked Akash.

'This time I would visit Mount Abu, Udaipur and Chitorghar and Jodhpur. I have not set my foot in these places before,' stopped Sandip and began after a while, 'I hope that by the time I come back to Bombay you will accept Maria's proposal. And I have a hunch that today or tomorrow your liking for her would turn into love for her.'

'I hope so,' said Akash absentmindedly as he saw Jasvinder Singh entering Udipi alone. He looked visibly disturbed. There were dark patches beneath his eyes. Though he was as handsome as before but had an air of loneliness about him.

'See, Jassi is there; do you think he looks disturbed?' Akash asked Sandip in undertone.

'Yes, he does. But why? He has a pretty sexy wife who must be giving him a good time. I thought getting a pretty girlfriend or wife solves all problem s of life,' said Sandip, somewhat sarcastically.

Akash ignored the acid in Sandip's remark.

'They are constantly bickering since they got married. Twice I had seen Sujata running down the stairs of our building. She was agitated and her eyes moistened. It occurred to me that Jassi often beats her. Late at night as I go for a walk sometimes I hear heated argument going on between them and followed by muffled crying of Sujata.'

'Women in the neighbourhood flats must be very happy as Jassi and Sujata's spat give them enough material for idle gossip,' Sandip said disinterestedly. They both stole stealthy glance at Jasvinder who was drinking coffee, sitting alone at a table in a corner of the restaurant. He was gazing at the floor unblinkingly, lost in his own maze of thoughts.

'There are many unhappy people who do not know the real cause for their unhappiness,' Sandip said.

They were about to leave Udipi when Akash's eyes met Jasvinder's and he gave Akash a dry smile. Akash reciprocated with a friendly smile at him at once. Jasvinder thought for a moment and beckoned Akash to join him. Akash could sense that Jasvinder wanted to talk to someone for a while to cheer him up.

Though Jasvinder was staying on the second floor, just above Akash's flat the communication between them was never more than Hi and Hello. Akash was naturally silent and Jasvinder, for his own reason, never took interest in talking to other boys. Akash hesitated for a moment and asked Sandip in a low tone, 'I think I should talk to him for sometime. Are you joining us?'

'No man, why should he share his sorrow and pain with me while he can do it with a writer,' said Sandip playfully.

'Fuck man,' said Akash. 'No publishers care for my work. I often doubt whether I have any writing skill.'

'Well, you carry on. I will push off now,' said Sandip and left immediately.

As Akash reached Jasvinder's table he motioned Akash to sit opposite him.

'Tea or coffee?' asked Jasvinder, somewhat awkwardly.

'I already had two cups of filter coffee. Enough for today,' smiled Akash.

'Have one more, yaar. You have no one at home to guide you, to tell you what you should eat and what not ...' he wanted to say something more but stopped suddenly.

'Which shift do you have today?' he asked Akash after a few moments.

'Night,' said Akash.

'So you are not in a hurry to leave?'

'No, I am not. Have not you gone to office today?' asked Akash.

'I am on leave for a week. Sujata has gone to her parents place in Patna this morning. So I am alone now.'

'You did not go to drop her?' Akash asked casually.

'No,' replied Jasvinder dryly. 'Her father came to collect her. Actually she is expecting, three-month pregnant.'

'So soon you would become a proud father,' smiled Akash.

'May be,' Jasvinder said indifferently.

Akash did not say anything. He was surprised by Jasvinder's insipid reply.

'So when are you getting married?' asked Jasvinder after a short while.

'I have not thought of my marriage yet,' said Akash.

'What about your girlfriend? Is not she insisting you on marrying her soon?'

'My girlfriend?' Akash grinned. 'Come on, I do not have a girlfriend.'

'But I often see you hanging out with a small girl. I thought she must be your girlfriend,' Jasvinder said casually.

Though Akash was slightly miffed with Jasvinder's referring to Maria as a small girl he thought of ignoring it for now.

'We are just friends,' Akash said rigidly.

'I am not interested in poking nose into others' personal matters. But I have a small suggestion, friend. If one day she claims to love you and tells you that she could not live without you, remember, all girls are expert in saying such emotional words. If you are carried away by such words and marry her one day, you are screwed forever. Soon she would show you her true colour, expecting you to behave every moment the way she wishes to and soon your life would be hell. Every time you talk to some one, laughing over phone, she might get suspicious. In short, you will lose your freedom completely. So do not marry, Akash, for after marriage you would terribly miss your bachelorhood. All day and night you would be with only one woman whose nagging would make your life living hell,' Jasvinder stopped.

His anguished face told Akash that Jasvinder was actually telling him about his own married life. It was apparent that Sujata and he did not get along together.

Akash did not say anything but was lost in his own thoughts. He remembered Maria and everything she had told him over a year to express her love for him. Who knows, she may change after marriage, thought Akash with a shudder. Now she is ready to do anything to earn my love but how much time will it really take her to change from a doting lover to a domineering and meddling spouse? A long train of thoughts passed through Akash's mind about the unpredictability of marriage and fragility of love.

'What are you thinking about?' asked Jasvinder.

'Nothing in particular,' said Akash, forcing himself to smile.

'I think one of the funniest things is that we man are very sentimental as we think that woman consider it as a virtue. Little do we understand that they make use of our being emotional.'

Akash remained silent.

'Let's go,' said Jasvinder, rising to his feet. 'In a way I am bachelor for next few months. I want to enjoy my forced bachelorhood to the fullest.'

'Bye,' said Akash as they left Udipi.

Akash did not leave immediately but stood near Udipi's entrance for sometime, observing the parents and daughter selling Mogra flower on the pavement near Udipi.

Many a time he had seen them before. He had also used them as the characters of one of his stories. They always drew his attention for the deep love he witnessed between the husband and wife.

How lucky they are as they do not doubt each other's love, thought Akash as he kickstarted his motorbike. As he reached near Diamond Park something caught his attention. Jasvinder was talking with a girl, standing in front of Baskin and Robbins. No more did he look disturbed rather a disarming smile was playing on his lips. Sitting on his bike, near the traffic signal, Akash saw Jasvinder leading his partner inside Baskin and Robbins, draping his hand around her. Most probably, his promiscuity is one of the reasons for his regular fight with Sujata, thought Akash as the signal turned green.

6

He was sitting cross-legged on the floor. His elder brother was sitting by him, placing his assuring and comforting hand on his thigh. He passed a furtive glance at his father, clad in white shirt and trousers, sitting a few feet away from him. His hair dishevelled, shoulder stooped as he was looking at his wife's dead body in front of him. As he looked at his father he could see that there was no remorse or regret in his eyes, rather he wanted to get off this ordeal as soon as possible. Suddenly he felt like giving full vent to his anger by shouting, calling him the monster who killed his mother but then a fear seized him. What if later his father kicked him out of his place for shouting at him in front of so many people? Where will he go? What will he eat? He thought and decided not to say anything to his father so long as he was financially dependent on him. He then looked at his mother's body. She had died four ours before. Yet now he harboured a hope that any moment she might get up, proving the doctor who had certified that she passed away wrong. She seemed to be sleeping so blissfully without any sign of worry or agony on her face. For a moment he felt good for his mother as she had been set free forever from the suffering of her present life. A searing pain filled him as he remembered that he could not do anything to alleviate his mother's trials and tribulation. Again he looked at his mother's face. Her eyes closed, lips joined, hair properly combed. She looked so calm and tranquil. A wisp of perfumed smoke rising up from a bunch of agarbatti placed in an agarbatti-stand near her mother's head. Her whole body was covered with a white cloth except for her face and feet. He looked at her toes where beneath her nails there accumulated a think layer of dirt. How much she cared to trim his fingernails, comb his hair, polish his school shoes, and wash his uniform. She also loved to spruce herself all the time. But, of late, she had lost interest in everything for, probably, she knew that her days were numbered, thought the twelve-year-old boy. That's why in the recent months she often said to me, 'When I would not be there do study harder, eat your food regularly and take care of yourself. Remember there would not be another mother in life.'

A sharp pain throbbed his being as he got up from his place. So far he had not shed a single drop of tears since his mother died. He went to his room and got the nail clippers. He sat by her feet and trimmed all her toenails. He then smoothened the edge of her nails with the nail file with extreme care as his mother had always done for his. Every time after cutting one his nails she would ask him, 'did it hurt you, beta?' After cutting her toenails he reached for her right hand beneath the white sheet. Nails in her right hand were properly cut though not well-shaped. He spread her palm on his lap observed it minutely.

One of the regular games between the mother and son was palm-reading. Whenever he found her in an unhappy mood he would sit by her and tell her in a serious tone of voice, 'Dear daughter, let me see your palm and I would tell you why you look so unhappy.' His mother would give him her hand without any protest. Keeping her palm in front of him he would pretend to read it and then started making all funny predictions he could remember to make her smile. He invariably ended his predictions by saying that, 'You have a very long life and you will outlive your younger son.'

This statement was enough to make his mother give him a playful spank on his back. 'Do not talk like this. I live only for you and your brother. Otherwise, long back I would have... ' her voice trailed off.

'I would never let you go anywhere leaving us alone,' he would say, hugging his mother.

He held her hand tight against his chest. It was cold and unresponsive. Slowly he placed her hand back inside the white sheet and, then placing his head on her he started weeping convulsively.

Somebody held him from behind, trying to take him away from his mother's body. From the rigid touch of the fingers he knew that it was his father. Never before was he so enraged with his father. With all his might he pushed his elbow back with an intension to hit his father in his ribs. But his elbow hit something very hard. He grunted with the stabbing pain and opened his eyes. For a moment he was in a state of puzzlement. He was sitting in a recliner, resting his legs in a plastic chair in front of him. Beside him on the table a laptop was lying open. It was in sleep mode. He understood that he got hurt for hitting the edge of the table. Although the room was specious it was bare save for a divan, a chair and a table. How have I reached here? Where is my mother? Thought Chirag and soon understood that he was in ICL colony, in his flat on the fourth floor, all alone. A pang of solitariness filled him that he always found difficult to shake off.

He got up from his chair and went to his bedroom. This room often accentuated his sense of loneliness but now he felt a sense of comfort as he saw a pair of Maina's jeans, sleeveless T-shirts and flimsy lingerie hanging from a nylon rope. Maina had left one set of her cloths at his place on her last visit to his place.

Maina was the first woman in his life with whom he often talked about his deep-seated love for his mother. She was ready to lend an ear to him. Slowly he realized that she understood him much better than he imagined. Though he never mentioned his loneliness to her she could easily sense it. She had her ingenious ways of helping him to stave off his loneliness. Sometimes she would deliberately left her used cloths at his bedroom. The smell emanated from her cloth was enough to give him a sense of her presence around him. She was extremely good at drawing and often drew something with crayons on the walls of his flat before leaving.

'How do you find it?' she would ask him, displaying one of her small piece of drawing to him.

'It is a masterpiece,' Chirag would say, finding no better world to appreciate her.

He felt blissful in her embrace yet a fear always chased him. There was no commitment between them. What if one day Maina left him? It might not be difficult to get girls who would be happy to be his friend and share bed with him. But the idea of changing girlfriend every second month – something he always found so adventurous and challenging even a few years back — did not excite him anymore.

He walked across the room to the nylon rope and touched her delicate bra and panty. Touching her undergarments gave him a vague feeling that he was not alone in the world. Yet he knew such feeling was hollow and short-lived.

He left his bedroom and headed to the kitchen to get a mug of coffee for himself. Over the months he had developed a liking for coffee and he owed Akash for that. Apart form Maina, it was only Akash to whom he felt comfortable to talk about his vulnerable side.

He boiled the milk and was about to open the lid to coffee powder bottle when something caught his attention. He heard a woman's voice chiding her son affectionately for pulling her suitcase carelessly. But her son defended himself at once, 'Why are you so fussy, Mummy? These castors are very strong. Even if I pull the suitcase on a bumpy road for a kilometre it will not break the castors.'

'How do you know that? You always carry a backpack to go anywhere,' asked the mother, reaching the lift door.

'I know because I am the son of an intelligent woman,' said the son. The sliding door of the lift got closed as Chirag, speechless, stood in the kitchen, holding the coffee powder bottle with both his hands.

He knew that Sandip's mother was going back to her hometown and that Sandip was going to see her off. Every time he heard a lively and cheerful conversation between the mother and son he experienced a pang of jealousy within his being. At once he rushed to the bedroom, where, standing by the window, he could have an unobstructed view of the main road in front of his apartment building.

He waited for Sandip and his mother and around half a minute later he saw them walking. Sandip was trundling his mother's suitcase and his other protective hand was around his mother's waist. His mother was walking with considerable agility for her age. Chirag gazed at Sandip's mother, with a look hungry for maternal love. He did not know what really came over Sandip's mother as all of a sudden she slowed down and turning her head; she looked over her shoulder to Chirag's window. Involuntarily Chirag raised his hand and waved at her. She acknowledged it with a tender smile and then continued walking in her usual pace. The exchange of greetings took place within a second but it had a deep effect on Chirag. He felt as though after many years emptiness within his heart filled with love and affection for the first time.

Had he been on a speaking terms with Sandip, he would have rushed down the stairs now to reach Sandip's mother and requested her to stay with him for a few days. He stood by the window as long as he could see Sandip's mother.

Akash's heart palpitated with an unknown fear as he heard a confident footfall approaching the telephone. He pressed his cell phone tightly against his ear lest he might miss a single word she would say to him.

After repeated rejection from no less than ten publishers, slowly a belief grew up in his mind that due to some unknowable reason, no matter whatever he wrote, would never get published. No publishers would ever give him an explanation for not publishing his work. The editorial department of all the publishers always appeared distant and unapproachable. He desperately wanted some noted literary figure to guide him, help him understand as to how he could improve his work. And then one day he couriered a few of his stories to Shobhaa De, hoping that she might guide him. She, however, was unusually kind over phone. She confirmed him that she had been in receipt of Akash's courier and that she would look into it in a week's time.

For the next one week Akash counted the days and this morning, nine days later, once he phoned Shobhaa De, her home maid picked up the receiver.

'Tell madam that it is Akash from Chembur,' said Akash.

'Please wait,' said the maid, keeping the receiver down.

Shobhaa De came after a few seconds.

'Good morning, Madam,' began Akash.

'Yes, Akash,' said she. Her voice was measured and concise.

'Madam, did you read any of my stories?' asked Akash.

'Yes, I did,' said Shobhaa De. 'Your work is good. Your storylines are fresh and original and writing style lucid. But you are unlikely to find a reputed publisher who may publish a short story collection of a first time author.'

'Why, madam?' Akash asked anxiously.

'Because, Akash, short story collection does not have a market. So I suggest you try your hand at writing novel. It should be around 80 thousand words. You are on the right track. But do not be in a hurry to pen down a novel. Let an idea sprout in your mind naturally. From the characters, think on it and then only start writing. I think you can write a good novel.'

'Thanks, madam, thanks a lot,' said Akash gratefully. It was beyond his imagination that Shobhaa De would speak with him for so long.

'Only one question, madam, if I write a full-fledged novel will any publisher publish it?' asked Akash earnestly.

Shobhaa De smiled over phone. 'The future is unknown to everyone. If you love writing, keep doing it. My blessing and best wishes are with you.'

'Thanks madam, your words mean a lot to me.'

'Good luck, Akash,' said Shobhaa and replaced the receiver.

For a moment Akash was floating on air. Shobhaa De praised his work – it meant his works had some literary worth. He must talk to someone about his discussion with Shobhaa De and Maria was his obvious choice. He called Maria at once.

'Hi Maria, just now I had a talk with Shobhaa De,' said the excited Akash as Maria received his call. She was in her office.

'Hold for a moment, Akash, let me go out. Signal is not good here,' said she and then Akash heard her walking a few steps.

'Now tell me what are you saying?' said Maria.

'Maria, Shobhaa De loved my writings. Can you imagine that she took time out to read my work. She suggested that I write a novel.'

'When did you send your work to her? Why did not you tell me?' she sounded somewhat depressed over phone.

'I couriered my work to her around two weeks back. I am feeling very good, Maria. That's why I phoned you.'

'I am always happy when you are happy, Akash,' said Maria but there was no excitement in her voice.

Akash was silent for a moment as he felt a sense of guilt inside. Every time he felt happy or a new storyline struck him he invariably phoned her to share his exhilaration but had he ever really cared for her happiness? Now it was more than one and a half year since she had proposed him. He desperately wanted to help her, make her feel good yet he was never sure whether he loved her not.

Over phone he heard her drawing deep breaths and knew that she was feeling sad and disheartened. Suddenly he felt he must do something to enliven her mood.

'Actually I phoned you to ask something else. Are you free day after tomorrow, I mean, this Saturday?' asked Akash.

'I am always free for you, Akash,' she said in a weak voice.

'I want to take you to Elephanta caves. For the whole day we would be out but only if you are okay with this plan,' he proposed, hoping to cheer up Maria's mood.

'Elephanta Caves,' said Maria after a while. 'It would take around three hours to reach there. We have to leave by eight or nine in the morning.'

'Yes, will you come with me?'

'Yes, Akash. One hundred time yes,' she said when her voice throbbed with emotion.

'And this evening I will meet you at Tastings at 7 pm provided you leave office on time,' said Akash, desperate to make her happy.

'I will reach before that.'

'Okay, bye.'

A short pause and then she said, 'You know something, Akash?'

'What?' he breathed.

'Love you,' said she and cut the phone.

'I do not mind going there but remember we should not waste more than half an hour on breakfast. It is already ten,' said Akash, consulting his watch.

'Okay sir, your wish is my command,' Maria smiled merrily.

They were standing outside Café Kyani and Co, a respectable Parsi café near Metro theatre. Akash looked at Maria and knew she had spent long time in the morning to make her look beautiful. She wore a sleeveless kurta with a very fancy stole around her shoulder and a pair of denim Jeans. Her hands and face looked slightly fair. Probably she had spent an hour in a parlour last evening, thought Akash.

Her eyebrows properly plucked and the line of thin hairs, sometimes he saw above her upper lips, was delicately removed. She had generously applied kajol to her eyes. After every few seconds she was rubbing both her lips against each other to spread the lip gloss evenly. With her two-inch-heel shoe she reached just above his shoulder.

He knew that she had taken all pains to smarten herself up only to draw his attention.

'You are looking good,' said he, looking into her eyes. Her eyes were moist, full of love for him.

She gave him a smile, 'Are you saying it to please me? I know very well, Akash, that I have no physical beauty.'

Akash felt that she emphasised on the words 'physical beauty'.

'Good,' he said amusedly, raising his eyebrows, 'what are the other types of beauty?'

'What is the use of talking of the thighs which are to be felt?'

'Wow, that's really philosophical. Let's go to the café,' said Akash and holding her delicate wrist crossed the road.

She had a penchant for Parsi food and ordered all her favourite dishes for Akash.

'How have you come to know of this place?' Akash asked Maria as the waiter left two glasses of water for them.

'First tell me have you liked this place?'

Akash passed a cursory glance around him. The café looked no less than 50 years old. Straight-backed wooden chairs were place around the round table. A transparent glass of round shape was kept on each table and beneath the glass menu card was on display. The room was very spacious with a very high ceiling and from the ceiling old fans were hanging above each table. A few of them were running in a languorous pace, with bothering to throw enough air down. In one corner of the café a three-feet-tall coin operated weighing machine was standing with a sulky face. An A4 sized hand-written paper attached to its display screen. It said: Out of order. On the wall there were age-old sepia glass-framed photograph of Jesus Christ, Zarathustra and Mother Mary. Two old grandfather clocks with long pendulum must have seen better days, yet ungrudgingly, they were showing right time.

The restaurant was crowded still the respectable distance between the tables afforded all its visitors to make personal talk. The most beautiful thing about the restaurant was that it was adamantly reluctant to be touched by a tinge of modernity.

'It's an ideal place for creative people,' said Akash after a few moments. Meanwhile custard was served in glass bowl. It was yellow in colour, thick and topped with a red cherry.

'So I have brought the right man to the right place,' Maria smiled, putting a piece of custard into her mouth.

Within five minutes the table was full with plates, containing Chicken Pattice, Mutton Pattice, Chicken nuggets and two cups of Irani Chai.

'Do you think after eating so much we could climb those long steps to reach Elephanta?' asked Akash, enjoying delicious custard.

'We do not come here everyday. Moreover, this tea will help you digest everything you eat here,' smiled Maria.

'Never did I hear that tea should be consumed for better digestion.'

'Just kidding, you know they serve excellent pudding too.'

'Should I ask them to get pudding for us?' proposed Akash.

'No, no,' Maria protested vehemently.

'Why no, if you really like it so much?' asked a puzzled Akash.

'You order anything you wish to but no pudding please,' she gave an enigmatic smile.

Akash shrugged his shoulders. 'Well, I do not want anything else. Already stuffed.'

Once the waiter left the bill they both struggled to grab it. Very obviously Akash succeeded in snatching it first. He checked the bill. It was one hundred thirty-six.

'The place is very reasonable, considering its location,' said Akash. '

'But it is not just. I have brought you here. We had a pact before entering here that I would pay the bill,' Maria said with an affected anger, reaching into her backpack for her purse.

'I do not remember any deal like that,' grinned Akash, getting on his feet, walking towards the counter with determined stride. Maria silently followed him.

Behind the counter, sitting on a comfortable swivel chair was a big fat man. He was unusually fair and on the wrong side of seventy. In spite of his alarming obesity and older age he was constantly munching something. He was almost bald, bespectacled and with flabby hands and a prominent double chin. His face considerably resembled that of the celebrated astrologer Bejan Daruwalla. What really drew Akash's attention to him was a twinkle in his eyes as if even at this age he was very much in love with life.

Akash gave the bill and a five-hundred rupee note to him and said with a courteous smile, 'One-thirty-six.'

The fat man paid a brief glance at the bill, tossed it to a basket and took the five-hundred rupee note with a disapproving frown on his forehead. He held it up against the light and inspected it for a long moment while Akash and Maria stood by the counter, somewhat astonished by the old man's behaviour.

'Do you think that this note is not a fake one?' asked the old man. He possessed a baritone voice that demanded an immediate attention.

'Positively not,' Akash said confidently. 'Yesterday only I got it from ATM.'

'How do you know that it is a genuine note?'

Though Akash was a bit angry with the old man's annoying question he kept his cool and explained to the old man as to why the currency note was not a fake one.

The old man chuckled, 'Young man, you do not even know how to check a note,' he said to Akash and took the note from him.

He folded the currency note in two and then again in half. He now placed the folded note on the table and whacked it several times as though he was swatting a mosquito which had sucked enough of his blood. He then unfolded the note and inspected it for a long moment.

'It is not a fake note,' he announced with a smile at Akash, displaying his strong pair of teeth.

'How do you know?' asked Akash, completely bowled over by the old man's technique of checking the genuineness of a currency note.

'See, I slapped it hard no less than five times, yet his glasses has not broken. It means it is not a fake note,' he said seriously, indicating the imprint of bespectacled Gandhi on the currency note.

Akash laughed uproariously at once as he was so unprepared for such a joke. Maria, however, took a bit of time to grasp the whole thing and once she understood the jokes she gave a hearty smile. For the next few minutes Akash and the old man talked to each other, sharing jokes to one another. The ending of each joke worked as the beginning of a fresh joke.

Looking at them, finding Akash's inexhaustible supply of good jokes and his power of presenting them with good humour, a sense of pride filled Maria. She inched towards him and held his wrist, looking at the old man with manifest pride. She wanted the whole world to know this young man was her and only her.

The old man was shrewd enough to understand her feelings.

'Are you guys married?' he asked Maria with a glint of fun in his eyes.

'Not yet,' she replied confidently.

'Well, invite me on your marriage,' said the old man, giving the change to Akash.

Akash left ten-rupee tip for the waiter and left the restaurant. This time Maria was holding his wrist, leading him to cross the road. A ten-minute-ride brought them to Gateway of India. Akash parked his bike behind Taj hotel, near Bade Minya, one of the most famous roadside eateries in the metropolis of Bombay.

On weekends ferries for Elephanta was easily available and within fifteen minutes they were in a well-built ferry. It could accommodate no less than one hundred people easily.

'Let's go up, on the roof,' Akash said to Maria, indicating the wooden stair, leading to the roof. A burly, dark-skinned fellow was standing by the stair and collecting ten-rupee from each one who wanted to go to the roof.

'Wow,' Maria exclaimed, reaching the roof of the ferry. She went near the iron railing and looked far. The sea was silent and tranquil, dotted with ferries, small fishing boats and speedboats. Behind them was the majestic Taj hotel and the splendid monument of Gateway of India.

'Bombay cannot look more beautiful from anywhere else. I can vouch for it,' said Maria. She was brimming with happiness. In the centre of the roof there was a small room where the ferry driver sat and controlled the speed and the direction of the ferry. They sat in a bench in front of the driver's room. Soon the engine grunted, the boat shook and glided forwards while a fresh and crisp wind kissed them.

'Happy?' Akash asked Maria after a while.

'I was never so happy. I desire everyday of my life to be like this day,' she paused and gazing at the distant island of Elephanta added, 'with you.'

'Which birds are those? They look like dove,' asked Maria after sometime, pointing a bird, flying for a few moments and then suddenly swooped down to the sea to catch a fish.

'It is not a dove, stupid,' smiled Akash. 'It is a seagull. One of the seabirds.'

'See, a flock of seagulls,' exclaimed Maria, trying to get camera from her bag. Rarely did they see such a magnificent view. In front of them no less than twenty seagulls were sitting comfortably on the shining seawater, rippling by the morning breeze.

'I have never seen something so beautiful,' said Akash. They both gazed at the flock of birds as long as they could.

Akash had come to Elephanta many times before but it was Maria's maiden trip. She loved the roadside shops selling trinkets, fancy jewelleries, small monuments, hats. After every five or six shops there was a straw-thatched eating place from where the aroma of freshly-fried vada pav, bhajiya was emanating. The owner of all these roadside eateries kept a strong and long stick with themselves to save their produce from the ruthless attacks of the monkeys. Some shopkeepers had slingshots with them and over a period of practice they had earned a sure aim of shooting stones at the monkeys. It was the only tourist destination near Bombay where the foreign tourist outnumbered the local tourists.

The steps were made by cutting the stones and they were no less than one feet in height yet the small Maria was climbing the flight of steps with considerable ease and alacrity.

'Have you liked this cave?' Akash asked Maria as they entered the first cave.

'It's awesome,' said Maria. ''I feel that I am in a far off land, thousands of kilometre away from Bombay.'

'Then why did not you come here before?'

'Why did not you bring me here before?' she beamed.

After visiting the last cave they sat beneath a tall Banyan tree when two big monkeys with red posterior looked at them disapprovingly and then baring their teeth to them for several times they left, wagging their prehensile tails.

The shadow beneath the tree was soft and pleasant. There was a soothing murmur around as the dry foliage was rolling on the ground by the gentle breeze.

'We should come here once a month,' Maria remarked.

Akash nodded absentmindedly. A young man who had a passing resemblance with Jasvinder Singh captured his attention for a moment. A pretty young lady accompanied him. It reminded Akash of seeing Jasvinder at Chembur station the previous day. He looked full of energy and was his original self. His partner was a beautiful young woman in her early twenties. She dressed with taste and had her hair permed. As Akash eye's met Jasvinder's, with a distant nod he hinted Akash that he did not want to talk to Akash now. It occurred to Akash if Sujata and Jasvinder's marriage was going through a bad phase, Sujata had many reasons to be suspicious about Jasvinder's lifestyle.

'What are you thinking about Mr. Philosopher?' asked Maria.

'Well, Maria, what will you do if one day you find that your husband is cheating on you?' asked Akash.

'Why do you ask such an irrelevant question? I am in a good mood now. Please…. No such talk like, cheating, suicide, infidelity, death and all that.'

'Okay, sorry. I feel like having something,' Akash said casually.

'Then have it,' said Maria, reaching into her bag and taking out a tupperwell Tiffin box.

'What is it?' asked Akash, taking the Tiffin box from Maria.

'Can not you open it and check?'

'Sorry, yaar,' smiled Akash and opened the Tiffin box. He was silent for a moment as he found a big heart-shaped pudding was inside the box. It could be easily understood that it had been prepared with utmost care and attention. Soon he realized as to why she had not ordered pudding at café Kyani and Co.

'Have it before monkeys snatch it from you.'

'I would let any monkey snatch it from me for it was made with so much love,' said Akash. He was deeply touched by her love.

'Eat it now,' ordered Maria.

Akash nibbled at it. 'It is delicious,' he said.

'I spent two hours last night preparing it.'

Akash, indeed, loved the pudding. It was soft inside and its edge crusty. She had generously added small pieces of cashew nuts, kismis to the pudding.

'Will not you have it?' Akash asked Maria.

'No, I do not like pudding prepared by me,' smiled Maria and continued watching Akash enjoying the pudding with a satisfactory look on her face. Akash was about to put the last morsel of pudding into his mouth when Maria stopped him. Without uttering a word she took the small piece from him and ate it.

'But you told me that you do not like pudding made by you?' Akash asked.

'Yeah.'

'Then?'

'I ate it because it touched you, your teeth, your tongue and your mouth.'

'Let's go,' said Akash, holding her hand.

They walked down the long steps in silence and stopped near a small shop selling monuments, metal bust of Buddha, Hindu God and Goddess, crystal balls and so forth. Akash got a small statue of Mother Mary and Infant Jesus for Maria.

When they caught the ferry it was 3 o'clock. They directly went to the roof and settled near the driver's room.

'Will we go to Kyani again?' asked Maria.

'Do you want to?'

'I do not mind a cup of tea and a bun maska.'

'Okay, then we will go.'

There were no more than fifteen passengers on the roof of the ferry and three young boys among them were smoking. They were in early twenties, strongly built, with an air of arrogance about them. Akash found their presence near him and Maria disturbing. Mainly one of the boys with long hair and bloodshot eyes was looking at Maria every second minute. His face was full of malevolence. Every time Akash saw him ogling at Maria an unknown fear filled him. He was never good at fighting and always preferred avoiding boys who were in a combative mood. He was not sure whether Maria could see any worry on his face but she placed her small assuring hand on his knee.

The ferry had barely cruised two kilometres while all of a sudden a wicked fancy seized the bunch of boys. One of them got a slingshot and a handful of small marble balls from his bag. He carefully placed one of the marble balls in the centre of the rubber band attached to the slingshot and pulled the rubber band towards him, aiming at a flock of seagulls, swimming and ducking under the water. In Elephanta Maria and Akash had seen the owners of roadside eateries keeping such slingshot with themselves to ward off monkeys' attack. The boy had a sure aim with the slingshot and the marble hit a seagull. The seagull released a painful crock at once. Opening its beak it struggled for breath for a few seconds before it succumbed to its pain. As its lifeless body floated in the water all the seagulls around it sensed danger and started dispersing soon by flying in different directions. A seagull flew in the direction of the ferry and was welcome with a sudden hit of a marble ball. As it made a helpless fall to the sea Akash felt anger boiling within him. The exhibition of such a cruel act in front of him made him extremely courageous. Without a second thought he walked towards the three boys in a determined stride. One of them was placing a new marble ball in the slingshot when Akash snatched it from him and threw it at the sea.

'It is not for killing innocent birds,' he said, without thinking of the consequence of his audacious act.

For a moment all the three boys were surprised by Akash's temerity and then they smiled as if they were amused by Akash's brave deed.

'Really, so you would like to teach us how to use a slingshot?' asked the tallest boy among the three while the other boys held Akash by his wrist.

No sooner had the boys held Akash's arm than Maria almost jumped near him with feline agility.

'How dare you touch him?' she spluttered. Her otherwise innocent eyes were flashing fire. She was trembling with fury. She held Akash by his arm and released him from the boys' grip.

'How dare you touch him?' she shouted again. Never in his wildest dream had Akash thought that Maria could ever be furious. As her whole body throbbed and she breathed heavily, staring angrily at the bunch of boys, she looked like a ferocious cat whose newborn kittens were troubled by a mischief-maker.

Suddenly finding an aggressive Maria in an attacking mood all the three boys got confused. Meanwhile the other people on the roof extended their supporting hand to Maria and Akash.

'He has done a right thing. You cannot make poor seagulls the victim of your ugly game,' said a few of them to the boys. The boys did not utter anything continued shooting angry glances at Akash and Maria.

By that time Maria led Akash to the other corner of the roof, holding his hand. Once she was alone with him a concerned look came on her face.

'Did they hurt you?' she asked him in an anxious voice.

'Not really,' Akash said. It was the first time he had seen a protective Maria who would put herself on the line for his safely at any time. She looked into his eyes for a moment and said to him, 'Do not worry. I am always with you. And no one can touch you as long as I am with you.'

She did not release his hand for the rest of the ferry ride. Though she was a small woman without much physical strength Akash felt safe and secured as she held his hand. Yet a fear remained within him.

What if those boys attacked him and Maria once they reached Gateway of India.

They got down from the ferry as soon as it anchored off Ferry gate no – 2 near Gateway of India and walked fast towards Bade Minya where Akash had parked his motorbike. After every few steps he looked back over his shoulder to check whether those boys were following them. Maria could sense Akash's worry and said to him time and again, 'Do not worry, Akash. I am with you.'

Akash's bike reached the traffic signal near Regal theatre when Akash saw those boys on a motorbike. They were few meters behind his motorbike. The rider of the bike was the tallest boy among them. Akash's heart escaped a beat at once. As he adjusted the rare view mirror to avoid eye contact with the bike rider, by chance, their eyes met and the bike rider recognised him at once. His eyes were full of malice as he gave a devilish smile at Akash. Immediately he tried to reach closer to Akash's bike, manoeuvring his motorbike through the other bikes. Akash's heart was thudding against his ribs. He did not want Maria to know that those miscreants were just behind them. Luckily signal turned green at once and Akash shifted the gear and took a sharp turn towards D. N. Road at a breakneck speed. On the rear-view mirror he could see that those boys following him in the same pace. As the bike reached near D. N. Road flyover an idea struck Akash in a flash. Two wheelers were not allowed on this long and winding flyover since some racing bikers had met with fatal accident on the flyover on many isolated occasions. The two-wheeler drivers had to take a detour around Crawford market to meet the highway around two kilometres away near Richardson and Cruddas Building. As Akash was very close to the flyover he dodged the boys. He pretended to take the street to Crawford market but at the last moment caught the flyover. After catching the flyover he drove for a couple of minutes and checked on the rear-view mirror for those boys. Fortunately, they were nowhere close by. Akash heaved a sigh of relief as he felt safe. He did not care to be caught by the traffic police on the flyover for breaking the law.

'So you have befooled those bastards?' asked Maria after a while.

'How did you see those boys?' asked the surprised Akash as they reached the next traffic signal. Luckily there was no traffic constable on duty.

'I did not see those boys but as I saw you scared I knew those boys must be around. Besides you suddenly swerved the bike to catch the flyover.'

'Yes, I was scared of those boys; chiefly, because you are with me. Your safety is my prime concern,' said Akash. The signal turned green.

'Nothing can hurt me so long as my Guardian Angel is with me and no one can touch my Guardian Angel as long as I am with him,' she said, bringing her mouth close to his ear.

'Thank you,' said Akash.

'I am always with you Akash. Please do not feel scared of anything,' she said, holding him from behind with both her hands, pressing her little bosom against him with a hope to infuse courage into him. And strangely enough, Akash felt himself extremely safe and comfortable in her embrace. For the rest of the way there was no communication between them but Maria kept holding him tightly from behind. She released him only after they reached ICL Township. Once Akash stopped the bike in front of Maria's building she got down and gave him a smile, 'Thanks for the beautiful day.'

Akash saw the Kajol in her eyes smudged, beads of sweat on her forehead and nostril. After the tiring day she looked even smaller. She possessed no feminine beauty but for once, Akash saw something else in her which was beyond all physical beauty and attraction. It was her deep courageous love for him.

'Rather I should thank you,' said he.

'For what?'

'For everything, I never knew that you are so different from other girls.'

Suddenly she took his hand and held it closely against her. She closed her eyes as two drops of tears formed at the corner of her kajol-smeared-eyes.

'You do not know, Akash, what you mean to me. I do not know whether you would ever feel it,' she said and slowly and carefully released his hand. Once she opened her eyes they were moist. Without uttering anymore words she walked towards her building.

That evening after reaching his flat Akash felt himself terribly empty. He was always secretly proud of his intellect and creativity but now it occurred to him that in spite of all his intrinsic qualities he was incapable of loving someone as wholeheartedly and ardently as Maria loved him.

No doubt he often displayed love to people but it was only when the entire situation around him was favourable. A real test on love was once the lover was ready to surmount all the obstacles that might come on the way to win his or her love. And in this true test of love Maria was much ahead of him.

He sat in silence for a long time while a searing pain gnawing at his heart and once the pain became unbearable he cried loudly, for no less than ten minutes, and stopped only when his cell phone beeped twice. It was a text message from his PUCHU.

Akash read the message: you have the blessings of so many seagulls for saving their life. Love you.

Feel safe when you are with me: typed Akash and sent the SMS to Maria. There was no response from her.

7

Sandip leaned back in the chair and stretched his legs. He placed his hands behind his head as if to hold it from falling back. Akash studied his face and posture. His whole bearing said to Akash that Sandip was completely at ease with life. His face was as calm as usual but the skin slightly tanned. Two days back he returned after spending two weeks in Rajastan. A mutual silence between both the friends ensued for a full minute and then Sandip began again, after slurping coffee noisily; something Akash disliked about Sandip. They were in Udipi near Chembur station.

'So started working on a novel?' asked Sandip to Akash after a while.

'No, no, it is not easy to write a novel. You have to devise many characters, have to show emotional display between them and what was more, the readers should able to identify themselves with the characters of the novel.'

'Though I am not much into reading fictions like you, so far I know, most of the authors' first novel is usually autobiographical.'

'What will I write about myself?' Akash gave a self-effacing smile. 'It sounds ridiculous that I am writing on my life. Anyway forget about novel writing. So far it is not my cup of tea. Tell me about your trip to Mount Abu and Udaipur.'

'It was good as usual. But certain encounter etched in my memory and you may love hearing those,' Sandip stopped, waiting for Akash's reply.

'Pray to continue,' Akash smiled. He was all ears to hear Sandip.

'One morning while I was having tea from a wayside stall, I saw a small boy scavenging something from a heap of garbage lying near the road. Soon I found that he was searching for a discarded shoe. He had already found one of the shoes and now was searching for the other one. Bad smell was issuing from the heap of dirty garbage but the eight or nine years old boy continued his effort for no less than twenty minutes. And he was beside himself with joy once he got the other shoe. You should have been there to see the expression on his face. It could melt the heart of the cruelest man of the world,' Sandip paused. His eyes were moist. He began again, 'Next evening I saw the boy again. Standing out of a plush restaurant he was looking at it expectantly. Hollywood Bollywood was the name of the restaurant. That evening I offered him having dinner with me and then got a leather jacket for him. But the strangest thing was that never did he talk to me. Every time I asked him anything he would look at me fearfully. But he was definitely not deaf or dumb. Once I gave him the jacket and ruffled his hair affectionately suddenly he cried, holding me tightly. It was so shocking. He then left without uttering a word. I was in Mount Abu for three more days but did not see him again. I do not think I would ever forget that orphan boy.'

Both the friends remained silent for a long time; Sandip, thinking about the boy and Akash's mind already started working to devise a story on the lonely boy with a surprise ending. He spoke after a while, 'Where are you going for your next trip?'

'For next two months I am going nowhere. Anyway, how is Maria?'

'She is fine,' Akash said slowly, lowering his eyes. He always felt sense of guilt in front of Sandip for not accepting Maria's love yet now.

'It is more than two years you guys know each other?'

'Around two and a half.'

'Are you scared that your parents would not accept a Christen girl for their only son?'

'I do not think so,' Akash sighed. 'I do not know as to why sometimes I feel myself so confused.'

'It is the negative side of being too much imaginative,' Sandip smiled dryly. 'She had already shown enough patience. If someday her mind changes and she falls for someone else do not blame her. We are all human being, Akash. Do not expect one-sided eternal love from someone forever.'

For an instant Akash imagined Maria walking, hand in hand, with an unknown guy and at once felt a stab of jealousy within him.

'She told me that I can take as much time as I want to let her know of my decision,' Akash said rigidly.

'She said so because she respected you too,' said Akash.

'Let's go,' said Akash, rising to his feet. He wanted to put a stop their discussion as Sandip's words touched him in the raw.

'Okay,' Sandip gave one of his enigmatic smiles and they both left Udipi.

'But what will you achieve by shifting to Singapore for good?' Chirag asked in a tone of desperation.

'It is not a question of any tangible achievement, Chirag. It is like a test to me. I am entrusted with more responsibility and now it is up to me whether I want to take it or not,' said Maina in a collected voice.

'And you have decided to take it?' Chirag asked helplessly.

'So far that's what my decision is. Besides, Chirag, the world cares a shit whether we have a goal in life but for our own sake we all must have a positive goal. And my simple goal is to dare the unknown. I may settle in Singapore for good and who knows one day I may quit the job with Warner Brothers.'

Chirag did not reply but continued inspecting his fingernails. As present he could not imagine his life without Maina. His life appeared hollow without her. Over last two and a half years a strange relationship developed between them. They were like best friends who shared many things between each other and often made love but yet there was no emotional commitment between one another. On many nights they slept together, holding each other tightly, without having sex. She would discuss the phoney pretenders from the film industry she encountered everyday while he used to tell her about his childhood and his occasional flings since his school days. Every time after a protracted discussion with her he felt himself cleansed. It was such an ecstatic feeling that he often desired for having her forever.

'Why cannot we stay together forever, Maina? We can start a new life, a new relationship from scratch,' he suggested once, evading using the word *Marriage*.

Mania smiled and gave him the most unexpected answer, 'You know, in a beautiful garden of Eden there were two flowers in two different plants. As the wind blew, the birds chirped, the sun shone, the flowers often touched each other, laughed together. One day one of the flowers thought how nice it would have been to be with the other flower forever. God heard her wish and fulfilled it at once. The gardener plucked both the flowers and kept them in a flower vase in his drawing room. The wind did not blow there, the sunshine did not reach there, the birds did not chirp there and within a day both the flowers wilted,'

Maina paused and gave a small smile to Chirag. 'I hope you have got what I meant.'

'But without you I would always be in a flower vase, all alone,' said Chirag.

'No Chirag, you are very much in the garden. Most probably, you belong to a wild tree. But it has its own beauty,' she kissed on his forehead and then pressed his hear against her bosom.

'Will you miss me if you leave Bombay forever?' Chirag asked Maina like an innocent boy. He desperately wanted to know whether he had succeeded in making a place in Maina's mysterious heart.

'Yes, I will. Because I care for you.'

'Why do you care for me? What is so special in me?'

'Because you have opened your heart to me with trust,' she replied as she felt Chirag crying hiding his face between her breasts. She did not utter any soothing words but let him cry.

That evening when Chirag returned his flat after seeing off Maina he felt himself drowsy. As he dozed off, lying on the bed, he had a pleasant but unanswerable dream.

He saw himself as a small boy, walking across a verdant terrain. He did not know how he had reached there or where he would go. There were many wild animals around him but none of them seemed to be interested in attacking him. A herd of cows sitting beneath a tree, ruminating lazily, not very far from a huge lion with an impressive mane, lying near its den. There were herd of deer, a pack of tigers, bunch of monkeys around him but a peaceful harmony prevailed as though all the wild animals had become herbivorous for a day. How strange this place is, thought the little Chirag, how can this animal world be so different from what I was taught so far? Why do all those ferocious and wild animals look so silent and peaceful?

The little Chirag did not feel like leaving this undisturbed animal kingdom. Finding a comfortable place near a tree he sat down, leaning against the trunk of the tree. How did I reach here? If I knew the way to come here I would visit this place very often, Chirag's chain of thought was active while an assuring hand touched his shoulder. Just from the mere touch Chirag knew that it was his mother. His heart leaped with joy.

'Why did you leave me for so long, mamma? I have not seen you for such a long time,' he said, keeping his eyes closed, feeling blissful by his mother's touch. He kept his head on his mother's hand.

'Get up, my son, I will show you the way to reach this unknown world of peace and joy,' said his mother, leading him by holding his hand.

'Yes mamma, I will go wherever you take me,' said Chirag. He did not want to leave his mother's hand lest he would lose her again.

They walked hand in hand while Chirag asked his mother, 'Why did not you bring me to this beautiful place before?'

'Because you have never asked me, beta,' said his mother and turned her face to give a smile to him. Chirag was surprised and shocked at once. This lady was not his mother yet he was sure that her motherly face was very familiar to him. He tried to remember her face when his sleep broke.

He remained on his bed, gazing at the ceiling for a long time. There was a vacant expression on his face.

'It would not take you more than twenty minutes to read,' said Akash to Sandip, giving him a few A4 sized paper stapled together. They were in Akash's flat this Sunday afternoon. Sandip took the papers from Akash in silence, as he knew these papers contained nothing but Akash's new story, which had been, probably, based on his experience on Rajastan trip. Without any delay he started reading the paragraphs typed in Ariel Narrow under the heading *A New Sunrise*.

A NEW SURISE

PRECIOUS GEMS ARE PROFOUNDLY BURIED IN THE EARTH AND CAN ONLY BE EXTRACTED AT THE EXPENSE OF GREAT LOVE AND AFFECTION.

- ANANDAMAYI MA -

Sandip, the best friend of mine, recounted this singular event of his life to me one evening. He was on a long-waited vacation for a couple of weeks for he wanted to be all alone for a few days. Being a busy doctor he always had a hectic schedule in Mumbai. One of his friends suggested that he go to Mount Abu for it was one of the most beautiful hill stations near Mumbai. And he indeed loved that place. All day he would wander aimlessly, often feasting on Gujarati and Rajasthani thalis.

One morning while he was having steaming coffee and bread omelette from a wayside stall, a few hundred metres off Nakki lake, something arrested his attention.

He saw a small boy, wearing a worn-out oversized leather jacket and tattered full pants, scavenging for something from a pile of garbage heaped on the other side of the road. As he was searching for something with the utmost attention, removing the smelly garbage and filthy rags, Sandip wondered as to what the boy was looking for. He continued observing the boy with evident interest and a sense of guilt while he discovered that the boy was searching for a shoe. He had already found the shoe for the right feet in the heap of garbage, and now he was searching for the other shoe. Soon the boy found the shoe. He cleaned the pair of shoes with evident pleasure while my friend was shaken to the core to discover how a pair of discarded school shoe could bring so much happiness to such an innocent mind.

Sandip walked across the road to the boy. The boy was no more than eight years old with close cropped hair. He was small for his age.

He was dark and beads of perspiration were glistening on his foreheads. His eyes were large and the whites of his eyes were extremely white which accentuated his innocence. Sandip smiled at him and the boy reciprocated a sheepish smile. His teeth were regular and white. Sandip remained silent for a few moments, taking in the boy's vulnerable features, feeling a sudden upsurge of emotion within him.

'Do you want to breakfast with me?' he asked at last, finding nothing else to say.

The boy studied him for a long moment and then rocked his head to say yes. Sandip took him to a roadside stall and the boy breakfasted on bread omelette and tea. He was unusually silent for his age.

'What is your name?' asked Sandip.

'Lalit,' said the boy.

'Where do you stay?'

'There.' The boy vaguely indicated somewhere with his fingers.

'Don't your parents stay with you?' Sandip asked Lalit, trying to get into conversation with Lalit.

This time Lalit did not reply. He looked at Sandip for a few seconds, and then, all of a sudden got up and left the stall without a word.

Very obviously Sandip was intrigued by Lalit's behaviour and all day the innocent face of the boy kept visiting his mind. All he wanted was to meet the boy again and persuade him into talking about himself.

Next evening he was lucky to see Lalit again. Lalit was standing outside 'Hollywood Bollywood', an expensive restaurant in Mount Abu, looking at the occupants of the restaurants through the see-through glass. There was a sombre expression on his face.

'Do you want to go inside, Lalit?' asked Sandip, nearing the boy, keeping his hand on the boy's thin shoulder blade.

Lalit recognized him at once.

'Yes, I do,' said the boy and then added, 'but you should not ask me anything about my parents.'

'Well, I will not.' Sandip promptly agreed. This evening Lalit was wearing a pair of oversized shoes, without proper lace, that he had collected the previous morning. Unlikely last morning Lalit was wearing a hat now. It was wrinkled, torn and washed out.

Suddenly a desire to squander money, gifts and affection on this stray urchin filled Sandip. He led the boy to the restaurant where he ate with gusto under many pairs of curious and disapproving eyes. He did not ask Lalit anything nor did Lalit utter a word. On and off Lalit would cast a doubtful glance at Sandip. Most probably he was wondering as to why an unknown man was suddenly so kind to him but Sandip's assuring smile always encouraged him to concentrate on eating. He evinced a good appetite and ate everything that my friend offered to him.

Once they left 'Hollywood Bollywood' Sandip took him to 'Modern Men's Wear' and bought him a leather jacket and a pair of jeans, and then from 'Hillside footwear' a pair of sport's shoe for Lalit. Lalit accepted the gifts with a natural ease. Once they left the shops Lalit stood in front of Sandip, looking intensely at him with his large eyes as though he wanted to say something and then suddenly he disappeared in the milling crowd. Sandip walked towards his hotel in silence, knowing that Lalit had already stolen his heart for some inexplicable reason.

For the next two days his searching glance did not find Lalit anywhere. However, on the third day a pleasant surprise was in store for him.

That afternoon once he was walking along Nakki Lake, suddenly a small and wet hand held his wrist. Turning on his heels he found Lalit, all smiles, looking at him. He was proudly wearing his newly-earned possessions.

'Would you come with me?' this time Lalit asked Sandip.

Sandip looked at the boy. Hope and expectation were glinting in his limpid eyes.

'Sure,' replied Sandip, as he felt his voice quivering with emotion.

The boy led him, holding his wrist, to a small garden, overlooking Nakki Lake, where they sat cross-legged on the grass.

Lalit remained silent for a few minutes, running his fingers against blades of grass as though he was not sure how to begin and then suddenly said, 'My father died three years back. We were not poor when he was alive.'

Sandip looked at Lalit affectionately, remaining silent, knowing that this time Lalit would speak about himself.

'We stayed at Abu Road. My parents loved me a lot. They loved me very very much,' Lalit paused when a pensive expression came to his face. He continued after a long moment. 'But things changed after my father's death. My grandparents and my uncle started torturing my mother, calling her the instrument of my father's death. She endured their torture for many months before her patients gave in and one night I and my mother fled from my parental home with her little gold ornaments. Since then we had a tough time for my mother could not find any suitable work. We lived in a dingy two-room house on the outskirts of Abu Road. Though we were living like the poor I was really not unhappy for I knew that my mother loved me more than anything. I also loved her more than anything. I never dreamed of parting from her. But one night all my hopes shattered. As my sleep broke suddenly, I found that my mother was not on bed beside me. I was about to call her but before that I heard whispering sound coming from the next room. I tiptoed to the door and found it latched from the other side. Soon I felt that my mother was talking to some man in undertones. Curious, I peeped through the chink in the window to the other room. Though the room was almost dark soon I could see that my mother was lying on a mat, panting, and a man was lying on her. I could not see his face but I knew for certain that I had never seen him before. Soon the man dismounted from my mother and immediately she got up. He sat by mother on the mat talked to her in a low tone. Sometimes he would try to hold my mother's cheek and pull her towards him. I felt as if my mother was unwilling giving in to his fondling. I felt very angry but could do nothing. Before leaving the man brought out a few notes from his purse and told my mother, 'First tell me that you love me the most.'

'Yes, yes, I love you the most,' repeated my mother impatiently, trying to grab the notes.

'Say it again, more sweetly,' ordered the man, keeping the notes beyond my mother's reach.

'I love you the most,' repeated my mother.

'That's like a good girl,' said the man and gave her the notes, patting her cheeks.

'I will come next week,' he said to my mother before leaving.

'OK,' said my mother and bolted the main door once the man left. I knew that she would come to my room now. So I immediately went to bed and pretended to sleep. My mother came to me, checked whether I was sleeping. She then kissed my forehead and climbed the bed cautiously. But I could not sleep that night. It broke my heart to think that my mother loved an unknown man more than me. Soon it occurred to me that she loved him more because he gave her a lot of money every time he came to meet her. The more I thought on it the more convinced I was.

So far I had never thought of doing something to earn money. But now I thought about it and next morning I left home with a hope that I would return only when I could give my mother more money than that man used to give her. I heard that Mount Abu is a tourist place where a lot of rich people come. It is a one hour journey from Abu Road by bus. For the last three months I have been staying here but could barely accumulate only three hundred rupees. But I do not want to go back to my mother before I earn enough money for her. That's why I do not like anyone asking about my parents.' The boy stopped his long monologue. Nonplussed by the boy's revelation Sandip gazed at the boy. Strangely enough, there was no sign of pain in the boy's eyes as if he had accepted his life happily.

Sandip was never so shocked in his life. Being a doctor he had witnessed many tragic deaths but nothing moved him so much. He understood that the innocent boy had no understanding that his mother was into prostitution to make the both ends meet. He felt an ungovernable desire within him to send the boy back to his mother.

'How much money do you want to give to your mother?' he asked Lalit.

'Two thousand, I should earn it within a few months. I miss my mother a lot,' said Lalit.

'Come with me,' gasped Sandip and led the boy to the nearest ATM and handed him five thousand rupees.

'Go and meet your mother tomorrow. And remember I have no doubt that your mother loves you more than anyone else. She may have her own reasons to say something to someone. But nobody can take your place in her life. So never leave her alone again. She must be crying for you everyday,' said he as he saw Lalit's eyes brimming with tears, lips trembling. Suddenly he dissolved in scalding tears, holding Sandip. He remained in Sandip's embrace for a long moment. Most probably, all the pain and humiliation stored in his little heart for last few months came out of his eyes as hot tears. Soon he left without any words with Sandip.

Sandip was in Mount Abu for another one week but did not meet Lalit anymore. But life returned his generosity in a strange way. On the way back to Mumbai when he reached Abu Road to catch Rajdhani Express a pleasant surprise was awaiting him. That afternoon in the marketplace near the railway station while he was having Rabri - something very famous in Abu Road - he saw Lalit with a woman whose face greatly resembled with Lalit's. She had one of her protective hand around Lalit as if under any circumstances she would not let him be away from her. They were buying banana from a fruit vendor.

My friend, Sandip, had saved many patients from the jaws of death but nothing had given him as satisfying a feeling as the sight of mother and son's reunion gave him.

AKASH CHATTERJEE

After finishing the story Sandip carefully kept the pages on the table nearby as though it was some priceless object and then looked out through the open window. His forehead puckered and lips pursed as he remained completely silent. Akash did not want to break Sandip's silence though Sandip's comment meant a lot to him.

Sandip spoke after a while, 'It is often said that *A man can be known from his work*. Do you think this statement is correct?'

Akash found the question somewhat irrelevant.

'I think this statement is correct to a great extent,' said Akash, after thinking for a moment.

'Do you know what impression your story would develop in someone's mind? The story is so heart-warming and soul-wrenching that any sensible reader may feel like hugging it's creator at least for once. Do you know why?'

'No.'

'Because the story gives an impression that it's author's heart is brimming with love. No one experiences love as intensely as he does. But they can not even imagine that the same man may take two years or even more to understand whether he loves a woman or not.'

'Every time you say something about Maria to me I have a guilty conscience,' Akash said after sometime.

'It is because deep down you also know that you can never be in peace if you spurn her love one day.'

'You are correct in a way, Sandip,' began Akash thoughtfully. 'To write about love, to talk about love is very easy. In fact it is very easy to show love to someone if it does not hamper your freedom anyway.'

'I think you are correct. All the same, the story is excellent,' said Sandip, rising to his feet.

Once Sandip left Akash thought of calling Maria to show her his newly-born daughter (that was how he referred to his stories) but before that his cell phone beeped. It was an SMS from PUCHU. Owing to Akash's shift duty he often slept in the afternoon which was why Maria was always considerate enough not to phone him in the afternoon. Akash checked the test message: Are you sleeping? He called her at once. Over phone he could feel that she was elated at hearing his voice.

'What are you doing?' she asked him.

'Nothing in particular, Sandip had left just now, was talking to him,' said Akash.

'Free in this evening?' she asked him.

'Yeah, very much, in fact wanted to meet you.'

'Why? Have some surprise up your sleeve?' she asked.

'Sort of,' he smiled over phone.

'Then it must be a new story.'

'How do you know?' asked a surprised Akash.

'Because you are not going to say I love you to me to surprise me,' she said playfully.

There was a brief silence on Akash's part. Very playfully, she had said something she was yearning to hear from him for a long time.

'When would you meet?' he asked her after a while.

'At 5.30, it is okay.'

'Yeah, perfect,' said Akash.

There was a pause while Akash felt Maria was hesitating to say something to him. He heard her voice after a few seconds.

'You know, Akash, love you very much,' she said slowly, spacing the words with determined gaps. She then cut the line without waiting for his reply. Akash kept the cell phone down with a deep sigh. He stood by the window, looking down at the road while his mind clouded with a maze of thoughts.

Since Maria had discovered that Akash was a foodie like her, she often prepared pudding, prawns Biriyani, Ceramal Custard and cakes for him. Never before her mother had witnessed her daughter preparing food with so much love, care and attention. Helen would stand by the kitchen door and watch her daughter in silence. She was not sure whether her daughter had a love affair with Akash or it was an one-sided-love. Yet she was hopeful that soon her daughter and Akash would get married. She often said to Maria to bring Akash home but felt that Maria had a natural reluctance to introduce Akash to her. She, however, often gave her mother interesting information about Akash. From Maria, Helen had come to know that Akash was a voracious reader and that he also wrote heart-touching English fiction. Sometimes she would give her father, Daniel, to read Akash's story. Once Daniel praised his imagination and style of writing she would bask in the reflected glory of Akash's creativity.

'Why does not he try to get his work published? His stories are good enough to be published,' Daniel would say.

'May be someday he would try,' Maria would say. She hated telling anyone about Akash's failure of getting his work published.

This evening, however, Maria had not prepared any new dish for Akash but brought him to Only Rolls – a take away famous for serving Paneer Rolls, Egg Rolls, Chicken Rolls, Egg-Chicken Rolls, Mutton Rolls and the list went on at a reasonable price. Every evening teenaged couples thronged there, making the street outside Only Rolls a lively place.

'Did you come here before?' Maria asked Akash once he parked the bike near Only Rolls.

'No, I have not heard of this place,' Akash lied. He knew that his stating the fact that he had visited Only Rolls several times before would puncture Maria's excitement to a great extent.

'That's why I have brought you here,' she enthused with a smile, displaying her small teeth. This afternoon she had shampooed her hair and it was giving off a mild fragrant perfume. She wore the earrings that Akash had presented her a couple of weeks back from ethnic jewellery section in Cottage Emporium near Regal theatre. Her salwar Kurta was also a gift from Akash. They had got it from Tata Textiles on the eve of her birthday. Akash gazed at her for a long moment. Her Kajoled-eyes were riveted on him. There was a sheepish smile on her lips for no particular reason.

A wave of affection swept over Akash again. 'You are looking good,' he said to her slowly.

'I know I am not good-looking. But before I met you I had never cared so much for my look,' she smiled. 'Now let's go.'

She held his hand and they crossed the road.

Soon they polished off five Rolls with relish. After his every bite to a new Roll she would ask him, 'Have you liked this Roll?'

He would nod in the affirmation as his mouth stuffed with mouth-watering Rolls.

'Why did not you bring me here before?' he asked her once he had done with the third Roll. Maria had two.

'There are many more beautiful eating places in our city. One life may not be enough to go to all those places,' she replied. She did not let him pay, claiming that she had brought him there.

As Akash was getting his bike from the parking area suddenly Maria held his hand.

'Akash, I want to say something to you,' she said to him.

Thinking that she was about to say '*love you very much*' he replied, 'I know it very well.'

'No, you do not,' she said calmly. 'Once I lied to you.' She lowered her eyes.

Confused, Akash asked, 'About what?' while hundreds of eerie thoughts filled his mind in no time.

She did not reply immediately. Every passing second was an agonizing moment for Akash.

'It was about my salary,' she said after a while. 'Once I got the job in the school I told you that my salary was around twenty thousand. Actually it was a measly seven thousand per month. And now I am paid eight thousand five hundred. They pay me in cheque at the end of the month.'

Akash sighed with relief. He was scared that she would reveal some secret event of her life that might disturb him. Yet the seriousness with which she had declared her secret touched him deeply.

'By the way, why did you lie?' Akash asked her, wearing a mask of sobriety.

She raised her eyes and looked at him. Her moist eyes were so limpid and honest that he could see her bare, innocent soul through her eyes. Her lips quivered as she tried to reply.

'In fact once we met I did not know you at all. I was scared that if you know my actual salary you might laugh at me, thinking that I do a petty job. I was afraid that you might start avoiding me. And I did not want it at any cost,' she paused and dabbed her eyes with her handkerchief. She began again, 'But this lying to you always remained as a burden in my heart. Now no more am I scared to reveal the truth to you.'

'Why?' asked Akash, completely moved by Maria's words.

'Because now I know you very well. I know you do not care about the kind of job I do or the salary I am paid.'

'I like you more than ever before for what you said, Maria. Even if you quit your job tomorrow you would remain the same Maria for me,' said Akash, looking loving at her.

'Thanks,' she smiled.

'Anyway, after you make a confession to a priest he is supposed to reward you. And I reward you with this one.' Akash handed a copy of '*A New Sunrise*' to Maria. Maria carefully rolled the papers and kept it inside her bag.

'I will read it tonight, thank you very, much.' Suddenly she became very lively.

'Let's have Kulfi,' she proposed.

They went near Grand Central and had Malai Kulfi on teak leaf from a roadside Kulfi-seller. Once he dropped her in front of Aryabhatt it was half past eight.

Around a couple of hours later he got a call from Maria.

'Disturbed you?' she began.

'Why do you always try to be so formal?'

'Because I heard that creative people often go into a trance to get ideas for their work,' she smiled. 'Loved the story very much. It is very soulful. But did not Shobbha De suggest that you should work on a novel?' she said almost authoritatively and Akash loved it.

'It is very difficult to write a novel, Maria. You have to build up many characters and have to do justice to all of them. What is more, it must have a satisfactory ending,' said Akash.

'I think you can write a successful novel. It is only a matter of time,' said Maria encouragingly.

'Why do you think I can write a good novel?' Akash asked amusedly.

'Some day an inner force will compel you to write a very long story. You need not have to devise characters for that. That's what I feel.'

'What will I name that very long story?'

There was a very long pause while Akash could hear Maria's breathing. When she spoke again her voice was almost hypnotic, 'Please name it *Life is Always Aimless .....Unless You Love It* because these few words say so much of our life.'

'I loved the name.'

'And I love everything about you, bye,' she cut the phone.

Akash kept the cell phone on his study table and went to the window. On the left side of the table he meticulously kept all his rejected proposals and manuscripts. Looking at them often gave him an impetus to work harder. He stood by the window for a long time, lost in his thoughts, while he saw Chirag taking a walk. He looked thoughtful and silent, so unlike the Chirag most of his colleagues knew. Remembering his occasional long discussion with Chirag while Chirag talked about himself at length, he agreed with what Sandip often said to him, '*We are all so different from what we appear to.*'

Maina draped her arms around Chirag's neck as a bunch of her friends, standing a little distance off, watched them in silence.

'I would not say anything to solace you. All I can say that once I met you never did I imagine that one day we would part like this and that the parting would be so heart-rending,' Maina said to Chirag.

'But the parting is heart-rending only for me,' said Chirag, staring vacantly at the bustling international Mumbai airport.

Maina gave a small smile. 'You know very well, Chirag, it is heart-rending for me too. But probably this parting would help you know yourself better. May be soon you would start talking to yourself. And everyday I would be available online.'

'Thanks,' said Chirag as Maina removed her hands after giving him the final hug. He wanted to hold her tightly against him for eternity but felt no energy in his hands. Maina hugged and shook hands with rest of her friends, shared jokes with them and then with a final wave at all of them, headed towards the 'Checking' section with her luggage trolley in determined stride. After Maina disappeared Chirag waited for an hour, sitting on his motorbike with a delusive hope that Maina might change her mind at the end moment and squash her plan of settling to Singapore for next few years. She, however, did not come back, rather he received an SMS form her.

will switch off the cell soon. Thanks for all your love.

Chirag did not reply. Sitting alone he watched the passers by for a while. They all seemed to be preoccupied, busy, moving with a purpose. But his existence was purposeless, without any past or future. Just with an unbearable present where every passing moment was as long as eternity.

Heavy-hearted, he kick-started his motorbike after sometime. He rode past Sakinaka, Kurla and once he reached Ghatkoper his bike slowed down. These streets and lanes were very much known to him. This was where he grew up, played street-cricket with his friends. He consulted his wristwatch. It was eleven-thirty. As his bike coasted down a flyover and reached in front of *Patel Paradise*, a fourteen-storey tower at Ghatkoper west, he brought his bike to a halt. On the sixth floor of this tower stayed his father, elder brother and his recently married wife. Rarely did Chirag visit his parental flat. His communication with his father was no more than once a month. Nor did he feel like meeting his elder brother, who was with his father with the hope of usurping his huge property after he passed away.

Chirag gazed at his father's flat for a few minutes with mixed emotions within him. He then started his bike and rode towards Chembur. He drove hardly a kilometre when something caught his attention and almost automatically his bike came to a stop near a bus stop. On the other side of the road there stood no less than four Bars and Restaurants separated by Paan bidi shops. All these restaurants were in a peaceful slumber throughout the day and awoke not before eight at night. As night worn on, exhausted business man, builders, corrupt party workers, policemen and men from many other walks of life went to the bars like Hot Spot, Aditya where expert seductress helped them enjoy all forbidden pleasure at the cost of money.

No sooner had Chirag seen a Honda City, bearing a nameplate MH-05-J-4381, than his heart escaped a bit. It was his father's car! His father was sixty-two now and Chirag nurtured a hope that his father must have stopped frequenting Ladies' bars since he had married off his elder son. But his father had proved him wrong. Now he saw his father at least four months later, an obese man with a considerable paunch. He was almost bald. He was very fair and the heavy gold chain around his neck glittered as he walked towards Hot Spot. For a moment Chirag was seized with a desire to go inside the bar and occupy a seat close to his father's. Let his father drink and do filtration with a bargirl, young enough to be his daughter, in front of his son.

Somewhat undecidedly, he took a right turn from the nearest road divider and reached in front of Hot Spot. He was in a dither now as a feeling of let-go filled him. What would he achieve embarrassing this old man? Let him lead a rotten, deplorable life. He would not be in the immediate vicinity once he was on his deathbed. His heart was brimming with vindictiveness as he thought of starting his bike again. At the very same moment the strong teak wood main door to Hot Spot opened and a pretty young woman came out. She had a slim and supple body with thick long curly hair. Unlike other bargirls who usually wore sari or chaniya choli for dancing, she put on a pair of Demin jeans and a sleeveless T-shirts, small enough to expose her deep navel. Chirag found that she had had a navel-piercing. Her lips were painted with colourful lipstick. She had applied some shining objects beneath her eyes. Her eyebrows were carefully plucked and she wore her hair in a stylish bun. Though she looked young it was difficult to guess her age.

'Leaving early ma'am?' smiled the darwan at her, ogling at her bare hand.

'Not feeling well,' she replied casually, deigning to look at the darwan.

'Should I get a taxi for you?' asked the darwan.

'Not required. I will find one myself,' she said resolutely when her eyes met Chirag's. There was some mysterious magnetic pull in her eyes and Chirag found if difficult to drag his eyes off her. He was not sure as to what she had read on his face for she walked towards him.

'Where are you going?' she asked him directly.

'Where do you want to go?' Chirag asked her back.

'Vashi.'

'I can drop you there if you wish to.' Chirag said. For once he did not care where this strange escapade might lead to.

'Start your bike,' she commanded, sitting astride behind him.

As Chirag started the bike he saw the darwan outside Hot Spot looking bewilderingly at them.

It took him twenty minutes to reach Vashi. Throughout the ride none of them exchanged a word.

'Where should I drop you?' asked Chirag, taking a turn to Vashi main market.

'My flat is not very far, take this left,' she said.

Chirag followed her instructions and soon they were in front of Maryland apartment, a ten-storey building.

'Thanks,' she said, getting off his bike as the engine continued whirring.

'It's okay,' smiled Chirag dryly.

'Are not you coming up? You may like my place,' she said plainly.

Is she a sex-starved woman, hunting for a gigolo, a fear crossed Chirag's mind yet he felt an unknown force drawing him towards her. No matter how seductive she might be at this moment he had no carnal desire. But he was attracted towards her for more than a physical need.

He parked the bike on the pavement, near the entrance to Maryland and went inside with her. There was a dog coiled by the staircase. It looked up as they reached near the lift and seeing his companion it sprang to its feet and, coming near her, sniffed at her. Bending down she patted the dog when Chirag had an unobstructed view of her deep cleavage.

'They understand the language of love better than us,' she said once they entered the lift.

Chirag had not expected a bargirl to speak like this. They entered her flat on 6th floor. It was a small flat, decorated with taste.

'Sit,' she said to him, indicating a sofa.

'Thanks,' said Chirag, passing a quick glance around the room.

She went inside and Chirag could hear the sound of splashing water, blowing nose and the click of the gaslight. She entered the drawing room a few minutes later, carrying a tray with two mugs of steaming coffee and some chip cookies.

'Coffee at midnight?' asked Chirag, amused in this unusual situation.

She gave a smile, 'Accustomed to remaining wake till late at night.'

Chirag saw her teeth were irregular and as she washed her face, removing all the layers of make-up she looked like a next-door girl. She untied the bun and her thick hair lying around her shoulder. She had changed the revealing outfit and put on a comfortable kurta and pyjama.

She sat cross-legged on the sofa and asked Chirag directly, 'Why did you look so disturbed and helpless?'

Chirag was taken by surprise by her question.

'How do you know I was disturbed?'

'It is not a difficult task for me. Every day I see scores of disturbed and frustrated persons who remove their mask in front of the women like us.'

Chirag did not speak but her words made him feel comfortable. An unknown fear within him disappeared partly. He smiled, sitting on the sofa in a relaxed manner.

'I saw my father entering Hot Spot,' he said after sometime, without looking at her. 'It was disturbing. Besides…' Chirag's voice faded away as he remembered Maina.

'Besides…what?' she asked him compassionately.

'The best friend of mine left Bombay for good this evening. I feel terribly lonely without her. Never did I feel so dejected. On top, I saw my father lurching into a ladies' bar. You can imagine my state of mind. In a way, I was out of my mind, otherwise I might not have agreed to drop you at Vashi.'

'It is good that your best friend has left for good. It gives you an opportunity to become your own best friend,' she gave him a wan smile as though she was tired of the battle of life. 'In our profession we have no choice but become our best friend. You never know who, when and how is going to befool you.'

Chirag did not respond but continued looking quizzically at the woman in front of him. It was beyond his imagination that an ordinary bargirl could speak so beautifully.

'And do not feel low for your father's frequenting ladies bar. He is trying to buy something with money there that can not be bought with money. In fact nothing beautiful in this world can be bought with money, yet money gives us an illusion that everything can be acquired with the help of it.'

Dumbfounded, Chirag looked at her with a pleasant surprise. Some rare instinct told him that he had taken a very wise decision by giving a lift to the woman, sitting in front of him now.

'What do they want to buy? So far I understand they want easy sex.'

'That's what it appears superficially. But in truth, they frequent ladies bar because they are all disturbed in a way. Actually, talking to a bargirl, fondling her or having sex with her are just the means to pacify their troubled mind. The presence of a bargirl might help but such help is short-lived. You cannot buy a peaceful mind or love with money. These words are very commonplace but very true,' she paused and added thoughtfully, 'Probably, no one experienced this truth as I did.'

'Means?' Chirag asked curiously.

She did not reply at once but looked at Chirag for a few seconds as though to size him up and then began, 'Once I tried to buy love with money. My intention was good but the means was, probably, wrong,' she stopped. There was a woebegone expression on her face.

'Do you know who that girl is?' she asked Chirag suddenly, indicating a framed photograph of a five to six year old girl whose face strongly resembled her.

'I think it is your childhood's photograph,' Chirag commented.

She gave a dry smile. 'So you have found some resemblance between this girl and me. Good. She is my elder brother's daughter. Renuka is her name.' She stopped and heaved a deep sigh. 'It's a long story but I would finish it in short. When my parents died my elder brother was nineteen and me eleven. Our father did not leave any property and my brother struggled hard to bring me up. As soon as I reached marriageable age he married me off, to set himself free from all responsibility. Very obviously, in a hurry he compromised with a bad catch for me. As a result I was regularly assaulted by that brute. Even now I feel ashamed of calling him as my husband. Many a times I wanted to go back to my brother's place once the torture became unbearable but my brother denied to keep me with his family. Always his stock answer was, 'After marriage husband's house is a woman's real home. And as a good wife you must make all efforts to change that brute to a good human being.' However, luckily he died after a few years of liver cirrhosis due to excess consumption of liquor. After his death this flat became mine. I was hardly twenty-two then. I did not seek any support from my elder brother and soon joined this profession where quick money was guaranteed. Once my elder brother came to know of my working as a bar dancer, he stopped communicating with me. For the next few years I knew nothing of him. He was staying in Bandra east and worked with BMC. Around five years later, one afternoon I bumped into him at Hill Road. Like most of the bargirls I used to go to Hill Road market at Bandra to buy sexy lingerie, fancy T-shirts and jeans.

He looked so despondent that it concerned me. I was the first one to speak. Soon I understood as to why he looked so despondent. No more than a couple of weeks back he had lost his wife. Now he had none but his five-year old daughter, Renuka. The daughter was standing by him, holding his fingers tightly, looking at the crowds of the bustling market of Hill Road fearfully. As I looked at his daughter I was so shocked that my jaw dropped for a full minute. She was a carbon-copy of a five-year-old me. It is beyond words to express the joy of seeing a child who looks exactly like young you. As I looked at her face I forgot everything else for a while. Perhaps, amazement was written on my face and my brother could read it easily.'

'She looks like you, does not she?' he said to me with a small smile.

'Yeah,' replied I without taking my eyes off Renuka.

We chatted away for a while. On and off Renuka asked her father some disturbing questions about her mother as my brother tried his best to give befitting answers to her. Hearing the father and daughter talk it occurred to me that Renuka did not understand what death was and was under a false hope, obviously given by her father, that soon her mother would come back.

The more I talked to Renuka the more I was touched by her innocence. I devoured her eyes, small fingers as everything about her reminded me of my childhood. I had an irrepressible desire to flourish her with love, affection, care and whatever I had. I forgot my strong resolution not to set foot in my brother's flat. The present situation of my brother worked in my favour as he thought that I might fill Renuka's emotional vacuum created by her mother's death.

Since then I visited his flat no less than thrice a week and every time I went there I always carried a gift for Renuka. Sometimes it was a frock, sometimes a dollhouse, a book or a chocolate. She received everything I gave her with an innocent smile. All I wanted was to occupy her mother's place in her little heart and I was ready to do anything for that. After coming from school she would spend a long time with me and I told her all the fairytales I remembered.

I flourished her with gifts and always cherished a hope that gradually she was forgetting her mother and that soon she would love me as much as she loved her mother.

But one day my dream shattered,' she paused and looking at Chirag gave a distant and forlorn smile. Chirag uttered no words but continued looking at her sympathetically. Never in his wildest dream did he imagine that a bargirl might have such a touching story.

She continued after a while, gazing at the floor, 'That afternoon I asked Renuka to show me all her toys. By that time I was convinced that I had almost achieved my objective and that she had forgotten her mother to a great extent.

'Come with me,' she said to me, leading me to her room by holding my finger.

She had kept her dolls and other toys in two big plastic containers.

'Here is all my toys,' she told me, indicating both the plastic containers in front of us. 'In one container I keep all the toys given by my mother and in the other one, toys given by others.'

I was so shocked by her words that for a long moment I was speechless.

At last I asked her, 'Why do you keep the toys, your mother gave you, separately?'

'How can I keep other toys with the toys mamma gave me? Those are very special for me,' she asked innocently but her words rooted me to the spot.

Slowly I understood that no matter how expansive toys or dolls I presented her I could never take her mother's place in her heart. It cannot be acquired with money or gifts. That afternoon I learnt one of the most precious lessons of my life. That is nothing precious can be bought with money because all precious things are priceless.'

They both remained silent for a few minutes while Chirag experienced a strong feeling of warmth within him. Her narrative worked as a soothing balm for his anguished heart. He gave her a friendly smile.

'Do you go to meet Renuka now?' he asked her.

'Yes, I do. I do carry small toys, frocks for her. But no more do I dream of occupying her mother's place with the help of gifts. Have you understood as to why I told you this Renuka episode?'

'Thanks,' said Chirag and asked her, 'Do you ask for a lift from any unknown young man late at night? Does not it scare you?'

'No, I never ask for a lift from anyone. But tonight once I looked at your eyes outside Hot Spot all I could read frustration and loneliness there. At the same time you did not seem to be one who visits ladies' bar to stave off loneliness. So I thought you might like talking to me,' she shrugged her shoulders with a simple smile.

'Do not you think that you are in a wrong profession? Do not you feel that you can help people in a much better way?' asked Chirag with sincerity.

She looked at him intensely. For a moment Chirag felt that her eyes were moist. She then averted her glance and said, 'I am perfectly okay as I am.'

Chirag checked his watch. It was a quarter past two.

'I have got to go now. It is already very late,' he said, getting to his feet.

'You can sleep here tonight. I have no problem,' she said plainly.

For a moment Chirag was in a dilemma. Did she have any devious ploy to trap him? He wondered but then told himself that he had nothing much to lose.

'Well, I will sleep here,' he said finally.

He took a wash and she gave him a pillow and a bed sheet. Soon after he lied on the sofa a deep sleep overwhelmed him. Next morning once he got up it took him a few minutes to realize where he was. Last night's sleep was very rejuvenating.

She showed him her small flat before he left. Her bedroom was a tiny 10 feet by 10 feet room designed with taste. Near her bed a small poster caught Chirag's attention. A few lines were written on it.

It said: *In life we all have an unspeakable secret, an irreversible regret, an unreachable dream and an unforgettable love.*

'Have you pasted that poster there?' Chirag asked surprisingly as the beauty and truth of those lines touched him.

'Yeah, sometimes I feel very low. Sometimes I think as to why bad things happen with good people. On such occasions these lines give me courage.'

Looking at her for a long moment it dawned on Chirag how little he knew of life.

Once he left her flat he felt himself a more collected and composed self. As he started his motorbike as unsmiling smile played on his lips. After riding a few kilometres he remembered that he did not even know the name of the woman whose meeting with him affected him so much.

'Can you imagine we have completed almost four and a half years in ICL?' said Akash, slicing the Idlis on his plate into pieces. Sandip and he were sitting in Udipi this afternoon.

'What about your novel-writing?' Sandip asked.

'I am yet to zero in on an interesting idea. The other day Maria was telling that one day I would naturally hit upon an idea of a novel,' said

Akash with a dry smile.

'So tries her best to tell you not to lose hope.'

'I think I should not continue one relationship in this uncertain way anymore. Now it is more than three years we know each other.'

'Why are you telling me all these?' Sandip asked tersely. 'If I tell you to take a quick decision repeatedly you would think that I am poking my nose in your personal matter.'

'I never said so. Rather I always seek your guidance whenever I feel confused.'

'But how long will you live with this confusion as to whether you love her or no? If you ask my opinion your this eternal delaying to take a final decision is an act of a coward. You do not have courage to say to her 'no' as you are afraid of losing such an artless girl at the same time you do not understand if you love her or not. Strange. Sometimes I do not understand what you really want from life.'

Akash remained silent for a while and once he spoke his voice was resolute, 'Well Sandip, before 31 December of this year I would take the final decision. And then no looking back.'

Sandip observed him critically, '31 December, 2011, means you have another four months to take the final decision. By the way, why do you need so much of time? Are you going to know her better in the coming four months?'

'No Sandip, I am definitely not going to know her better in anyway. Rather I think she knows me very well, much better than my parents know me. Yet I need this coming four months for my sake.'

'Good, you take your own time. But now it's my time to go for a small trip. Since my last trip to Lakshadeep I have not gone anywhere. I am sick and tried of this bloody mundane job.'

'Where will you go this time?'

'I went to Lonavala once but could not see Karla and Bhaja caves the way I want to. I can spend a full day in one of these caves. There is so much mystery about them. Just imagine those Buddhist temples are no less 2000 years old. How did they cut rocks so perfectly at that time? Whenever we go to such caves we do not take more than five minutes to look around it. But every carving on the rock speaks so much. In fact this name Lonavala is derived from a word, Lanovi, means a place surrounded by caves. I have planned to be at Lonavala for a week,' said Sandip. His eyes were shinning with joy, which the thought of travelling always brought to his heart.

'When will you leave?' Akash asked.

'Next week.

They were about to leave Udipi they bumped into Jasvinder Singh.

'Hello Akash,' Jasvinder greeted Akash when Akash thought of ignoring him. During last few months Akash had seen Jasvinder several times with no less the three girls in different cafes and restaurants in Chembur. It seemed to Akash that he was reliving his colourful bachelorhood in his wife's absence. Every time Akash's eyes met Jasvinder's he invariably averted his glance. Since then Akash made it a point not to look at Jasvinder or greet him once he met him.

'Hi,' said Akash, somewhat coldly.

Jasvinder passed a brief glance at Sandip and was in a dither for a moment.

'Are you busy? I mean, going anywhere?' he asked Akash at last.

'Not exactly, why?' Akash asked curtly.

'Joining me for a coffee?' Jasvinder asked casually yet Akash felt some desperation in his voice.

'Okay, but I already had two coffee.'

'Never mind,' said Jasvinder.

Sandip left at once, knowing that Jasvinder wanted to see Akash alone.

'We are meeting here after a few months,' Jasvinder began hesitantly.

'Yeah, may be after six months.'

'Yeah, time passes so fast,' said Jasvinder.

'Yeah.' Akash was determined not to ask Jasvinder anything or show any curiosity about his present life.

'In fact I was out of Bombay for a while,' Jasvinder began again, haltingly. 'I had been to Patna. Sujata's parental home is there.'

Akash nodded slowly, remembering the girls with whom he had seen Jasvinder in his wife's absence.

'I became father two weeks back, Akash. It is a small lovely girl with curly hair,' said Jasvinder as his voice quivered with emotion, his eyes shone with joy. 'I am just counting days for their returning Bombay.'

'Congratulation, but I remember you telling me that you wanted to be alone for sometime.'

'Yeah, I said so and you know very well what I really meant. The chief reason of my occasional tiff with Sujata was that she never tolerated my mingling with other girls. I always thought of her jealous and nosy for the same reason. A few months after our marriage as Sujata tried to control me and wanted my life should revolve only around her, my mind started revolting against her possessiveness. Obviously it caused a lot of trouble in my marital life. On and off I deeply regretted my decision of marrying. So I welcomed my forced bachelorhood when three-month-pregnant Sujata went to her parental home. I secretly prayed that she stayed with her parents for good. Unlike many other guys I never considered the idea of becoming a father as a matter of pride. Once I had been informed that I became father of a small girl I went to Patna somewhat reluctantly, mainly to discharge the parental duty. Once I reached Patna Sujata and my daughter were at the maternity ward in Mahatma Gandhi Memorial Hospital. Sujata was difficult to recognize as she looked more like a mother now. Her eyes were clam and face tranquil. Then my attention was arrested by a small thing wrapped in clothes, lying beside her, sleeping blissfully. Her pink lips were slightly contorted. Her eyes were closed. She had long eyelids and nose a bit large, most probably like my nose,' Jasvinder paused and smiled absentmindedly. His eyes were moist. Akash knew that with his mind's eyes Jasvinder was seeing his wife and daughter in front of him and did not want to break his ecstatic mood. Jasvinder continued after a moment, 'She is the prettiest little thing ever I have seen. Suddenly I forgot everything and sitting on a stool near Sujata's bed I devoured the beauty of my daughter. I do not remember how long I sat by her bed but at one moment of time I felt like touching her. It is unbelievable to see a living thing in whose creation I also had a merger contribution. But the three-day-old girl cried as soon as I touched her. She opened her eyes and for a moment my heart missed a bit. Her eyes were hazel like mine. Sujata silenced her daughter at once, giving her a feed. The mother and daughter looked so perfect together that I felt myself useless and unwanted. I understood how terribly I was ensnared by my selfish thoughts.

As tears of remorse ran down my eyes I placed my hand on Sujata's feet, hoping that she would forgive me. Believe me, Akash, I was ready for any retribution. For the first time it occurred to me that my loving wife and beautiful little daughter were much more a precious thing than scores of girlfriends I might have. Her feet were slightly cold. At first I was afraid that she might retract her feet, recollecting my unkind indifference for last many months. But she did not. She, however, did not speak to me. I was in Patna for four more days and all the days I was with her and my daughter so long as hospital authority allowed. I had no appetite nor did I feel sleepy or exhausted. On the third when all her relations left she held the baby with both her hands and gave it to me. It was a divine feeling to hold that little thing against my heart. Again I cried soundlessly, regretful and repentant. I wished I could bare my heart and let Sujata know how much sorry I was. I did not know what she read in my eyes, for on the day of my departure from Patna, once I went to her cabin and sat on the stool near her feet she asked me to sit by her pillow. Almost mechanically, I followed her instruction and as I sat by her she told me slowly, 'Your tears said more than your words could. Let's start our life afresh with our daughter.' She placed her assuring hand on me. I was never so grateful to life.'

Jasvinder was crying now. He got a handkerchief from his pocket and hid his face with it. After a few moments once he controlled himself, he looked straight at Akash. 'The reason I said everything to you, brother, is that once I suggested to you that you must not marry and that you should enjoy your bachelorhood to the fullest. But I was grossly wrong. Marry someone who deeply loves you, Akash. It is an advice from your erring brother. And always remember sex without love is always bestial but love, with or without sex is divine. It is not a saying that I read somewhere but my own experience. So marry someone who loves you, brother. Your life will change completely.'

Their meeting ended as abruptly as it had started. Jasvinder's revelation made Akash feel strangely happy. He wanted to narrate to Maria about reconciliation of Jasvinder and Sujata. At least it would remove her doubt that love was gradually getting diminished from the world, thought Akash.

The steps were long and as Sandip climbed down from Karla cave it struck him that probably the monks of 200 BC were much taller than twenty centuries' Indian. He checked his wristwatch as his feet touched the dusty reddish earth. It took him seventeen minutes to reach down from the cave. Sandip sat on a stool near a stall, selling cold drinks, dosa, vada pav, bhaji pav, for sometime before he started walking towards the highway. While coming to the cave he got down from a ST bus near Waksai and walked around six kilometres to reach Karla caves. It was one of the best walks of his life. The roads towards Karla caves were narrow but tarmaced. On both sides of the road there stood long trees through which shafts of morning sunlight fell on the road. The air was fresh and crisp. Sometimes speeding cars, crammed full of tourists passed him while some lively tourists waved at him. Sandip always reciprocated such hearty greetings at once.

As he walked around a few hundred meter and Karla caves disappeared behind the windings lanes, Sandip experienced a sad feeling churning within him. This feeling was his faithful companion every time he left a place that he loved. Yet Sandip was happy with his day. The road was almost deserted barring the passing cars. Sometimes he saw villagers on their ox-carts. They looked completely contended with life.

The place was no more than hundred kilometres off the metropolis of Bombay yet life is so slow, peaceful and idyllic here, thought Sandip.

He was around two kilometres from Bombay-Pune highway when a panoramic view on the right side of the road arrested his attention. A little distance off the road there was a large lake and behind it was a wide paddy field, meeting the horizon at a far distance. A water pump was running, standing close to the lake, squirting water to the green lush paddy field. The lake was ill-maintained and its' water was well-covered with a green slime. Close to the water pump, were a few broken stone steps, reaching down the water. There was no one in the immediate vicinity and for a moment Sandip felt like being transported into a magical, surreal world. As the wind blew and the luxuriant rice plants danced with it, whispering with its neighbours in an hushed silence, Sandip felt as though the verdant rice field, tranquil lake, gentle wind were inviting him to be with them, to appreciate their beauty, their contribution to make the earth beautiful. Sandip did not waste any time. Finding a narrow pathway, partly covered with undergrowth he reached the lake. At first he sat on the top step to the lake but soon felt the water of the lake, yearning for human touch for ages, requesting him to touch it, to feel it. The stone steps were old and cracked at places. Sandip carefully went a few steps down and sat there with his feet in the water. The water was cold and slowly Sandip started playing with water, raising his flip-flop up after every few seconds, letting the water pass through the gap between his feet and flip-flop. On and off there was a splash in the water for the fish in the lake made occasional jumps, just to get off the underwater boredom.

Sandip looked around gratefully as a pure peace descended upon him. Suddenly one of his flip-flops slipped off his foot and floated away a few feet. Folding his jeans up, Sandip carefully placed his foot on the next step under water and then by stretching his hand out tried to grab his flip-flop. His fingers almost touched the flip-flop when his foot under water missed its grip for the step was slippery and covered with algae. Instinctively Sandip's feet searched for the next step only to find with horror that there was no more step down and that the lake bed was much beyond the reach of his feet. For the first time he was really scared to death as he remembered that he did not know swimming and that there was no one nearby to rescue him. Yet, as a possessor of an indomitable heart, he struggled hard to reach the last step to the lake, only a few feet away from him. He was floundering continuously though he could feel that gradually he was wilting. Twice he drank water. Again and again he tried to float and at last he gave up as a very pleasant ecstasy filled him. The last thing he could see was a *Disha,* the rare bird that he had seen on his way to the valley of flowers that was known for showing the right direction to the lost travellers, hovering over his head.

Around an hour later when Sandip's body was floating on the water, the fishes of the lake swarmed towards it, hoping to feast on human flesh.

Late in that evening when a farmer from the nearby village came to stop the water pump he witnessed a horrifying sight.

The room was overcrowded and it gave Akash a stifling sensation. He wanted to go out but there was no less than ten ICL employees were standing the main door to Sandip's flat. He looked around helplessly, his face streaked with tears; the burning pain within him was unbearable. The dead body lying in front of him was that of his best friend, his closest *yaar*, who felt his feeling even before he uttered a word. The place he occupied in Akash's heart was irreplaceable. His world became poorer without Sandip.

Motionless and listless, Akash sat in corner of Sandip's drawing room. Soon they would take his body for cremation. Akash, too, would go with them, knowing that burning pyre would also burn a part of his being forever, making it empty and void.

He kept his eyes closed for he was scared to look at Sandip's body, covered with a sheet. There was a wad of cotton, stuck with some adhesive, on each of his eyes. Every time Akash remembered that the fishes in the lake had nibbled at his dearest friend's body and eyes, left it bloodied, his body gave an involuntary shudder. Keeping his eyes closed was also unendurable for sweet memories came flooding into his mind, making him heavy-hearted and distraught. He opened his eyes again. He knew almost all the faces around him. There was a sombre expression on everybody's face. Akash then stole a stealthy glance at Sandip's mother. She had not dropped a single drop of tear. She rather was self-possessed and completely reticent. Whoever had visited Sandip's flat to express his or her condolence could not muster courage to utter a single word of sympathy or empathy to his mother. She was gazing at her son's body with a vacant expression on her face. Her son's death made her virtually alone for several time Sandip had said to Akash that they had had no close relation. He then saw Chirag, sitting cross-legged, his shoulders stooped, close to Sandip's mother. His otherwise styled hair was dishevelled, face colourless and his demeanour distressed. Looking at him one might think that the death of Sandip was a huge personal loss to Chirag. After every few seconds he was looking at Sandip's mother as though he was waiting for some instruction from her. However surprising Chirag's sitting next to Sandip's mother with a sad face might be, at present situation Akash ignored thinking about it.

Time dragged terribly slowly as Akash remained sitting at the same place. At last when ambulance came to take Sandip's body to the crematorium he budged. Chirag helped Sandip's mother stand. He seemed to be concerned about her. In spite of some neighbour's trying to dissuade Sandip's mother from attending the funeral ceremony, she went inside the ambulance and sat by her son's body, placing her hand on it. Chirag and Akash accompanied her.

When the pyre was set ablaze and the greedy tongues of the all-consuming fire was devouring her son's body, she folded her hands and, closing her eyes, prayed for a long time.

But Akash was not as strong as her. Every time a new flame flared, determined to turn anything to ashes in no time, he felt something within him burning. It was an excruciating pain which could not be expressed in words. Once it became unbearable he silently tiptoed to a small temple, close to the crematorium, and sitting on a step there, cried uncontrollably. He was not sure whether he was crying for Sandip, his mother or for himself.

Akash rang the doorbell and waited. Chirag opened the door after a few second and asked Akash to come in.

'Come inside, Maa is in the bedroom,' he said slowly.

Maa – Akash was shocked by the word Chirag had chosen to address Sandip's mother. He looked at Chirag. A strange transformation had taken place on his face. No more did he look restive rather an agreeable calmness dominated his face.

Since Sandip's death, around two weeks back, every time Akash went to Sandip's flat, Chirag invariably opened the door. It struck him that Chirag spent better part of the day as Sandip's place though he was not sure what exactly he did there.

'Which shift do you have today?' Akash asked Chirag.

'I have not gone to office since his death,' Chirag said in a low voice.

'Why?' Akash asked and his question sounded foolish to his own ear.

'There is no answer to why, yaar. I simply did not feel like leaving her alone,' replied Chirag, a bit frostily.

Sandip's mother was sitting on the bed, propping against the pillows, reading newspaper.

Seeing Akash she gave a tired smile.

'Sit, beta,' said she, folding the days' newspaper and keeping it aside.

'Disturbed you?' asked Akash courteously. Since Sandip's death Akash did not find much thing to talk to his mother. He went to Sandip's place just to find if he could help her anyway.

'Not in the least,' she smiled. She had taken a bath a few minutes ago. Her hair was wet, plastered to her skull. A drop of water was glistening near her earlobe. She looked tired but not broken.

'Coffee?' she asked Akash as Chirag sat at the other corner of the bed.

'No, no aunty, please do not prepare anything for me,' protested Akash at once.

'I need not take any pain, Akash. He will prepare it,' she said, indicating Chirag as Chirag gave a satisfying grin. Suddenly, for no reason, Akash experienced a pang of jealousy. It was clear that just within a span of two weeks Chirag had developed a mother-son relation with Sandip's mother. But why should I be jealous of it? Akash tried to rationalize his feeling, yet for the first time he looked at Chirag with envy, not for his enviable feature but for his closeness to Sandip's father.

As Chirag left for Kitchen Akash asked Sandip's mother, 'Did the administrative department give you any date to vacate the flat?'

'Yes, I am supposed to vacate it within three month's of my son's death,' she said slowly, looking at the floor. 'Anyway I would vacate it within a couple of weeks.'

'Should I talk to Movers and packers for shifting the furniture to your place at Nasik?'

'That will not be required, Akash. My son did not have many pieces of furniture. For the time being I will leave them here. All I want to take with me is his laptop, camera and clothes and for that one suitcase should be enough. Whenever I miss him I could see his photograph on the laptop. My son lived his life to the fullest. He lived everyday, every moment of his life. In a way he lived life more than a seventy or eighty-year–old man.'

'You know, Akash,' she began after a pause. 'Every time I recollect his death I feel inconsolable and devastated. But then as I remember his face, his love for life, I feel, if I remain low and distressed I would rather show disrespect to my son's soul.'

Akash remained silent. What could he say to a mother who drew inspiration and courage from her deceased son?

'But how will you keep the furniture here?' he asked after sometime.

'I will leave them at his flat,' she said, indicating Chirag, entering the bedroom with two cups of steaming coffee. Again Akash experienced a stab of jealousy but this time he recovered fast.

'Thanks,' he said to Chirag, taking the cup from him.

Chirag gave him an affable smile and walked to the bed.

'Hold it carefully, it is hot,' he said to Sandip's mother with filial affection.

She held the cup by its brim and took it from him. She took a small sip at it and said to Chirag, 'One more spoon of sugar.'

'Wait for a moment,' said Chirag and rushed to the kitchen. He returned with sugar in no time. He took the cup from Sandip's mother and stirred the sugar into coffee.

'Is it okay now?' he asked Sandip's mother, handing her the cup.

'Perfect,' she patted Chirag's hand as he sat by her.

Looking at them, completely at ease with each other as if they were mother and son, Akash understood that he could not be of any help to Sandip's mother. Chirag would do ten times more than what he could do for her.

As he got to his feet to leave Chirag came to the main door to see him off.

'Thanks for taking so much care of her,' Akash said to Chirag, forcing himself to smile, finding nothing else to say.

'Do you remember, Akash, once I told you about a recurring dream of mine?'

'Yeah, I do. You have dreams about your mother.'

'Exactly.' A thoughtful pause and Chirag added then, 'I think I will not have that dream again.'

'Why?' asked Akash, a bit foolishly.

'There is no answer to why, Akash. I just feel it,' Chirag gave a dry smile.

'Bye.'

'Bye, thanks for coming,' said Chirag and closed the door.

On the evening of Dipavali, towards the end of November, Maria an Akash met at Tastings. Since Sandip's death, about a couple of months back, Maria had observed a distinct change in Akash. Most of the time he looked downcast. He became more silent than before and she found his silence disturbing. Sometimes he would say something after a prolonged silence and whatever he said, usually revolved around the futility of life. Besides, since Sandip's death Akash seemed to have no go to pursue his literary activity.

She desperately wanted to say something to him to cheer him up, to let him feel that life could not stop with anyone's death. She, eventually, tried once but his reply silenced her at once.

'Maria, please, no commonplace philosophy. I know, you want to see me happy but I have lost my brother, my best friend. One would understand my state of mind only if one loses one's sibling.'

Maria remained silent and no more did she try to bring him to a good mood. Time and again she remembered what Athrava's grandfather had told her once – *Shradha and Shaburi* – Respect and patience are the keywords. Time is the greatest healer. She was patient and knew that as time elapsed slowly Akash would get over the shock.

This evening Akash was playing with the straw, moving it in the cold coffee mug absentmindedly. Maria looked at him. His face was covered with stubble of several nights. Two moles on both sides of his lips had grown slightly bigger. Chiefly the mole beneath his lower lip looked more like a wart. Very recently he had trimmed his hair with a hope that it would reduce his hair fall. His face looked slightly small and eyes brooding. Once his eyes met Maria's he gave a short smile, 'Do not you feel irritated to sit in silence by me?' he paused and continued without waiting for her answer, 'You may think how can I be so indifferent and silent to my friend who cares so much for me?'

'But I never said so, nor do I ever think like that,' Maria replied.

'Well, finish your coffee fast. We will go to K-stars then.'

'But the mall would be very crowded today.'

'Never mind,' said Akash.

K-stars was the only shopping Mall in Chembur. It was a huge three-storey building that boasted large multiplex and no less than 50 retail outlets, selling branded shoes, apparels, food, electronic goods. Most of the young couples go there to do some window shopping or to have some refreshments from MacDonald's, Domino's Pizza, KFC, Dosa centre and so forth, housed on the top floor of the Mall.

The mall was no more than ten-minute-walk from Tastings.

As they reached the first floor of K-stars suddenly Akash saw Chirag and Sandip's mother coming out from Food Bazaar. The shopping trolley, Chirag was pushing, contained two large polythene bags, apparently full with monthly provision. With his left hand he was holding Sandip's mother wrist protectively as though she might get lost in the crowd. Without a shadow of doubt they looked like mother and son.

'Hello Akash,' Chirag was the first to greet Akash as their eyes met. Then he gave a courteous nod to Maria.

'Hi,' said Akash to Chirag and paid his attention to Sandip's mother. She looked her original composed self.

'When did you come to Bombay?' Akash asked her.

'This morning,' she smiled. 'How are you two?'

'Good,' said Akash and Maria almost in unison.

'How long will you be here?'

The reply, however, came from Chirag, 'Mamma will not leave here for next two months.'

Somewhat shocked, Akash looked at Sandip's mother while she gave an indulgent smile at Chirag.

'Even if I leave, he will come to Nasik with a car to bring me back here,' she said, ruffling Chirag's hair affectionately. Chirag smiled sheepishly.

'Do come to his flat whenever you feel like,' said Sandip's mother to Akash.

'Yes, I will,' said Akash.

'Bye beta, Bye Maria.'

'Bye,' said they.

'Happy Diwali,' Chirag greeted them and headed towards the escalator, leaving the shopping trolley nearby, carrying the polythene bags. Though Sandip's mother wanted to carry one of the bags Chirag refused to give her one. Standing a little distance off Akash watched both of them. Once they reached the ground floor, they bumped into a young married couple. Akash saw the young lady introducing her man with Chirag and Chirag shaking hand with them. They young lady was around twenty-five and was one of the prettiest women Akash had ever seen. It occurred to him that he had seen her before.

Once Chirag and Sandip's mother left the Mall, walking out through the automatic sliding door, Akash turned to Maria.

'Let's go to KFC. It's a long time I had Chicken Finger from there.'

'But it is very expansive. Besides, I am already stuffed,' said Maria, heading towards the escalator to the second floor.

'Okay, then sit by me and watch me eat,' smiled Akash. 'I want to tell you something and for that we must sit somewhere.'

'Okay baba.'

After a few minutes they were sitting on two swivel stools outside KFC counter.

'I feel good as I saw them together. I mean, Chirag and Sandip's mother,' Akash said after a while.

'I could read it on your face while they were leaving the Mall.'

'There is a reason behind it. After Sandip's death when I found Chirag getting closer to Sandip's mother, calling her Mamma, I was very jealous of their closeness. Sandip was my best friend and now all I have is my memory. The only living person, I know, who was very close to Sandip was his mother. So Chirag's closeness with her gave me a feeling as though somebody was secretly snatching away my best friend and his memory from me. Obviously I was very jealous of Chirag.

But this evening as I saw them together I felt very happy and contended. No more do I feel jealous. Rather I feel grateful to life.' Akash paused and continued again, 'Do you know why? This evening once I saw them together for the first time I understood as to why it is said that L*ife is full of compensation.*

They looked perfect together, Maria. A young man, craving for mother's love, got it at last. And a mother, who had lost her son recently, got another boy, most unexpectedly, who loved her no less than her son did.'

'I immensely loved what you said,' said Maria, looking loving at Akash, and then stretching her hand across the table she placed her hand on Akash's, just to tell him that she was always with him.

'Do not you think that these two bags are too heavy for you? You can give one to me,' Sandip's mother said to Chirag.

'Am I mad? People around would say that an old mother is carrying weight while the young son is not bothering about it.'

'I am not an old mother,' smiled Sandip's mother.

Chirag was about to say something but before that a sweet voice called him by his name.

'Hello Chirag.'

Looking at his right Chirag found a ravishingly beautiful woman smiling at him, showing her pearly white teeth. Standing next to her, holding her hand was a tall, handsome, clean-shaven young man with wavy hair. Together they epitomised newly married happy couple.

For an instant Chirag could not recognize her and then a strange emotion surged over him. He recognized her. It was Kritika.

'Hello,' Chirag smiled at her, making a walk down memory lane for a short moment.

'He is my husband, Prashant, and Prashant, he is Chirag. Once we worked together in Epicentre.' Kritika's voice was concise. She seemed to be so happy with life that the bitter past experience with Chirag did not vex her at all.

'Hello, Prashant,' Chirag said to Prashant affably.

'Hi buddy,' said Prashant. His voice was crisp and he spoke English with an accent. 'Did you invite him on our marriage?' Prashant asked his wife.

'No,' stammered Kritika with a sheepish smile. 'In fact I forgot to invite many of my friends in a hurry.' Then turning to Chirag she said, 'Actually our marriage was planned all of a sudden. Prashant has come only with one-week leave. He is leaving for the US day after tomorrow. Soon I would settle there for good.' Kritika's eyes glinting with joy and, as Chirag thought, greed. There was no remorse or regret on her face.

'Congratulations,' said Chirag. 'Best wishes for your happy married life.'

'Thanks,' said they both and then Kritika asked, 'How is life?'

'Life is treating me well.'

'Well, bye Chirag.'

'Bye,' said Chirag.

Once Kritika and Prashant left Chirag was in a state of shock for a minute. During last many months whenever he had been in a reminiscent mood and had remembered Kritika, he experienced a deep antagonism towards her. But this evening once he had bumped into an ebullient Kritika he was not at all angry with her. He rather genuinely wished good for her. Suddenly Chirag felt himself free, as he was no more burdened with hatred towards her.

Most probably true freedom means you do not have an iota of hatred towards anyone on earth, thought Chirag with an inward smile.

'Who was that girl? She was very beautiful,' said Sandip's mother once they caught an auto rickshaw from outside K-stars.

'She is Kritika, Mamma. I told you everything I know about her.'

'Yes, I remember,' said Sandip's mother. Unlike her own son this boy was very voluble and poured his heart out to her without any fear, shame or awkwardness.

'Meeting her this evening was very educative for me.'

'Why?'

'Because no more do I have any bad feeling towards her although I remember her nasty deed with me. I think, I am becoming a better person,' Chirag's voice was distant.

'You are a very good person, my son,' Sandip's mother placed her had on Chirag's shoulder. Chirag held her hand and looked at the Diwali-lit street in front of him with hope and expectation.

On the morning of Christmas, 2011 Akash's cell phone buzzed persistently while he was in deep sleep. Somewhat irritated, Akash checked the cell phone though the mist of sleep. He was a bit surprised to find that it was a call from Maria. She was never inconsiderate to call him in the morning for she knew that he was a late riser.

'Hello,' said Akash over phone. His voice was heavy with sleep.

'Sorry to disturb you, Akash. I got through WNS,' she said excitedly.

'What is that?' Akash asked wearily, without comprehending what she meant.

'*Aree yaar*, it is World Networking System. It is in Vikroli. They have offered me a pay package of 5.2 lakhs per annum,' she paused and added, 'This time I am not lying about my salary. I am very happy, Akash.'

'Congrats,' said Akash, trying to bring some exhilaration to his voice.

'Are not you happy, Akash?' she demanded.

'Yes, I am. But did not you know of it last night?'

'No, I did not. Just now I have received a courier. You are the first one I phoned though I knew that I might have disturbed your sleep.'

'Congrats again, I will call you later, Maria.'

'Wait a moment. Are not you coming tonight for dinner? Dada told me to invite you for Christmas dinner. Please do not fail him this time,' she implored.

Akash was in a dither. He always felt a sense of awkwardness to go to Maria's flat.

'I will let you know, Maria. Please let me sleep now for sometime. I will call you later.'

'It means you will not come. Okay, your wish,' she said in a pained voice and added as an afterthought, 'Akash, I often regret loving you so much. You care so little for someone for whom you are everything.'

She cut the phone without waiting for his reply.

Somewhat guiltily Akash kept the phone. Rarely did Maria talk to him like this. He wanted to call her but some hollow pride within him forbade him from phoning her back. She cut the phone so if she wishes she should call me back, he told himself and tried to sleep again but doorbell rang a few minutes later.

Once he opened the door, yawning and rubbing his eyes to get rid of the remnants of sleep, he was taken by surprise.

It took him no time to recognize the tall handsome youth, standing in front of him, with a condescending smile on his lips.

'Hi dude, what's up?' asked Aniket Mahapatra, Akash's roommate in ICL hostel.

Clean-shaven, hair gelled, Aniket was beaming with confidence.

Akash forced a smile though he did not like to see Aniket standing on his doorsteps.

'Please come in,' he said courteously.

'Thanx,' said Aniket with an accent.

They sat in Akash's bedroom while Aniket observed everything in the room critically.

'Actually I am here just for a few days. Day after tomorrow I will fly back to States. So just come to meet you guys.'

Akash forced a smile again.

'I was under an impression that none of our batch mates is left in ICL anymore. But then I came to know of you and Chirag.'

'Sandip was also here. Most probably you have heard of his death.'

'Yeah, I did. I felt very sorry for that,' Said Aniket casually.

Akash looked at Aniket. Success made him brass and haughty. He knew that the purpose of Aniket's visit was to let Akash know that he had left Akash far behind in the battle of life.

Soon Aniket proved Akash correct by launching into a lengthy account of his successful career, colourful lifestyle and his occasional flings with the chicks from the other side of the pond. His long monologue was peppered with derogatory remarks about ICL and its poor work culture.

'This fucking organization does not deserve graduate engineers from reputed colleges and universities. Please do not think that I want to hurt your feelings, Akash. But if you leave this wretched place and join a reputed IT company you would understand what you are really missing. Man, a boy of your talent deserves much better a job,' Aniket paused and asked Akash, 'Are you in Facebook? I tried to find you but did not find you there.'

'I am not in any social networking site. For some reason I do not like it,' Akash said dryly.

'Register yourself today itself. You will get to know what you friends are doing. It may encourage you to seek a more satisfying and financially rewarding job.'

'Thanks,' Akash said shortly.

After Aniket left Akash was silent for a long time. Though he found Aniket's condescending attitude irritating, he could not forget what Aniket said to him. The more he pondered over Aniket's words the more it occurred to him that he had deceived himself for last few years, dreaming of becoming a successful author one day, spurning the repeated opportunity to get a better job which could be financially more rewarding. How much has he saved in last few years? He asked himself. It was not more than a measly few lakhs whereas Aniket had hinted that he had already saved no less than 50 lakhs of rupees which he preferred to say in terms of million. His three-year stint in the US made him financially very strong.

I could have left this job for good had I had fifty lakhs of rupees in bank, a long chain of thoughts passed through Akash's mind while his forehead puckered and lips pursed. I devoted all my energy, intellect and love to create new stories for last four years but what did I get in return? Not even a single story of mine had got published so far. Forget about dream of making a living from writing. What if after another ten years not a single piece of my write up gets published? What will I do? How long will accept rejection from publishers and work on new stories with renewed enthusiasm? What will I do on the day when my patience might wear away? I will be left with no choice but continue doing this boring and monotonous job in ICL. Is it worth living such a dull and vapid life?

Akash sat in silence while his fertile imaginative mind conjured up pictures of Aniket's prosperous life in the US. Suddenly he experienced a twinge of regret and disappointment within him. Most probably, he had deceived himself for last few years of his life by chasing an unreachable dream. The more he compared his present life with that of Aniket's the more he went into depth of depression. All his intellectual inputs could not help him to revive his mood.

Around half an hour later he got up and opened the laptop. Never had he felt like registering himself to Facebook. Never had he felt like knowing the present status of his collegemates and ex-batchmates in ICL. He was perfectly lost in his own world. But for now he wanted to know how they were doing in life.

He made a quick registration under a pseudonym and searched for the boys whose name he remembered. Soon, to his utter surprise, he discovered that most of his batchmates were the members of Facebook. They uploaded their photographs, shared their thrilling experiences, wrote about their achievements. Most of them were settled in the US and looked very confident self on the photographs. At last when he logged off it was 1.30 in the afternoon.

All his collegemates and the boys who had left ICL seemed to have made their life a success story and it was only he whose all effort doomed to failure. For a moment he was seized with a desire to tear all his manuscripts, lying on the study table. Well, material success did not matter much to him but could he deny the fact that he needed money to lead a comfortable life? Yes, all his friends and ex-colleagues were more matured than him for so far he lived in a make-believe world from where he had always dreamed of becoming successful and famous in future. His mind always dwelt upon a rosy day of future while the present had always slipped out of his hand. How fool he had been to believe firmly in an old saying that 'what comes from heart touches heart.' Yes, so far he lived in a house of cards, he told himself, that's why meeting with Aniket had worked like such a strong blow to his belief. Never had he felt so low and depressed in life, not even after the death of Sandip. What was more, his sense of dejection was coupled with his feeling of self-deception, which brought him almost to tears.

Crestfallen and heavy-hearted, he went to the window and stood by it for a long time. After sometime he saw Sujata and Jasvinder walking down the narrow lane, hand in hand, in a blissful peace. Jasvinder was pushing the pram with one hand. The little thing lying on the pram was one of the cutest babies Akash had ever seen. Sujata and Jasvinder were talking in undertones and it could easily be seen from their bearing that at present they were one of the happiest couples of the world. As yet Akash had never seen them together walking so peacefully and lovingly. He gazed at them as long as he could. But for some strange reason, at this present moment, this happy reunion between Sujata and Jasvinder, threw Akash into the depths of despair, in an abyss of loneliness.

Afternoon dragged on slowly while Akash remained in a bitter mood. Around five in the afternoon his cell phone rang. It was a call from Maria; the first call since she had cut the phone abruptly in the morning.

'Hello,' said Akash in an icy voice. He was not in a mood to talk to anyone.

'Have I disturbed you, Akash?' she said slowly.

Suddenly Akash found himself extremely angry with her. Had she not loved him so much he would have felt himself more free; he would have left ICL and gone somewhere to seek a better job. But she had always given him a feeling that she would literary expire in his absence, a chain of thought ran through Akash's mind in no time. He felt Maria and her love for him was a burden on him.

'Will you cut the phone if I say that you have disturbed me?' Akash asked petulantly.

'Why are you getting so rude to me? I am sorry for what I have said in the morning. I did not want to hurt you. In fact...'

She could not complete as Akash cut in on her, 'You need not be sorry. If you regret loving me so much please stop loving me. I do not beg for your love.' Akash cut the call.

Though he felt that he was unusually rude with her, at present, he could not control his actions. Now again Akash found himself extremely angry. It was as though he had messed up his life so terribly that there was no way out now. He walked across the bedroom several times before he felt that staying all alone in the flat was getting on his nerves. He changed his dress and went down. He kick-started the bike and drove aimlessly for half an hour. And then an idea struck him. Immediately he turned the bike and reached in front of Ashish theatre in a few minutes. But unfortunately, a sheer disappointment was awaiting him there.

More than four years back, during his hostel days, Akash used to have boiled egg in the evening from an old lady, sitting near the main gate to Ashish theatre. He did not meet her since he had shifted to ICL Township. In the evening of Christmas when a mood of deep melancholy descended upon Akash he wanted to talk to the old lady. But she was not there. In place of her there was a middle-aged man, sturdily-built, selling pani-puri and sev-puri. Akash passed a searching glance around but she was nowhere around.

Disappointed, Akash started his bike. He parked the motorbike near ICL hostel and moved about aimlessly for an hour or so, whiling away the time, trying to get away the mood of despondency. Around 8 at night he made do with vada pav before returning to ICL Township.

As his bike rode past Maria's building he passed a cursory glance at her flat. Outside the window of their drawing room, a big star, made of some colourful and bright cellophane paper, was hanging. Their drawing room looked brighter than usual.

He parked the bike at the parking lot beside his building and hurried to the staircase as he saw Chirag and Sandip's mother coming out from the neighbouring building. He did not want to talk to anyone now.

He entered his flat and slammed the door behind him. But soon he felt himself more restive for the silence of the flat was extremely insufferable. It again and again reminded him of that his 27-year-old was nothing but full of failure. With his mind's eyes he created a picture where he could see all his college mates and Ex-colleagues were leading a successful and fulfilling life, time and again he remembered those photographs he had seen on facebook. All their girlfriends and wives looked gorgeous on the photographs. They were all smiling, wearing fashionable outfits, celebrating life to the fullest. His own life appeared so drab and dull compared to their colourful and exciting life.

As the clock ticked away minutes Akash felt himself more and more disconcerted. He checked the watch. It was ten past twelve but there was no sleep in his eyes. He passed a vacant glance around the walls of his bedroom. Suddenly it struck him that those walls had witnessed his anguished mind and was laughing at his miserable plight, his so-called intellect, creativity and his care-a-shit-to-material-success attitude. No matter what I do, I can not hide my feelings from them, thought Akash and felt himself terribly claustrophobic as though the walls of the room were gradually inching towards him from all directions, determined to crush his being, his pride and confidence forever. An unfathomable fear gripped him all of a sudden as if he was on the verge of insanity.

He picked up the cell phone and door key from the table and rushed out of his flat. He entered the elevator and went to the sixth floor. From there he climbed the stair up to the roof. And there he was – beneath the open starlit sky. The wind was crisp and fresh yet there was a chill in it. He stood at the edge of the roof, holding the parapet. No matter whether anyone knew or not he would never forget that his life was a complete failure.

He looked down for a while. How difficult it was to live life with a heavy burden of failure in his heart for the rest of the life. It was like dying everyday but how easy it was to get away his affliction forever. Just a jump over the parapet, a travelling on the air for a second or two, an intense physical pain for a few minutes and then a state of permanent bliss. He did not know where he would go after that but one thing he knew for certain that he would be faraway from all the worldly pains.

Yes, what was the use of leading the kind of life he was living? He looked down again. The area between Akash's building and the next apartment where Chirag stayed was cemented and a part of it was used as parking area. Gazing down for a long time, while a train of depressing thoughts ran through his mind, his mind became almost demented. He felt as though the cemented floor, right down there, was inviting him, alluring him with its assurance to wipe off all his pain and agony forever. The more he looked down at the semi-dark and silent cemented area near parking lot, the more it drifted Akash into a state of pleasant lunacy. Why was he wasting time when breaking away from this unbearable pain was so easy, thought Akash, and holding the parapet in a determined way stood on it. A gentle breeze was blowing. Akash took a deep breath and looked down for the last time.

He was about to take the final and the most crucial step of self-annihilation when, like a providential coincidence, his cell phone beeped twice. It was an SMS. Standing precariously on the parapet of a six-storey building, Akash checked his cell phone. It was a quarter to one. No one ever sent him a message at such an odd hour. He opened the inbox. It was a message from PUCHU!

He read the message while his heart palpitated involuntarily.

Had a bad dream. Saw you on a roof. Thinking of ending ur life. If so wait for me to join u. what will I do if you gone forever?

Akash read and reread the message when his whole body trembled by a strange emotion that hitherto he had not experienced. Her SMS was like a sharp needle that burst the balloon, filled with pain and frustrations, making them disappear into nothingness. Just in a span of a few seconds a chain of new thoughts ran through his mind.

How does she know that I am on the roof? Even if she is on the roof of her building she cannot see me. Does it mean that she had really seen me in her dream? But it is so unexplainable, thought Akash when his heart missed a beat. Suddenly he remembered long ago Maria had told him that she had had a dream about the death of Atharva's grandfather just before he died. That time Akash ignored her words, thinking that she was fabricating a story to impress him. But now he did not have the liberty to think in the same way. He remembered her innocent face and telling him with teary eyes, 'You know Akash, I loved him very much. More than I love my own grandfather. And probably we get connected to our loved one, once they are in serious crisis, in a way that cannot be explained scientifically.' Though Akash had not said anything to her, he silently laughed off her proposition. Now he had no doubt that she had not lied to him.

So many stories he wrote on love but never had he experienced such a depth of love. Her pure love for him was not a piece of fiction but real. Yet it was more unimaginable than a fiction work.

Suddenly all the layer of frustration and sense of failure obliterated from his mind where remained only love and bliss. All the disturbing thoughts which troubled him so much walked in front of him, trying to cast their depressing spell on him but, Akash smiled absentmindedly, for he know that they would always fail to torment him again.

How fool he was not to realize that no one was as fortunate as him to receive such an unconditional love which travelled beyond the boundaries of reason and science. Yes, he was not only fortunate but also blessed. But ignorant was he not to realize it as yet. Tears trickled down his eyes as for the first time he wanted to cry, hiding his face in Maria's small bosom. He wanted to embrace her so tightly that she would merge with his being. He wanted to flourish her with kisses. Now he realized that his life could not be a failure for her love would always show the light; the light that could lead anyone to a state of pure ecstasy because it was the light of love.

Carefully he climbed down on to the roof. He kept his eyes closed for sometime. For him it was like a rebirth.

Slowly he typed an SMS and sent her: *ur love saved me. Be with me forever. Love u.*

Almost at once his cell phone buzzed. It was Maria.

'Hello,' said Akash as his voice quivered with emotion.

She did not respond but he could hear her crying. He waited till she spoke.

'It took you so much of time to say *love u,*' she said.

'We will get married whenever you want,' Akash's voice was firm and decisive. 'Even if you want it tomorrow I do not care.'

A silence.

'Merry Christmas, Akash,' she said at last.

'Merry Christmas,' Akash responded.

'They said Jesus was born on this day,' she said after a while. 'I feel it is very correct because love is born in you tonight.'

'But not in a stable,' smiled Akash. 'But standing on the parapet dangerously, about to end my life.'

'Hush, do not say it to anyone. Now go to sleep,' she paused and asked, 'Can you meet me tomorrow, ten in the morning?'

'Of course, I can,' said Akash. All of a sudden he was in a state of elation.

'Go to sleep now,' instructed Maria.

'Love you very much, Maria.'

'Love you too. Now go to sleep,' she said and cut the cell phone. Holding the cell phone tightly Akash stood on the roof for sometime. He looked up at the whispering stars and the crescent moon and felt very grateful to life. Suddenly he had an intense urge to record his feeling of deep love for Maria and life. He wasted no time and ran down the stairs...........

EPILOGUE

'**A**re you ready?' A direct question from Maria made the drowsy Akash remember that he was supposed to meet her at ten. It was already ten minutes past ten. Owing to his writing last night till the wee hours, his heavy sleep did not break although he had set an alarm call at 9.

'Got up just now. In fact by your call,' said Akash, recollecting the last night's ordeal.

Her excitement damped slightly. 'So you are not coming to meet me?'

'Of course, I am coming. Just give me fifteen minutes.'

'Take your time, Akash. I have already waited for a few years to get you. I do not care if you take an hour even to come down.'

'Just fifteen minutes, and I will be down.' Akash kept the cell phone on the table and hurried to the bathroom.

Once he left his flat around twenty minutes later and went out of his building something very strange struck him. This morning appeared much more beautiful, quiet and calm than any other morning of his life. It seemed as though in this morning the whole nature was in a peaceful harmony, celebrating everything. *Falling in love is so different from writing on love...* thought Akash with an inward chuckle.

He then saw Maria, standing at the bend in the road. As he neared her, he was taken by a pleasant surprise.

She looked smaller than usual. There was no lip-gloss on her lips, no *Kajol* in her eyes. She was virtually without any make-up. No more was she wearing a 2-inch-heel to look taller. Her wet hair was plastered against her skull, making her face look smaller. For the first time she had come to meet him without smartening herself even a bit. She wanted him to accept her as she was. No more did she want to hide her natural look behind any make-up or elegant dress. Yet Akash felt, with a trembling in his heart, that never had she looked so beautiful. Their eyes riveted on each other for a long moment. There was a strange glow in her eyes. It was a glow of love. He did not know what Maria had read in his eyes as all of a sudden she asked him, 'Last night you wrote for a long time?' Her voice was soothing.

'Yeah, but how the hell do you know?' asked an astonished Akash.

She gave a benign smile, 'I saw it in your eyes. And no matter whatever you wrote, Akash, it will get published if at all you want, take my word for it.' There was so much sincerity and love in her voice that it brought Akash almost to tears.

'Why do you think so?' he asked her at last.

'Because now you know what love is. Let's go,' she said and held his hand.

'Where?'

'We will go to Mount Mary church. Long back I lit a candle there, praying for the publication of your book. Now I want to go there to express my gratitude to god.'

'Let me get the bike.'

'No, we will go by an Auto Rickshaw.'

'Why?'

'Because today I want to sit by you, not behind you.'

'As you wish,' said Akash with a smile. He did not care at all where she might lead him.